DECLARATION
DETERMINATE
Book 1 of the Declaration Series

jdgray1425

DETERMINATE

This is a work of fiction. All of the characters, names, incidents,
organizations, and dialogue in this novel are either the products
of the author's imagination or are used fictitiously.

iUniverse books may be ordered through booksellers or by contacting:

iUniverse
1663 Liberty Drive
Bloomington, IN 47403
www.iuniverse.com
1-800-Authors (1-800-288-4677)

ISBN: 978-1-5320-5342-9 (sc)
ISBN: 978-1-5320-5341-2 (e)

Library of Congress Control Number: 2018909242

Print information available on the last page.

iUniverse rev. date: 08/10/2018

To Kim.

My love, my muse, my couch buddy:

try to remember it's just a story.

"Tell us a story," they said. And so it began ...

Darkness

In the beginning, God created the heaven and the earth. And the earth was without form and void, and darkness was upon the face of the deep.

Toby began anxiously flapping his hand as Randel Hull and his brother Bobby eyed him shuffling past the general store. Randel began to have that gnawing feeling once again. Randel had seen the kind of games Bobby liked to play and knew he could no longer condone his brother's actions. "Chase Toby" was one of Bobby's favorites—he chased him like a dog would chase a squirrel, never quite sure what to do with the prey once he caught it. Maybe he'd call him a retard. Maybe push him down hard on the ground so his hands and elbows bled. Maybe hit him with a stick and send him crying on his way back to the dirty little shack of a house that he shared with Andy and Penny. Amid the brothers' silent stares, Toby began to run, not swinging his arms as might be expected to balance the strides but flapping them erratically. As Toby fled down the dirt road, he muttered, "Could not. Would not, no, no, no …"

Bobby smiled. The Hull brothers both knew where Toby was headed. If Toby got close enough to home, the threat of Andy would protect him. Like reaching base in a game of tag, that was the rule. Once he crossed the fence line, game over. If he got too close to home with Bobby still pursuing, Andy might fire his double-barrel at Bobby and give him a scare for a change.

Toby wasn't fast. So Randel understood when Bobby said, "Wait till he gets to the bend." Bobby was giving Toby a head start because Bobby liked the chase. Bobby would let Toby run, let him get within sight of freedom, and then snatch it away at the last minute.

But today, Randel didn't give a shit about what Bobby wanted. This time, they'd play for keeps. Randel waited as Bobby had asked, but not because Bobby had any real control over him. It was the idea of giving Toby false hope that pleased Randel.

Bobby was the eldest, almost eighteen, and the biggest, but Randel planned to do things differently today. Randel thought that he'd trip Bobby as the path narrowed, sending him ass over teakettle down the ravine and over the long drop onto the rocky creek bed below, just so Bobby couldn't spoil his prize this time. Bobby always spoiled it. Randel knew Bobby would let Toby go free afterward, like catch-and-release fishin'. What was the point if you just set 'em free afterward?

But Toby wasn't the fish. Fish might escape the cold deep of the water. Toby was the buzzin' fly disturbin' the surface of the water. Randel ran his tongue along the edge of his teeth, imagining them to be sharp and predatory. He wanted to take the Toby fly down into the Darkness. To Randel, this creature was not worthy to be anything more than prey.

Randel was fixated on this thought when Bobby suddenly took off running. He could see that Toby was past the bend now, but that wouldn't change the outcome. The brothers lost sight of him, but his path was obvious. The dirt road turned sharply down into the valley, toward Knoxville and civilization. But Toby ran upward, through the corn rows. He would flap his way down the winding access road to the Coopers' farm. Once across the bridge, Toby would turn into the woods, taking the narrow path along the edge of the creek and over to the Coopers' southern border. If he made it past the fence, he would be home.

The general store sat halfway down the lowly mountain. Toby was scrambling uphill, away from the little store, which was run by their uncle Billy. The Hulls and their kin overlooked this smaller mountain from the north face of their larger domain. They sat like unchallenged kings of the hill atop their snow-pinnacled peak. Vast green pastures spread out along the base of their mountain, below and between a tangled ribbon of trees and creeks, where their ancient herds of cattle and horses grazed undisturbed. Their kin had dozens of businesses, farms, and ranches between their ancestral home and Knoxville—or Yankeeville, as their pa liked to call it.

Randel began to gain ground on the skittering Toby fly. He would overtake Bobby at the bridge. They would both catch the Toby fly in the woods on the narrow path, within sight of the fence, unless Randel threw Bobby down the ravine first. As the two boys ran, Randel decided he had a better use for Bobby. Randel considered the weight—the Toby fly would be the biggest so far—and he knew he would need his brother's help.

Long ago, Bobby had been the one to show Randel the Darkness for the first time. It had been Bobby who finally sent him in and left him there. But it was the Darkness that had then returned him, all those years ago, reborn to await his destiny.

In those days, Bobby often took little Randel fishin', anytime Pa went on a drunken rampage. Ma took the worst of the beatings, and the boys went fishin'. The creek they fished had a clear, deep, bottomless hole in one of the slow-moving bends.

Randel had watched himself grow up through the reflections in those waters, following the changes over time. In his younger days, he had seen a towheaded, fat-cheeked cherub. More recently, his hair had gone brown, and his pale face had become drawn and lean. It was difficult for him to reconcile the two images, except for the sharp blue eyes that endured, staring back at him from the water's reflection.

The area around the dark hole was not cloudy, since

it was fed not from the creek upstream but from deep underground springs that merged into the stream. This hole had few nutrients to offer, so it wasn't good for fishing. The fish preferred to be near the aerated, bubbling flow that bounced down the faster-moving rock beds. But Bobby had told him about the underwater hole. "That's where the river monster lives. If you get too close, it comes out of the depths and grabs you."

Little Randel had always stopped to look. He had imagined letting himself fall into it, imagined the river monster pulling him down into the darkness. On occasion, he had thrown in a dead bird as an offering. Once he had thrown in a dead fawn they had found in the woods.

But that wasn't the only place where the Darkness lived. It ran throughout the mountain and could access openings not only in creek beds but also in small holes and caves. If you dug a deep well, you could see it too. But to really feel it and have it lick you like a wet, sloppy, cold tongue, you could walk right up to the edge of the Darkness along the western side of the mountain. There, an enormous crack in the rock face opened into a low, tree-covered crevice.

"It looks like a giant nigger's cunt," Bobby had said, squeezing the young prince's shoulder.

"What's a nigger?" Little Randel had asked, looking up at Bobby. He'd respected Bobby then. Bobby had seemed able to navigate any situation and to know just about everything there was to know. Bobby's early teachings had constituted much of Randel's education and his view of the world.

"It's like a person, but with black skin. Used to have lots of 'em around, a long time ago. Used to have 'em work the fields before the Yankees took away our rights."

"I saw one once," said little Randel, proudly proclaiming his understanding to his teacher.

"Don't be ignorant."

"I did. His skin was dark, and he had lines on his face."

"That was just a Yankee. They all got brown skin, and most have those blue lines all over. I'm talkin' 'bout really dark skin. They raped all the white people and made the Yankees. Any that were left died off a hundred years ago. So there ain't no more, at least not around here."

"But if Yankees come from niggers, ain't they niggers?"

"Well … maybe," Bobby concluded.

"Told ya."

Bobby shook his head. Little Randel felt he had won a small victory. The complex realities of his families own mixed heritage would not be understood until later in life. Even then such issues would be overlooked as the dominant beliefs of their ancestors continued to be perpetuated through the following generations.

Bobby had spoken of the cave many times before, but this had been the first time Randel had actually seen it. "So," Bobby had encouraged him, "are ya goin' to impregnate the bitch or just tickle it a little?"

Little Randel didn't understand.

Bobby had to restate the question. "Are you goin' in or not?"

Little Randel had felt drawn to the opening from the beginning. It was quiet, with not even the chirping of birds or insects. He walked in unafraid. The Darkness seemed to beckon him forward. It felt refreshing, and he accepted the invitation. Bobby followed him in but then tried to turn back. They had not brought a light, and had only the faint glow from the opening, so it was difficult to see. If the sun went down, they would be left in complete darkness.

Little Randel had continued blindly, feeling his way along the cold, slimy, narrowing walls with his feet and hands. Then, only little Randel had been small enough to fit in the ever-tightening tunnel, leading into the mountainside.

"I'm goin' back," Bobby had said.

"Go on then," little Randel had replied.

Little Randel had felt like this was finally something he could do better than Bobby. His size had become an advantage. He had continued deeper into the cave, as if drawn in by a power he didn't quite understand. Bobby had gone. He had probably thought little Randel would leave when he did. But this had been fine for little Randel. It had been better than going home. Little Randel was surpassing his brother. He had graduated from those early lessons and become the master. Under the tutelage of the Darkness he could grow into something new, something powerful. Then he had felt himself falling.

He remembered later how peaceful the void had felt as he pedaled in midair—silence, weightlessness, darkness, and nothingness for a few beautiful seconds. The sudden cold of the water at the bottom had been enough to wake him from his falling daze. But then he had been pulled under. Though wide awake, he didn't struggle; he let the river monster pull him down, like a baptism.

For a long time he had drifted down, but then suddenly, there had been light, and he had been spit out of the mountain into a small creek. At first, he had choked for air, and his legs had been struck by rocks. But then the stream had widened and become shallow, and there hadn't been enough water under him to carry him further. Randel had lain in the flowing water for a moment, looking up at the sky. The sunset had been too bright for his eyes, so he kept them closed. He coughed up the remaining water in his lungs, like amniotic fluid. Randel had been reborn from the womb of the mountain.

Then Randel had instinctively walked home, dripping and drying with each step. He would need shelter and food if he was to carry out his new mission. Later that night, his resurrection had surprised his family. His mother cradled him and shook him and cradled him again, crying. But Randel knew the Darkness had given birth to him. This sniveling creature, with her warm caress, had become alien to him.

Bobby had looked worried. Perhaps he realized something had changed. Randel was not the same boy his brother had left in the cave.

Bobby's puerile motivations no longer interested Randel. In the years to follow, Randel, with his newfound sense of purpose, took the lead and the brother's exploits became infamous. Alone, Bobby indeed might have burned down one of the only remaining Christian churches in North America, out of boredom or orneriness. But as the people fled the little building, carrying their snakes and coughing from smoke, and as the ashes that had been lifted high into the sky began to rain down on the congregation, Randel had chanted, "There is no true god but the Darkness, and Randel is his prophet."

The consequences of the brother's action were weakly administered by those fearful of reprisals. Even so, the harshest of punishments would not have swayed Randel. He had committed himself to a greater power. What could others teach him now?

"Some have tried …" croaked Randel's Pa suddenly one quiet evening, awakened from a drunken stupor by a cool breeze. He had then interrupted his own response to light his pipe. The brothers had looked doubtfully at each other as they prepared for the impending lecture.

"We showed 'em all. That's your heritage, boys. You don't let no one take what's yours. Especially not no dress-wearin', computer-worshippin' Yankee. Those ignorant sons of bitches … say they got a computer that talks to God for 'em. Ain't that somethin'? I expect it preserves the knees. But what would you boys know about God? Y'all wouldn't go near a church, 'cept to burn it down."

Randel had heard this all before, a mix of advice, blithering nonsense, and a little chastisement layered in for good measure. Randel had wanted to argue, *What was it all for, old man? For the privilege of listenin' to your bullshit? So Ma can work on her knees for you and be your punchin' bag when you get drunk?* Randel was a prince of the mountain. He knew he would have to kill the king one day and take his place of honor.

Now, chasing after Toby, Randel was getting confused again about which boy was the actual prey. Randel came up fast behind Bobby. Toby was just ahead, sprinting down the narrow trail that ran along the top of the ravine. Toby didn't sound right. His breathing was vocal and loud, like a cat coughing up a hairball. "Huuuh, huuuh," he wheezed.

Before the two brothers could reach him, Toby fell onto his heaving chest. He landed on the narrow path at first, but then out of terror or accidentally because he kept looking behind, Toby either threw himself or toppled down the ravine. There were some trees he could have caught onto before reaching the edge, but he was rolling too quickly. Randel watched Toby's flushed, terrified face roll down under his legs, again and again, until Toby went over the drop. Randel couldn't see or hear him hit bottom.

Bobby ran up and down the trail. Was he looking for a way down the ravine? Randel was disappointed. He stood panting on the path, realizing that this had not gone as planned. He had wanted to dangle Toby upside down in a nearby well. Then, while Toby screamed, Randel would have held his feet and tortured him and finally dropped him, head first, into the Darkness, like he had done to the others. Killing Toby like this, with his prey falling neatly to his death, was not the same as feeding him to the Darkness. Randel had learned that the Darkness preferred to feed on the living. It fed on fear as much as the bodies.

Bobby's continued panicking annoyed him, and Randel didn't need his help with Toby anymore. Bobby was now yelling at Randel, something about getting help. Randel couldn't take it anymore. He pulled his knife and stabbed Bobby in the stomach—not so severely that he would die right away, but just enough to incapacitate him. Randel needed someone to feed to the Darkness, and Bobby, with all his dribbling nonsense about rescue, had just volunteered. Randel dragged his bleeding brother by his ankles toward the old well. He propped him upright against the old stone wall around the well and tipped him in. Bobby grabbed the other side of the well with his hands as Randel held onto his feet. Bobby yelled down the well. The Darkness immediately mocked his terror by echoing the sound back at him. Randel could see the Darkness below. He could feel Bobby beginning to fade from blood loss and pain as he tried to support himself spread-eagle across the hole. As Randel held his legs, Bobby finally went limp and slipped in, smacking his chest and head against the inside of the well. Randel dangled him there for a moment, and then let go.

Chapter 1

Augustus the Student

Augustus panted as he ran down the long hallway, evoking looks of surprise from his fellow students. Had they realized the time, they would have understood that he should be in Room 401. And that was nowhere near Room 420 … 419 … 418 … 417. He imagined they were shaking their heads in disgust, but it was difficult to be certain while jogging and weaving around the more slow-moving obstacles. There were not many students in the hallway at that time of day, just enough to get in his way and make the journey an erratic zigzag. The pale blue suit-jacket uniforms, indicating an affiliation to the county's school system, were durable, impossible to wrinkle, breathable, and easily cleanable. But they were designed to promote a sense of modesty in a way that made them a little too warm for this type of activity.

One last turn … 407 … 406 … 405. *No problem*, he thought. *Plenty of time.*

Just then the tone sounded for first period. Augustus hated that tone. It was not uncomfortably loud, but it did seem to rise above all conversation, and if you happened to be in the hallway, it resonated down and back, clearing students like a pulse of solid energy, knocking one and all through the doorways. Augustus's brain associated the tone with words: *Thaaaat's it. You're late.* Then he felt the building begin to focus in on him.

Augustus wasn't completely paranoid; the school building was controlled by artificial intelligence. Usually, any building complex the size of a city block had its own system. These AI systems could be counted on to faithfully mind their own business, such as ventilation, power usage, and automated custodial work. But the school programming seemed to have been modeled on the heart of an old schoolmarm. It had opinions and was judgmental. It measured each student's performance against an individual potential algorithm, which was partially based on diet, exercise, and the amount of sleep the students received. The school received much of its data from an internal human interface lining the hallways and rooms. Although the educational AI was technically isolated from other civilian or security networks, it could also receive information on student activity that had been designated as relevant to educational imperatives. Such information could be shared among many other artificial intelligence systems. When given an opportunity, the educational AI would share its concern about the data with the students under its protection.

The school's primary interface was through the sensor strip, visible as a silvery blue line seamlessly adhered to the wall, about three meters off the ground. The sensor strip ran along both sides of the hallways and around the interior and exterior of the building, creating a panoramic, multispectral, auditory, and chemical analysis of all things inside and out. It also functioned as a gigantic lie detector, drug screener, and watchdog. Complete honesty, zero drug use, adherence to dietary recommendations, completion of homework assignments, and punctuality were expected. The interface also allowed for two-way auditory or holographic communication with students or with the occasional visiting faculty.

"Augustus Mendelson, a tardy has been registered in—"

"Yeah, yeah," Augustus said, interrupting the tardy alert as he broke into the classroom, sweating and breathing heavily.

Just then, someone ran into him from behind, pushing into his backpack. "Oof," said the muffled voice as the second tardy alert of the day was also interrupted. Augustus turned to see Tiberius staring up at him in surprise through a pair of round glasses.

Tiberius's diet was of great concern to the school's educational AI. The educational AI had already spent a good deal of computing capacity in futile contemplation of improvements to reduce the boy's weight and increase his height. The tardy had just become yet another example of why a solution must be found. The educational AI went on about its calculations in silence as the two boys stared at each other with amusement.

"All right, you two, sit down," scolded Room 401. "Attention, class ... we will now begin our studies of post-Declaration civilization. I hope you will all find this an interesting and informative subject. All of you have successfully passed your studies of the twenty-first century, which have now led us up to this momentous milestone in human history. Please review the first article of file HPDC100 ..."

Augustus and Tiberius took their positions, which automatically activated each young man's Solid Particulate Holographic Interface Technology, more commonly known as a SPHIT, or Holo-Interface.

A SPHIT generated an energy field, which levitated small metallic compounds, from which light was reflected. It provided a superior display compared to other types of holographic imaging, but it also offered tactile sensation for human interface with the school's network. Children were limited to the more basic mode of the interface until they were enhanced later in life, but it remained important to familiarize students with the technology that they would one day master.

Phoebe had watched Augustus in amusement as he plopped unceremoniously into the empty seat beside her. Augustus knew before he looked at her that Phoebe was smiling at him. Phoebe smiled at him every day. But today, of course, the tardy would not go unnoticed—or unexploited.

"Don't break your face," said Augustus from inside the SPHIT.

"What happened?" Phoebe asked in a playful tone as

she leaned forward in her seat to catch his attention. "Did someone stay up late playing Stratos?"

Her tight curly brown hair bounced playfully as she talked. Augustus could see her deep brown eyes. They easily caught his attention. He sometimes found himself getting lost inside them. But then her button nose and the playful dimples in her soft brown cheeks broke his gaze.

He caught himself smiling in spite of himself. "No, the damn PT got rerouted through the Kalamazoo city center. I don't know what happened," whispered Augustus. He had to be careful to lower his voice. Phoebe seemed immune to reprimands from the educational AI, but Augustus was on the shit list. He would appeal the tardy later, citing uncontrollable circumstances, but Augustus didn't think it would help his situation very much. Augustus felt he must be triggering some sociological or psychological subroutine that produced behavioral concerns about him in the educational AI. If only he could just figure out what he was doing wrong, he would stop doing it.

Augustus and Phoebe had engaged in many long, circular conversations about matters such as why schools existed in the twenty-third century. Just last week Augustus had complained, "I don't know why we have to be here anyway. Artemis has a Holo-Interface at home, and he does homeschool. He's already signed up for a summer internship with Ceros."

"Yes," Phoebe had said, "but then we wouldn't get to see each other much. I don't ever see Artemis. The last time I spoke to him, he seemed very distracted, like he was too busy to be bothered. I think social interaction is a good thing."

Augustus knew she meant that interaction with him was good for her. He knew Phoebe had romantic designs for the two of them. There were few secrets between him and Phoebe. *To be honest,* he admitted to himself, *I really like Phoebe. We have been friends forever … and she is cute, and she smells nice, and we share a hatred of apricots, and she puts up with me. That should be enough.*

But then there was Julia. Julia sat on the other side of Phoebe. Every time he looked at Phoebe, he saw Julia. She wasn't just cute; she was gorgeous and surprisingly mature for her age. She was probably dating much older boys, Augustus thought. Julia was brilliant and looked bored all the time. She was emotionally distant, the complete opposite of Phoebe. This gave Julia an air of mystery. Usually, Julia took no notice of him, but today Augustus noted that she looked him directly in the eye.

Just my luck—the only attention I get from her is when I make a fool out of myself. Was that a good thing? Why didn't the school teach a subject on teenage girls? *I wouldn't want to be late to that class …*

"Augy, are you listening to me?" said Phoebe urgently.

"Yep … uh … say that again," said Augustus.

"I said there was an explosion at the Second Street PT power transfer hub. PT is calling it a faulty transformer, but there are reports of terrorism. You could have been killed."

"How many people were hurt?" asked Augustus.

"None," said Phoebe.

"Then they weren't very good terrorists," Augustus said, trying to calm her down.

"None that they are reporting," said Phoebe, sounding fully justified in her concern. "Maybe we should walk home tonight." Phoebe looked as if she should have a light bulb above her head as she said this.

"It's a long walk," said Augustus, remembering his early-morning sprint to class.

But Phoebe persisted. "The weather is just right for a walk, and we can stop off at Carlito's on the way and have some ice cream." She said this last part about ice cream in a kind of sweet singsongy way that melted all debate on the subject.

Augustus returned to his studies. Instructive voices that might have been generated from some soft, flying, invisible mouth were heard near his ears. Multiple images, such as, three-dimensional pictures, charts, maps, and written archives were displayed on the SPHIT around him. His responses to each dictated the emergence or disappearance of each. Augustus swatted, poked, and punched his way through the material. Using the SPHIT this way was like using training wheels on a bike. He knew it was a childish way to interact with a machine and longed for the day when he could be enhanced. Then interactions with images, sounds, and sensations would all be internalized in his mind and projected out again through pure thought.

ED Archive HPDC100-1002-2

Humanism: A philosophy that places importance on human interests rather than the supernatural. Humanist beliefs stress human achievement and human values. Following the Great Declaration, Humanism developed into an organized political movement. Humanist ideology emerged from the Great Declaration as the only organized opposing philosophy to the prevailing Forgist religious movement.

Forgism, or the Forge: A religious movement with Christian and Islamic origins. Forgism successfully merged the doctrines of these two ancient religions with a common theology. The name Forge, originating in Denmark as Smedje, came into existence by way of an unlikely source and its namesake, an immigrant metalworking society. This group became politicized over the issue of religion-based persecution. This metalworking society later developed into an organized religious movement. After the Great Declaration, Forgism emerged as the only organized religion on Earth.

The Great Declaration: A cataclysmic series of global pandemics in the early twenty-second century. Though it devastated the global population, it left a disproportionately large human population in North America. The global population was reduced from just over fifteen billion to two hundred million over the course of seven years.

- In comparison, the current global population is estimated at three hundred million, with one hundred million still living on the North American continent. Outside of North America, the remaining global population now consists of the descendants of native survivors of the pandemic and migrants from the North American continent.

- Forgists believe these pandemics were the will of God and named the event God's Great Declaration. As members of the only surviving, significantly organized religion on Earth, Forgists believe that they were chosen by God to bring all people together under a common doctrine.

- Humanist historical accounts indicate that human technology was responsible for saving a significant part of the human population on the North American continent due to several factors, including political and geographical isolation and the relatively advanced state of medical technology in this region, which finally produced a cure.

- During the late twenty-first century, and through the time of the Great Declaration, some of the largest recorded earthquakes in history reshaped the land masses of Central America and parts of North and South America. This had the further effect of isolating the North American population and inflaming Forgist dogma.

Room 401 continued its holo-projected lessons. "Forgist ideology changed dramatically as a result of ..."

"I hate studying history," said Augustus, interrupting the SPHIT. "It's worthless."

"But it's like listening to stories," said Phoebe. "Remember how we used to snuggle together during story time when we were little." She wiggled into her seat and pulled up her legs, demonstrating how to properly conduct a history lesson.

Julia flicked her hair back.

"But it isn't like math or even art," Augustus explained. "In most subjects, you are taught how to reproduce the examples so that you can then create new forms. What you learn from most subjects becomes useful. How are we supposed to create history?"

"Maybe you are just not studying correctly," Phoebe said as she wiggled a little further into her seat and patted the edge in a way that indicated there was room for Augustus.

Isabelle turned in her seat. "You two should get a room."

Several of the other students seemed to agree. Augustus was now conscious that they had been overheard. Hermes and Aries, the twins, had turned in their seats to join the chastisement. Prophetically named, they had become star athletes for the school's soccer team.

Also, Camila and Antonia seemed to be in agreement as they bobbed their heads up and down. "Uh-huh," they said in unison.

Other students who sat farther away, like Tiberius, apparently had not been able to hear the initial conversation but were made curious by the murmuring and insisted on being updated. Like an unstoppable wave, the update went through the seated students. "Isabelle said … about Augustus …"

Seeing that Julia had heard all this, Augustus blushed and then quickly returned to his studies. Time passed slowly for Augustus during history lessons. He couldn't wait to move on to the next subject.

ED Archive HMC104-7203-1

Derivatives of Polynomial Functions: The derivatives of third-order polynomial functions are explored interactively and holographically in the following tutorial.

Room 401 announced, "Please review the first article of file HMC104 …"

At last, Augustus thought, *a subject worthy of my time.*

Many of the studies required pairing together students to complete the various activities. According to the EI, Augustus and Phoebe were paired together 61.25 percent of the time. Even the twins had been matched together only 45.7 percent of the time. Julia was paired with Alexander 25.2 percent of the time. This latest statistic did not go unnoticed by Augustus.

Julia and Augustus had been paired together only one time. This had been rather uneventful, with Julia carrying the assignment to completion without much input from Augustus. Later that day, Augustus had built up the courage to speak to Julia at her locker. The pretext was that he wanted to follow up with her on some point in the assignment. He did this only after lengthy discussions with himself that resulted in an apparent shutdown of several areas of his brain that usually interfered with his ability to walk toward her. His standard leg control caused him to walk around any location that Julia inhabited, subconsciously avoiding contact. His only remaining brain function now, Augustus deduced, was at the very top of his head. He determined this from the lightheadedness in other parts of his brain, indicating localized shutdowns. As he walked toward her, he could feel the heat escaping through the top of his head due to this one remaining area of super activity in his brain. There was so much heat that the top of his head began to sweat.

"Hello," said Augustus, weakly.

She didn't seem to hear him.

"Hello," he repeated, this time in a louder voice that made Julia jerk her head to look.

Her face had been covered by her long, straight brown hair, but suddenly she was staring at him with those stunning gray eyes. She had paler skin than anyone else he had met. She stood out in a crowd, even when wrapped in a heavy robe. In the past, it apparently had been more common for people to have variations in skin tone and hair and eye color, and Julia had inherited this throwback to another era. Augustus had read about how simple differences in skin color had caused a lot of problems in early societies. Today, average people like Augustus had varying degrees of brown skin, dark hair, and brown eyes. The only distinctive feature about Augustus was that his hair was straight, like Julia's. But his hair would stick out in contrast to others only if he let it get too long.

He thought he would like to meet Julia's parents. He wished he could tell what she was thinking and get some insight into her psyche. He could read nothing in her expressions. After the initial surprise at her locker, she had returned to her perfect, beautiful poker face. She waited, apparently expecting more to be said, but Augustus couldn't speak.

After a moment, she prompted him with a questioning greeting. "Hello?"

"Just wanted to say thank you for your help on the last assignment," said Augustus.

"Sure, no problem," said Julia.

Augustus forgot what he had planned to say after hello. He had imagined a much longer conversation, but Augustus's partial brain shutdown had left him with nothing more to say. So he reengaged his standard brain function, which conveyed him quickly away from the area. Then he realized he was going in the wrong direction and turned suddenly.

"Okay ... see you later ... I guess," said Julia behind him as he zigzagged away from her.

After a short period of recovery from his self-imposed lobotomy, Augustus had remembered something from this interaction. Maybe that top part of his brain had blown a fuse, or perhaps he really had caught a glimpse of it as he was fleeing the scene. *Could it have been?* thought Augustus. *A necklace with two crossed hammers hanging in Julia's locker—the sigil of the Forge?*

CM Archive MBFRK687-0806-9

Maintenance bots used in the food service industry became popular before the Great Declaration. These relatively simple bots, controlled by a central AI processor, were found to be much more effective than humans at cleaning restaurants and food manufacturing facilities. These bots were related to the many types of repair bots and the more versatile automatons that could conduct a variety of tasks. But it was the early cleaning bots that achieved a first in human history: mandatory use by businesses of a system based on artificial intelligence. The cleaner bots became an industry standard, and regulations were established for their use. Although this displaced some human workers, it was seen as a food-safety imperative. In the latter twenty-first century, accounts of foodborne illnesses were rampant, and reports of restaurant inspections depicted apparent differences in the look and feel of any restaurant using the new technology. And they were statistically safer for the consumer. Those sites cleaned by humans were reported as distinctively dingy in comparison ...

Carlito's was a small restaurant that served many flavors of ice cream. They also served the best gyros in town, and it was a favorite place to stop for Augustus and Phoebe. Most of Carlito's competitors utilized holographic or automaton interfaces for interaction with the customers. But though many aspects of the business were controlled with automation, the face-to-face interaction with every customer was strictly handled by Carlito or his brother Pepe.

As promised, Augustus walked Phoebe home, ice cream in hand. The weather was good, but even if it hadn't been, it still would have been possible to walk most of the way without being affected by rain or snow. The city provided an extensive system of walkways that could also be used by electric carts or human-powered cycles. Many of these walkways meandered through covered tunnels or utilized overhead solar-glass canopies that could support landscapes and water features, with many types of evergreen and perennials. The solar glass doubled as a lighting source at night. But since the weather was cooperating and the sun was shining, the outdoor pathways were in use.

Many people were wearing various-colored dress robes. Augustus and Phoebe stood out in the antiquated, relatively dull jacket and suit pant style used as the school uniforms. The flowing robes and colors of the city's inhabitants created a beautiful parade among the curving pathways of the gardens through which Phoebe and Augustus walked.

CM Archive HTCD508-0053-4

Many types of human technical skills were lost to the Great Declaration. The textile and retail clothing industry compensated for these shortfalls by promoting those simple styles that could be easily manufactured and had already been adopted by so many around the world. As manufacturing technology recovered, advanced robotics were employed, but the trending style had now become part of the traditional clothing for the newly formed government and society of

North America. The robe had become an acceptable garment for many occasions and now came in a variety of colors and styles. The cassock, abaya, toga, tunic, boubou, and sari, to name a few of these styles, can be worn long or short, with or without pants, depending on the discretion of the wearer. The pellegrina is often added to a cassock uniform to designate a position of leadership within an organization. One significant change to the traditional garments was a deviation from the various types of fasteners that once existed. These were all replaced with a new solid chemical fastener. These fasteners function like a magnetic strip to provide a closure for garments, much like a cross between Velcro and a mechanical zipper. Such fasteners can also mimic snaps if preferred. Hats are optional but also come in a variety of styles. Though outlandish hats are frowned upon, women often have preferred to wear colorfully laced wide-brimmed hats to match their colorful robes for walks on sunny days. This ritual of promenading through the city in impromptu parades has become a favorite pastime. Often, hints of silvery blue material are used to accent enhancement technology commonly embedded in the skin ...

The exposed outdoor pathways were also heavily landscaped, and a little workforce of animals could occasionally be seen, planting or trimming the ornamental shrubs and grass. These animals were actually maintenance bots, disguised as small animals so as not to disrupt the natural setting. These bots used a network of small underground service tubes to prevent trip hazards for the people walking above. If you looked at just the right angle, you could tell the service bots from the native animals by the little bow ties pinned under their chins. The service bots wore the bow ties. Otherwise, it was challenging to tell them apart. Along the walk, Augustus and Phoebe reminisced about how as children they would try to catch the little landscaper bots in action. They would run as fast as they could, chasing squirrels up trees or groundhogs down holes. Neither could be 100 percent certain of what they were chasing, since both animal and bot not only looked alike but also would scurry away from such attention.

"I saw a penguin once," commented Phoebe.

"No, you didn't."

"Yes, I did. It had a little bow tie and waddled."

It might have been possible for a landscape maintenance bot to have been geographically inappropriate, but not a penguin, thought Augustus. That would be silly. And only Phoebe had seen it? She must be joking. It was probably a skunk or just her imagination. Unfortunately, Augustus's brain would now always be on the lookout for penguins wherever he went.

Chapter 2

Jerimiah

The night was cold, and the Pilgrim camp smelled of smoldering fires. Jerimiah was awakened roughly. In the broken darkness of the tent, a man's dark, bearded face loomed over him. His sister Esther was still fast asleep under the blanket next to him. She was a couple years older than Jerimiah but she was still under his protection. Jerimiah began to realize who the man was as the glint of his milky-white eye came into view. If that had not been enough, he now heard his father's familiar voice, telling him, "Put on your boots and follow me ... now."

It was late. There was no sign of the dawn. *This is different*, thought Jerimiah. He had grown accustomed to being awakened at dawn for drills—drills that included long runs, hand-to-hand combat training, and if they happened to be near a particularly cold lake, a swim. The cold plunges were particularly unsettling since one of the boys had drowned recently. This had had no effect on the practice of rousing boys out of bed and throwing them in the freezing water. It seemed that God favored strong swimmers.

A light mist lay across the field of tents. A gathering of Pilgrims was waiting along the roadway with torches in hand. The Pilgrims were made up of other boys Jerimiah's age, some younger men, Guardians, and armed soldiers. Each group was distinguished by the length of their brown and black beards. Jerimiah's face was too young to support a full beard. It was starting to grow, but its meager attempt seemed to inspire needling and ridicule from the more developed men.

The women were waiting back at the tents. If his sister was lucky, she would sleep through whatever this was.

No one spoke. One really did not want to be the first to break the silence, thought Jerimiah. A feeling of anticipation moved through the gathering crowd.

Then the procession began, like an unfolding accordion. The Pilgrims marched quietly along the road away from the camp, into darkness. After what seemed to be about a kilometer or so, Jerimiah heard singing. First, a few voices rose from up ahead, and then the entire procession broke out in song.

> Nearer, my God, to Thee, nearer to Thee!
> Even though it be a cross that raiseth me,
> Still, all my song shall be, nearer, my God, to Thee.

After a time, Jerimiah could hear in the distance the distinctive sound of machine-gun fire. The gunfire was sporadic but growing closer as the procession approached a fiery glow, just visible above the tree line. The smell of smoke wafted through the mist as the marchers continued their unwavering song. This smell was different from the smell at camp, a mix of burned rubber and cooked meat, which spoiled his previously growing appetite.

On the path ahead, he could see an opening to a little village. When Jerimiah arrived, he was stunned by the scene. A series of small homes and barns were engulfed in a raging fire. Bodies had been clumped together in shadowy mounds, their fresh blood glistening in the firelight. Some of the piles were on fire.

"They were people." Jerimiah had been afraid to say it out loud, but it came out anyway.

In the darkness, sporadic gunfire continued. The procession joined together in a circle around a wagon, on top of which stood a man in a white robe. The firelight danced in his eyes, and the Pilgrims fell silent.

"Our holy mission has brought us to this sacred land," began the man in white. "God has declared our right to these lands and resources."

Cheers rang out from the gathering Pilgrims. Many had just arrived on the scene from the long train of robed men and boys.

"These heathens tried to claim what is not theirs. We, the holy warriors, will not fail to make ourselves worthy of the task of cleansing all those who oppose God's will. The heathens may roam these lands, but they are weak, and God's wrath is almighty ..." The man was momentarily interrupted by some sporadic gunfire in the distance. "Many of you have brought your sons along tonight to bear witness to God's glory," he continued. "This journey will be long, and it is good and proper for you to teach the next generation about our holy mission."

Jerimiah felt sick. The man in white was the prophet John Murphy, a descendant of the prophet James Murphy. His voice and appearance were unmistakable and sent shivers of fear through the younger boys. The older boys and men seemed to be more enthusiastic and chanted, "God is great!" They repeated this in unison during deliberately timed pauses in the sermon.

Murphy went on to praise the bravery of the soldiers and chastised "the Humanist cowards that would soon pay for their sins against God."

Finally, the gathering was dismissed with a two-fisted salute intended to mimic two crossed hammers, the sigil of the Forge. The crowd returned the salute, making two fists and crossing their arms across their chests. The battle had been unexpectedly short, and so they began to re-form a line for the journey home.

Jerimiah's father, Colonel Gold, seemed somewhat disappointed. There wasn't any further singing on the way home because everyone was getting tired. Colonel Gold was the commander of the camp and a thirty-plus-year veteran of the pilgrimage. Starting out as a young lieutenant in the African campaign, he had earned his promotions, and the Africa continent had been won. He had been placed in this new position partly due to his age and partly due to an injury he had sustained, which had left him blind in one eye. But the main reason was the unexpected death of his wife, as well as his uncle's family, during an ambush of natives in the Bernina Mountain range. Jerimiah and Esther had been hidden in a small compartment of their vehicle, narrowly saving their lives. This left his two children without any other family members to take care of them.

Jerimiah's father had been resentful of the reassignment and had been looking for opportunities to rejoin the fight. Instead, it was now his reluctant duty as commander to prepare the boys for combat. And at the moment, they did not have the correct resources. The civilian camp was, by design, to follow closely behind the fighting forces. This close proximity to civilians meant that North American drones could not target the military forces without risking civilian casualties. However, it was noted, by way of the camp's gossip network, that Jerimiah's father was a little too eager to move the relatively unarmed camp close to the fighting.

Before the Pilgrims returned to camp, dawn broke over the horizon. Smoke plumes could be seen in the distance. Many in the crowd commented on how beautiful it was and chanted, "God is great."

Jerimiah overheard some of the Guardians discussing whether the villagers had been given a chance to join the Forge. "Cleansing should always be a last resort," said one. Others agreed but were quickly hushed, since they noticed they were being overheard by some of the boys.

Jeremiah's father grasped his shoulder firmly as they walked and said, "God has provided us with a new cache of weapons. Soon you will learn how to use those weapons. Get some sleep. I expect you up before noon."

Esther awoke, rubbing her eyes, as Jerimiah collapsed onto the blanket beside her. "Great," she said. "I guess I get all the chores this morning."

Chapter 3

Law Man

The local sheriff was technically a Yankee, but he was related to the Hull family by marriage to Randel's mother's cousin. He had made his excuses for the boys' behavior for years. But the sheriff had grown concerned after the church fire, insisting the brothers perform community service and help rebuild the church. Now he was dealing with a mounting list of missing people and animals in the area. It was his duty to try to do something about it.

He walked somberly to a locked cabinet in his office at the base of the mountain range. Inside the locker was a bulletproof vest, which he quickly strapped to himself. The next item in the cabinet was a wooden box, which he opened carefully. The Colt .357 Magnum glistened in contrast to the dark interior of the cabinet. He removed the revolver and held it for a moment, remembering its weight, remembering what it was to shoot, remembering the sticky legal issues surrounding the weapon. He loaded it carefully and tucked it into the hanging docker's clutch next to where the vest had been. He heard his deputy, Martin, bringing up his horse outside the office. He took a quick swig of courage from a bottle he stored in his desk as he looked at the open cabinet that still contained the hanging gun. For a moment he considered going with just the stun gun he always carried on his hip. But this situation could be serious. So he strapped on the Colt revolver and covered everything in a long, dark brown pellegrina with simple khaki lines embroidered around the edges. A star had been sewn over the heart. Like a poncho but better tailored, it indicated his ranking authority as sheriff. He topped himself off with a Stetson, mounted his horse, and began his long ride up the mountain to the Hulls' ranch home.

He planned to ask Bobby Senior about questioning Randel and Bobby Junior in regard to recent allegations. He had been wondering what to say to Bobby Senior. Upon reaching the ancestral home, he gently guided his horse up to the porch. When he arrived at the front door, he could see through the screen that something was wrong. Mrs. Hull was cradling Bobby Senior on the floor in a pool of warm blood. She was in shock, staring down at the bloody corpse in her arms, still reeking of alcohol. Seeing the sheriff walk in, she began to cry, not for her husband, but for her son.

The sheriff began to send out messages through his communication enhancement. The signals from his mind were interpreted and transmitted by the silvery blue antennae running through his skin. The signal was then amplified and relayed to the Carolina Provence security service via a mobile transmitter carried by his horse. This was at first completed in silence so as not to disturb Mrs. Hull. But then he had become frustrated and his voice began to inadvertently announce the messages he was sending, "No, you don't understand. I need security agents, plural, with an *s* at the end. Not just one agent."

"Why is that, sir?" The reply came through the enhanced communication being downloaded silently into his mind.

He replied more quietly this time, conscious of his previous outburst. He turned away from Mrs. Hull as she began a new round of weeping. "Well, it's a big mountain, and this boy knows the land. He's armed and dangerous. I got other people I need to protect and only one deputy. Your agent's goin' to get himself killed trying to handle it by himself."

"The responding agent is more than capable of handling the situation you are describing. He should be overhead now."

"He's where?"

Just then, the sheriff noticed a humming sound over the hills. It was getting closer. The security transport that had been sent from Knoxville to handle the situation at the Hull ranch came into view. The sheriff's horse, tied to the porch outside, was disturbed by the sudden wind and noise as the security transport hovered overhead by its four rotors. The sheriff left the house and the weeping, bloodstained Mrs. Hull to meet the flying machine and calm his horse. He tried to guess where the security agent would choose to land. Instead, a man was lowered from the transport on a long wire. He landed firmly on both feet, disconnected the cable, and walked the short distance toward the surprised sheriff. The transport began to lift higher and soon was out of sight.

"Howdy, Sheriff," said the man through a speaker in his helmet. The helmet had a face shield that prevented the sheriff from seeing his face. "Please give me as much detail as you can about these events. Start with a list of witnesses or acquaintances and where I might find them. I already have the missing-person report. Also, you will please relinquish your firearm. Lethal force has not been authorized for this operation."

The sheriff reluctantly gave up his revolver and began recalling what he knew about the ongoing developments. The man listened and at the same time removed the bullets from the sheriff's weapon. He then returned the gun back to the sheriff, unloaded. The sheriff just shook his head and holstered the revolver.

After the sheriff finished, the man went inside to talk to Mrs. Hull. This annoyed the sheriff because he could see that Mrs. Hull was getting tired after the trauma. She had just told the same story to the sheriff, who had just relayed this information to the man.

A still sniffling, blood-soaked Mrs. Hull restated the events. "They left together, but Randel came home by himself and killed his pa with a knife. Just walked up to him and stabbed him. He didn't say nothin' at first. Then he talked like he wasn't himself. He said, 'Randel, the last remaining heir, has come home to take his rightful place as king of the mountain.' I don't know where Bobby Junior is."

After the second interview, the man in the helmet said thank you and made several observations around the body. He then stood in the living area while men from a local hospital arrived in another flying transport. They were allowed to remove the body from the home, and soon they were soaring along the mountain range out of sight.

"Well?" said the sheriff.

"How can I help you, Sheriff?"

"Aren't you goin' to go after him?"

"I will stay here in case he returns. Rest assured, Randel Hull will be found."

"How are you goin' to do that standing here?"

"I can wait outside if you like."

Before the sheriff could answer, he began to get reports through his enhanced communications.

"There's a flyin' machine droppin' uniformed men in helmets all over the place …"

"This guy's askin' questions 'bout Randel and Bobby Hull …"

"Sheriff, there is a strange gentleman at my door asking about Marigold, my lost cat. Do you know anything about that?"

The sheriff confronted the man standing in the Hull living room again. "I thought you were alone? Now it sounds like you got a whole team out there."

"There is only one human operator. Technically, you are correct in both statements."

The sheriff was about to say something in response, but the man continued before he could.

"Sheriff."

"Yes."

"Several people and animals from your missing-persons reports have been located. You may wish to inform Mary Hull that her son, Robert Elis Hull, is dead. You may also wish to inform Andrew Vance that his son, Tobias Vance, is dead. You may also wish to inform James Anders that his daughter, Nancy Elisa Anders, is dead. You also may wish to inform Elouise Osborn that Marigold is dead …"

The list continued. The sheriff began to cross the names off the list in his notebook.

"Sheriff."

"Now what?"

"Randel Hull is now in custody. We will be taking him back to Knoxville for processing."

"Just like that? Don't I get to process him first?"

"All information will be shared with your office. And if you wish, we can connect you virtually or transport you to Knoxville for any further questioning. Please call if you want to conduct further investigations into other crimes he may have committed in your area. He will, however, need to be tried in the provincial court for his current crimes."

With that the man, or automaton—the sheriff was never sure which—walked out of the house and off the porch and was then pulled straight up into the air by the newly arriving security transport. The sun began to set as the sheriff and Mrs. Hull stood on the porch and watched the transport shrink into the distance.

Chapter 4

Enhancement

Augustus's father was not in the pictures that adorned their house. Augustus's mother Martina Mendelson, had wanted to have children, but Augustus's other mother Cecilia, had not been keen to go through with the process of childbirth, preferring instead to adopt her partner's child. So Augustus's mother Martina had been artificially inseminated.

The two women had had a rocky relationship over the years, and Cecilia was no longer living with them. She could, if needed, make herself available, but it was more common for Augustus to hang out at Phoebe's house, a few blocks away, anytime his mother was working late. Augustus had often thought about trying to track down his biological father, but this would be impossible without the man's authorization. Only medical and country-of-origin information would ever be available.

Mrs. Tuttle opened the door for Augustus and Phoebe as they popped the last nibbles of their ice cream cones into their mouths. They trotted inside, and Mrs. Tuttle greeted them with a smile. She displayed the common silvery blue enhancement technology subcutaneously embedded in various parts of her face, forehead, and arms. Although all enhancement tech was unique to the owner, Mrs. Tuttle had distinctive chin and eyebrow implants that moved along with her face in a way that somehow exaggerated her expressions. Her smooth, tan skin was otherwise uninterrupted. Augustus had always thought that she was very beautiful, and her smile always seemed sincere. Mrs. Tuttle was like a second, or third, mother to Augustus.

"Hello," said Augustus and Phoebe in unison as they immediately zipped upstairs to Phoebe's room.

The house smelled wonderful. It always did, but tonight, Mrs. Tuttle was obviously preparing her famous Italian burritos. The garlic, onion, and spices filled the home to a point that could cause your eyes to water if you went too close to the kitchen. Cooking was a duty that Mr. and Mrs. Tuttle shared joyfully. They took turns coming home early from work to meet the kids after school and prepare dinner, so that they could enjoy a family meal together. Augustus was always welcome. Sometimes Phoebe's sister and her friends would participate. Other times, some of the neighbors, whom Augustus had assumed were relatives, would join, and the house would begin to rumble with opening doors, footsteps, conversation, and music.

Today Mr. Tuttle was still at work. The Tuttles ran a small family business that made, among other things, PT components. After the so-called terrorist action earlier in the day, Phoebe had been quick to point out that they had not manufactured the transformers. She had said this as if being the maker of a component attacked by terrorists somehow would have implicated them in negligent activity, rather than implying that the incident might have been due to defective workmanship.

Mrs. Tuttle called after them. "Will you be staying for dinner, Augy? I hope you haven't spoiled your appetites."

CV Archive ETC92-0251-1

Human enhancement technology: Eighteen years is a milestone in North American society, the age of consent at which many kinds of enhancements become available. By age twenty-one most people have undergone the most significant modifications. The visible portions of human enhancement form sharp angular shapes made up of sets of silvery blue parallel lines, one to two millimeters in width. These subcutaneous antennae and sensor arrays extend along either side of the body, from the face and down the neck, torso, and limbs. The antennae and sensor arrays must be connected to external devices that support the technology. These devices are networked, but connectivity is strictly controlled by the North American Confederation. All enhancements are voluntary, but it is difficult to participate in certain occupations or access specific technologies without the characteristic silvery blue lines ornamenting the skin and propelling the owner into the next phase in human evolution. **Human communication enhancement** creates a direct interface with technology and new communication pathways with other humans. The interface signal is broadcast from local wireless relays. These signals can be received directly inside the human brain, via stimulation of a variety of synaptic pathways. This technology is a developmental progression from earlier nerve-stimulation technology, such as cochlear implants and sight-restoration technology of the twenty-first century. The latest technology stimulates synaptic pathways in the thalamus and cortex for extrasensory information transmission and reception.

One type of transmitted synaptic stimulation communicates simple messages. These are downloaded directly into the human brain, altogether bypassing the experience of sensation. This provides silent, efficient messaging between computers and enhanced humans.

Another common type of transmitted synaptic stimulation utilizes visual and auditory receptors to reproduce images or sounds in the user's mind. Utilization of the natural receptor pathways does not override or inhibit existing sensory inputs. Users may distinguish these transmitted signals from natural experiences by the inherent hollowness of sound or the slight yellow shift of the images. Tactile messaging has an electrical feel. Olfactory and taste messaging have a metallic tone and are therefore not very popular.

Each form of enhanced communication has limited bandwidth and may require the supplemental use of more traditional types of visual and auditory communications from physical displays and speakers. These physical interfaces, or hard interfaces, enable users to process extra information that would otherwise be limited by user tolerance to direct synaptic stimulus. To provide a more consistent transmission process, to and from the synapse, an antenna array is subcutaneously embedded in the skin. This provides a relay for internal and external transmissions.

All synaptic stimulation is voluntary, for both receiving and transmitting signals. Any signals that have not yet been received are stored in a central database, which provides an alert before the final relay unless an open channel has been established beforehand. For minors or those choosing not to be enhanced, hard interfaces of various types may be used.

Human medical enhancement provides real-time, comprehensive medical scanning capability. This technology is used for diagnostic purposes, as well as to direct repair of physical damage and biochemical imbalances, through nanotechnology circulating throughout the body. When combined with this technology, the human body is capable of miraculous feats of strength and speed. Vision and hearing are also improved, and the average life span is extended significantly. Due to enhancement technology installed in most people over the age of twenty-one, only significant injuries may overwhelm the repair functions. Incidents requiring more traditional medical attention are infrequent. Medical enhancement tech will also limit the effects of most drugs on the body. All forms of drug and alcohol are legal for use by anyone with enhancement technology.

Medical enhancement has evolved from early techniques involving stem cells. Natural stem cells are capable of changing into many types of cells in the body. The current technology utilizes reproduction of standardized cloned stem cells, capable of being used generically in animals or humans.

Genetic material from the host is introduced to the cloned stem cells before the stem cells' introduction into a host, to prevent rejection by the host's immune system. During the cloning process, synthetic electromagnetic-sensitive proteins are embedded in the stem cell, allowing for external control. Scans of the host can then be used to direct the activation or deactivation of enzymes, which in turn direct responses to specific abnormalities in the body.

Originally, scanning hardware used to control the cloned stem cell nanotechnology was external to the host's body. However, as scanning technology developed, it was recognized that the scanning hardware was more effective once it was able to be embedded as a series of internal sensors in the skin. The customizable, subcutaneous sensor and transmission array allowed for more consistent application of the nanotechnology.

Tissue regeneration may serve to nurture a fetus in the womb of a pregnant woman. However, internal genetic scanning may also direct immune responses that attack embryonic cells if they include deleterious genetic material. This has led to an elimination of genetic diseases in the children of enhanced humans. And a more recent development in the medical technology employs the building of super tissues to replace the natural varieties in the body. Overall, remarkable improvements in the human body have been achieved ...

It was expected that Mr. and Mrs. Tuttle conversed silently through a particular form of communication enhancement technology. This type of enhancement was specific for two-way continuous streaming of transmissions between spouses.

It took the form of subcutaneous silvery blue lines around their ring fingers. The antenna array of the enhancement tech could cover many areas of the body, but the use of the ring finger was deliberately reserved for marriage enhancement. Once, Phoebe's sister had suggested that Phoebe and Augustus should be enhanced in this way, as soon as they were old enough for the procedures. Phoebe had smiled at Augustus afterward.

Augustus had always felt comfortable in Phoebe's room. It was a little girly, but to him it felt like a place free from judgments. It was refreshing to sit and relax after a day under constant surveillance by the educational AI. Once they were safely inside Phoebe's room, the two sat on oversized cushions pushed into the corner of the walls and floor. As usual when Augustus came over, the plan was to complete some homework before he returned to his own home. This plan would traditionally fail, and they would end up debating something entirely off-topic or firing up a game of Stratos. Augustus wondered what would happen if instead he visited Julia's house after school. *We would probably end up doing homework,* thought Augustus.

"Augggyyyyyyyy!" The shout came from Phoebe's doorway. In a flash, Phoebe's sister Arria came bounding into the room and performed a cannonball. Though this maneuver was typically reserved for entering swimming pools, now the hurtling cannonball-shaped child splashed the cushions, scattering them along with Augustus and Phoebe. Arria hugged Augustus tightly before he could react, creating an awkward position in which his arms were trapped and his head was forced into her hair, itching his nose.

He noted that Phoebe and Arria used the same shampoo. Arria smelled and looked so much like Phoebe had when she was younger. This brought back memories of the "fluffy bumps," as Phoebe still loved to call it. Augustus's and Phoebe's favorite amusement park included a kiddie play area called Huffalumps. Superficially, it was a large, soft, fuzzy carpet. But once a play session started, small hills and valleys were generated through the use of expanding and contracting air bladders underneath the soft cover, pushing and rolling the children around and up and over one another. The children often collided with one another, and this naturally would have resulted in severe injury if not for the quirky animal-themed suits that they were first stuffed into as protection.

Of course, after young Augustus and Phoebe returned home, the fluffy bumps had had to be recreated through the use of pillows and blankets gathered from around the house. The children had to imagine the effect of the air bladder contraption, but they painted their faces with whiskers to mimic the suits. They used to roll around and giggle on top of the cushions and each other. They had on occasion cracked skulls, but with some practice, an injury could be avoided, and exhaustion would soon degenerate into their lounging next to one another, breathless and finally motionless as the imagined ride hissed to a conclusion.

Augustus could never be annoyed by Arria, not for long anyway. As a budding superhero, Arria wore a shimmering blue cape whenever possible. Her parents had to convince her that her superhero persona would be compromised if the general public found out who she was. Therefore, she had to take off the cape and pretend to be an ordinary person around other people. Augustus was an exception. He knew her superhero identity: Amazing Arria, or Mazy for short. Arria further embellished her amazingness and insisted on being known as Mazy Danger Tuttle. Mazy looked forward to the day she could be enhanced. She had seen the effects of enhancements on people. As she saw it, people got to be superheroes after they were enhanced, and she wanted to practice being a superhero now because she was definitely going to be a superhero when she grew up.

Room 401's homework assignment was to develop a three-dimensional representation of the geopolitical shifts between the twenty-first and twenty-second centuries. The students were to use standard homework tablets to write the initial code. This would later be loaded into the school's SPHIT for further refinements. The tablets at first glance were just flat squares. They controlled a small holographic projection, but much of the work was completed two-dimensionally. This compact interface did not allow for the same human interface that SPHIT provided, with access to the school's network. SPHITs were a customizable, physical interface that allowed one to actually grab or touch the virtual images that were being projected. Image control was supplemented by the educational AI, which meant it understood what you wanted and did a lot of things to assist. Once a user was enhanced, the interface between the technologies would become seamless.

"I can't believe they want us to work with this crap," said Augustus with renewed interest in the homework assignment. "These tablets use subroutines that are based on binary code running on a simple molecular matrix."

"Public schools just aren't what they used to be," chimed Mazy.

"No, just the opposite, Mazy. They aren't letting us work with the latest technology. I can't tell if this is even going to work until we get back to school and access a SPHIT. You know Artemis ..."

"Artemis has a SPHIT," said Phoebe and Mazy together, laughing.

"Okay, I guess I made that point before," conceded Augustus. "But the school operates on modern processors that allow for base 10 coding on a subatomic matrix. Why are we even messing with this antiquated garbage?"

Phoebe put her hand on his knee and answered cutely but gently, "Because the holo-interfaces are expensive. There not just projectors, you know? You have to have an AI or borrow time from one, and the registrations are difficult to get."

"How do you know all this?"

"My dad has one at work. I asked him about it."

Augustus had still been spending time with Artemis when his family received their first SPHIT. Artemis's father was the governor of the Great Lakes Province. This allowed Artemis's family to utilize the government-controlled technology in their home. The boys were instantly hooked and spent many hours "researching," as they called it. Augustus's best subject in school became programming. Artemis's family saw no need to take the risk of sending Artemis to school when his studies could be completed at home.

The boys still stayed in touch. Augustus liked to use the school's SPHIT to contact Artemis, but there were limits placed on the use of the networking technology connecting the holo-interfaces. It was not to be used for non-government-sanctioned activity. Interactive educational assignments were allowed, however. So Artemis and Augustus would pair up whenever possible. Lately, though, Artemis seemed to be getting too far ahead of Augustus for most assignments. On occasion, Artemis still relied on Augustus for insights into certain aspects of programming, especially those that required higher-level mathematics. Augustus, above all, liked math. These brief interactions with Artemis and Augustus's contacts with the Ceros Company allowed him to keep up with some cutting-edge technologies.

ED Archive HMGV-5002-2

Comparisons of Pre-Declaration and Post-Declaration North American Government Structures: The merger between the Canadian, Mexican, and US governments retained the three-branched structure common to each country's government: legislative, judicial, and executive. However, federal bureaucracy was nonexistent after the Great Declaration. Instead, following the devastating population decreases and the loss of most elected officials on both sides of each border, a new executive structure—a confederation—was formed out of the fourteen newly created provincial governments to govern all of North America. Although hastily constructed, these local governments successfully maintained essential services in the aftermath of the Great Declaration, at least within the major cities. The executive-branch leadership of the newly formed North American government now includes the governors of each province as representatives to the Executive Council. This council features one of the governors as an appointed chairman. Reporting to the Executive Council are several councils made up of subject-matter experts in various fields, including technology, education, security, agriculture, health, and commerce, each with its own appointed chairperson. The technology council, known as the Confederate Technology Council, or CTC, is dedicated to the development and regulations of new technologies ...

Chapter 5

Pilgrims

Instead of the anticipated weapons training, the Pilgrims broke camp and moved south, all before noon. The Pilgrims kept their heads down to avoid the direct light of the sun. With the exception of the Swiss campaign, they had quickly overwhelmed all opposition, although the German campaign was running into some surprising resistance. It was the first time that the Pilgrims had encountered an organized fighting force with weapons that matched their own capabilities. The Pilgrims were revitalizing the factories of old France, but the opposition forces had begun rebuilding as well. The next target for the Pilgrims was the heavily fortified city of Berlin. Hamburg had just fallen to the Pilgrims, which shifted the front line. The front line now consisted of the three city-states of Berlin, Dresden, and Prague.

The sun continued to be bright that day, clearly defining the distant smoke plumes behind them. With their packs loaded, Jerimiah took his sister's hand to help her over a ridge made of dirt and twisted, rusted-out automobiles.

The overgrowth had interlocked and buried the old pile of cars. Usually, the Pilgrims' path would have been cleared by bulldozers, but their camp was out of position. The only significant path cut through the road today was just wide enough for the vehicles, horse-drawn carts, and wagons. These were used to carry supplies, the sick, and the wounded. The people on foot could not wait for the long procession to clear the narrow passages and made the best use of their time by crawling over or around the blockages, utilizing the smaller pathways that could not support vehicles. From above, they looked like a swarm of ants. Neither Jerimiah nor Esther could read the old traffic signs that littered the roadway, so they had to follow the leader, their father, to get them where they were going. Esther and Jerimiah were old enough to remember better days of the Great Pilgrimage. They had started out long ago in enormous transports.

"Could really use the old Peace Maker about now," said Jerimiah. "It was so big, it wouldn't even notice this terrain."

"Of course, everything was bigger then," said Esther.

"Mother was with us then. God, she could cook. And she always had a calming effect on Father when he was around," said Jerimiah.

Jerimiah and Esther had been born in Spain while their father was away in Africa. Once he returned to the European campaign, and once the children were more capable of traveling, they had begun to follow the fighting Pilgrim units. Back then, a single transport housed each family of ten or fewer, and each family gave their transport a name. Their mother had named theirs Peace Maker. As resources began to run low, the transports had been given to the soldiers for military use. Occasionally, they saw these old transports roll by, and the two siblings would try to read the names as they rumbled along. One time Esther thought she saw old Peace Maker and jumped up on a rock at the side of the road. This ended badly because she had hiked up her robe to climb onto the rocks and in doing so had failed to provide for appropriate modesty. She was dragged down and spanked, which, ironically, proved to be more revealing than the rock climb as she kicked and struggled to evade the punishment.

ED Archive HPDC100-4010-9

Brigades of Pilgrim soldiers are followed by large groups of families that function to support the brigades but also to shield organized troop movements from attack by North American drones. Each camp contains around five thousand members, mostly composed of women and children. The current leader of the Forgist movement is the prophet John Murphy, a descendant of James Murphy, who was exiled for inciting terrorist activities after the Great Declaration. John Murphy operates as a supreme general for the European front.

Opposition forces are made up of a handful of native peoples who survived the Great Declaration, along with groups of North American Humanist pioneers who set out to colonize the newly deserted areas. Although some cities and factories have been rebuilt, both sides are dedicating much of their resources to military hardware production. Opposition populations are organized into several city-states. Many are built with large underground structures, to protect from Forgist attacks and to conceal the opposition forces' stockpiles of armaments from North American surveillance. Any detectable military weaponry is vulnerable to attack from the same North American drones.

In spite of the dedication to the suppression of armaments by North American military drones, the Forgist armies have assembled many forms of concealable mobile weapons. The Forgist military remains technologically superior to most opposition forces. Forgist and opposition forces may also maintain a limited hidden nuclear capability ...

Jerimiah had just helped his sister down from the latest obstruction when he tripped over an old tire. The fall was not serious, but he suddenly realized his hand was bleeding. He had tried to catch himself on the nearest object he could grasp. This turned out to be a piece of glass attached to an old window frame. It was not a small cut that could be ignored, more of a puncture. Esther flagged down a medical transport that was passing their position. They both were able to board while the medic prepared Jerimiah's hand for stitches. The medical transport continued down the narrow road. As Esther looked on in concern at her brother's injury, Jerimiah said to her quietly, "A least we get to ride again; it's better than walking."

Once the wound had been washed, the medic began to sew the skin back together. The damaged, bleeding white and red tissues underneath the skin of his palm were threatening to escape the wound. The medic resealed it, much the same way Esther darned their clothes. But this was different somehow; Esther couldn't stop watching, even though it began to make her sick. She stood suddenly and made a break for the back door of the transport. She had it partially open before she started to throw up. Feeling faint, she almost toppled out the back as the medical transport bounced down the narrow road. She squatted with her head between her knees and tried to wash the vomit out of her mouth with a bottle of water, spitting the water out the back of the transport. The truck following them backed off slightly, and she waved at the driver just to let him know she wasn't going to fall out.

Jerimiah said mockingly, "So much for your medical career." Esther had always talked about becoming a medic, which seemed a worthy occupation and an excellent way to contribute to the mission. Mother had also worked as a medic, and she would be following in her footsteps.

Jerimiah and Esther had quickly been excused from the medical transport and were now exhausted and sweating. They arrived at their new campsite as the sun began to set low over the large open field. A pack of dogs was still challenging some of the newly arrived campers. Rolling hills in the distance were just about to cast the last shadows of the day upon the Pilgrims. Between the round hills, the sun became an eye closing for sleep. Slowly at first, then unmistakably, the next issue of their journey overwhelmed them all.

The Pilgrims had not been the first to use this area. The

condition of the proposed campground was unbearable. Women huddled into small groups, with arms occasionally flailing overhead in a heated discussion. To Jerimiah, they resembled sea urchins as they pointed with their black-robed arms in all directions at once and the shadows made by the sleepy sun multiplied their spiky exterior. Men were dispatched to address the disturbances. Each man seemed to be swallowed whole by the urchin mobs, as the small groups surrounded the outnumbered men.

A smell penetrated the eyes and nose, like a sewer had opened up and spewed its corrupted contents onto what otherwise could have been a picturesque landscape. A sewer was just what had been needed by the previous occupants of the land. Instead, human feces and urine had been left to stew in the trampled grass. What food hadn't been consumed had been dumped in small piles as well, confusing latrines and garbage dumps and making it impossible to set up tents or organize the cook wagons.

A vast army had bivouacked here, not long ago from the looks of things. They had been wasteful, leaving more food than they should have. The packs of wild dogs had followed behind, taking advantage of the leftovers. During the days of the Great Declaration, it was the dogs, being more comfortable around human populations, that had picked at the bodies of the dead before they could be buried or burned. These new breeds were less domesticated, having taken back many of the traits of their ancestors, the wolves. They did not make good pets, and with no extra food to spare, no one encouraged them intentionally.

Usually, the bands of Pilgrims were very orderly and efficient. Care was taken not to contaminate living and eating areas, through use of a standard camp configuration. This allowed one band of Pilgrims to follow another without incident. They strictly adhered to camp discipline, establishing separate areas for washing, eating, and worship. The organization was drilled into them from an early age to help support each camp, which could consist of over five thousand people. Some soldiers provided security for the civilians, but the majority of the soldiers were moving across the countryside, engaging any native villages as they found them.

It might have been preferable to use some of the old buildings in the area to at least get out of the elements. But over the years of the campaign, they had learned that using such buildings for more than firewood might be more trouble than it was worth. Unmaintained buildings could be hazardous. Pilgrims had fallen through floors or had been crushed by collapsing roofs. Buildings that were structurally intact were confiscated by the military commanders on both sides. So a simple support camp of Pilgrims would not be allowed in, or they could be ambushed by opposition forces if they chose the wrong building. With limited security forces attached to the camps, this could end badly. But the main reason to stay away from old buildings was that many were haunted. This was an issue that most Pilgrims were not willing to challenge.

Who are we following? wondered Jerimiah. *The people who camped here could not have been of the Forge.* Equipment also had been left behind, another unforgivable sin. Jerimiah remembered how he had been beaten after his cup had fallen out of his pack during a march. A Guardian, following from behind, had noted the transgression. Quickly, a punishment had been exacted using the nearest available stick.

Esther was now holding the sleeve of her robe over her face and crying into it. But Jerimiah, who was among the many boys who had been deprived of sleep, collapsed on the ground in apathetic exhaustion. He then began to realize that he had fallen onto a small miracle. He quickly signaled his sister to start laying out the tent. Esther realized what he had found almost immediately and began to unpack, looking around to see if anyone else might notice. Once the task had been completed, Jerimiah fell asleep instantly, only to be awakened in the middle of the night by a nightmare in which he had been strangling his father. In his dream, while Jerimiah still had his hands around the man's neck, his father had somehow caught on fire and exploded suddenly.

Though they awoke very hungry the next morning, Jerimiah and Esther had slept better than most. The temperature, at least, had gone down from the previous day, and due to the small miracle, they had claimed a spot in the field that looked as if it had supported a large crate. Coincidentally, it had been about the size of their tent. This had protected the ground below their shelter from the filth of the previous campers. There was, however, no escape from the air. The morning light revealed the Pilgrims' plight. Jerimiah had never seen their camp in such disarray. Each Pilgrim family had staked claim to whatever random area was least affected by the grounds' forebearers.

"A pig sty would have been preferable to this camp. Wonderful animals, pigs," said Jerimiah as he contemplated where breakfast might be found. Esther was looking for the cook wagons also. Then the wind shifted, and the smell of freshly baked bread came wafting over a low hill nearby. The bakers had been up before dawn, getting ready for the morning meals. The two siblings quickly found one of the cook wagons. Because it had been near the rear of the previous day's caravan, the bakers had decided to simply stay on the road, just over the hill from where Jerimiah and Esther had slept.

Jerimiah loved the bakers. They always seemed cheerful, and they took the time to acknowledge their customers with smiles and conversation as they moved ingredients and the unbaked and baked bread to and from the different stations on the wagons. Although the bakery was generally open on two ends, these openings were dedicated to moving ingredients on one side and bread out the other. It was possible to see the bakers in action only through a large glass window that overlooked the interior of the little operation from the middle of the wagon. As younger children, Esther and Jerimiah had pushed their noses up against the glass. The bakers had responded by throwing dough at them. The dough had landed harmlessly against the inside of the window, but the suddenness had made them jump back. They were always surprised, and then they giggled afterward.

If he had a choice, Jerimiah would choose to be a baker. His father, however, would never approve. His father had once told him he had high hopes for his son to become a great military commander. But all his father's dreams had diminished after the death of Jerimiah's mother. He now comforted himself over his lost aspirations only by stealing sips out of the small flask that he carried wherever he went.

Chapter 6

The Assignment

In spite of the statistical improbability, Augustus and Julia had been paired together to complete the next phase of the assignment. Augustus had already programmed a beautiful three-dimensional model of the Earth. Time was expressed as cool blue waves washing over the continents, revealing the geopolitical changes, expressed as flags or sigils, for each of the native peoples. The population density was expressed as varying intensities of color.

ED Archive HPDC100-4003-8

As has been previously discussed, pre-Declaration Forgism originated in a region predominated by Christian and Muslim peoples. One of the first tenets of the Forge was that any true religion, ordained by God, should never lead people to look down upon or disrespect others out of a belief in their own superiority and must promote not just tolerance but justice for all. It was reasoned that if the purpose of this life was to prove worthiness for entry into the greater society, existing as heaven or paradise, then this should be achieved by demonstrating the ability to work together to improve the human conditions on Earth—and not just with acts of charity, but to provide a meaningful coexistence with all people. Many faiths, but most significantly the Christian and Islamic faiths, had been found wanting in this regard. An acceptance emerged that neither religion, despite having essential aspects, was worthy on the whole. It was reasoned that at some point in history, people must have subverted God's teachings to their own ends, and that this was the source of the conflicts that were then raging across the land.

Through much deliberation around the early hearths of the metalworking society, it was decided that biblical sticking points, such as the reference to salvation as coming through God who "became flesh," could be viewed in a way that applied to both Mohammed and Jesus Christ as prophets. This perspective accepted that God's salvation, not God Himself, became flesh. A prophet might lead his followers to salvation through God and, being God's messenger, could possibly be conceived through divine methods without necessarily being a god. For example, Adam and Eve were not considered gods but were created by God. Aligning the Forge with the Islamic tenet of a singular God, the new religion removed the awkward convention of the Trinity as taught in the Christian religion, making it possible for both faiths to be partially correct in their teachings. Once a common theological foundation was established and other passages of the Bible and the Quran were aligned, an effective merging of the two faiths was achieved.

The Forge also deemphasized the concept of personal benefits attained from service to God. Heaven was no longer an individual reward, and prayers for relief of personal hardships were deemed irrelevant. A broader worldview now included a dedication to God's teachings through works of public service. Forgist efforts focused on the creation of a great society through an understanding of science.

This was, for some time, considered heretical by both religions, and the Forge was attacked by members of both faiths. However, given that Muslims and Christians were also fighting each other, this battle proved ineffective in stopping the growth of the Forgist movement. The Forge had the benefit of inclusiveness of both faiths during a time in which mass migrations of Muslim people were creating disruption in traditionally Christian societies. With peaceful political solutions in short supply, the Forge was considered a necessary political compromise, was recognized as a legitimate religion by many countries, and was included as required teaching in public schools.

Later, however, the original tenets were lost to modern-day followers, and a new holy war began. The Great Declaration provided justification for Forgist radicals' belief that God had chosen them to rule the Earth. Radical Forgists, led by the prophet James Murphy, were frequently jailed for terrorist acts against the newly formed government of North America. Many were exiled, including Murphy, after the Great Declaration. The exiles, or Pilgrims as they call themselves, organized a new movement and have since assembled nearly one hundred million followers to retake the lands of Europe,

Asia, and Africa, which were otherwise almost entirely unpopulated following the pandemics.

For once, Augustus could read Julia's face. Julia was unimpressed.

In spite of his earlier complaints about the lack of appropriate resources, Augustus had been quite proud of his work and now wondered if Julia was playing with him. "Well?" asked Augustus.

"Superficially, it's quite nice," said Julia, failing to sound encouraging.

"Uh … yeah. I would have used your version, but it didn't make sense?" Augustus ended his response in a higher-pitched voice, turning it into a question rather than a statement of fact. He was trying not to sound too demeaning.

"Look here." Julia was undeterred and pointed to the North American continent. "Your estimate of the Forgist population is all wrong, and this seems to indicate the Humanist political movement originated from pre-Forgist capitalist culture."

"Uh …" Augustus was aghast. "The data was taken directly from the archive. What are you talking about?"

"You mean you took the data listed as having the highest probability of historical accuracy according to the school's educational AI, and you didn't bother to do any other research on the subject," said Julia. In a calm, slightly condescending tone, she continued, "I'm talking about the Forgist population on the North American continent, which was nearly 90 percent of the total population at the time of the Great Declaration.

The Forgist population wasn't reduced independently of the rest of the North American population. It was reduced in proportion to the rest of the population. There are quite a few more Forgists in North America now than this model would indicate. And the Humanist movement emerged from the Great Declaration as an offshoot of Forgist ideology, not as a precursor."

"Where are you getting your information?" asked Augustus. "Humanist ideology goes back way before Forgism, no matter what historical archive you use."

"But the modern political movement doesn't go back that far," she insisted. "It came after the Great Declaration. The Forge was split into three philosophically distinctive groups: Humanists, traditional Forgists, and radical Forgists."

Now it was Augustus's turn to look unimpressed. "Again, where are you getting your information?"

"Well, if you would really like to know, we could go together … just you and me, though. Tomorrow perhaps?" asked Julia, smiling.

"Are you asking me on a date?" Augustus was befuddled. He looked around, wondering how he had missed the two of them arriving at this turn in the conversation. Maybe she had been talking to someone else the whole time. *No, don't see anyone else around*, thought Augustus. The only others nearby were Phoebe and Aries off in the distance, staring disappointedly at a pear-shaped Earth hologram. *What the …?*

***

That evening the Capital County 400-level soccer team was playing its Upper Peninsula rivals. Augustus had promised Phoebe they would go together. Now Augustus was feeling uncomfortable as his date with Julia had been set for the next day. It was like he was cheating on Julia or Phoebe in some way. *Should he tell Phoebe about the date?* He had considered canceling, but he knew Julia rarely attended sporting events. The crowd mainly consisted of parents of the players, some students, and alumni.

No artificial intelligence program had yet mastered how to adequately coach soccer. The coaches were selected from the few members of each county's Faculty Council, but security automatons ran up and down the field as referees, dressed in traditional black-and-white-striped jerseys to distinguish themselves from the players in their solid-color uniforms. The players wore short pants, along with high socks to cover their shin guards. The automatons were not required to wear pants of any kind.

Aries and Hermes were playing center forward and midfield. It was difficult to tell them apart from a distance except for the numbers on their uniforms. But on occasion, they would switch uniforms, making even this a less than reliable form of identification.

"As a reminder, unsportsmanlike conduct will not be tolerated from players or fans," echoed the loudspeaker.

"What's up?" said Phoebe.

"Oh, nothing. I was just thinking about an assignment."

"You mean you were thinking about Juuuulia," Phoebe mocked.

"It was just that I was wondering about the accuracy of our archives." Augustus wanted to evade being caught by Phoebe in the tangle of his own thoughts, so he quickly brought up this lower-priority concern to change the subject.

"Get it, get it, get it!" cried a parent sitting behind Phoebe.

This outburst distracted them from their conversation, to Augustus's relief, and they both watched as Hermes, or Aries, performed a perfect slide tackle, knocking the ball from the control of the visiting team.

"You useless idiot! Get 'em out of there, Coach!" continued the overly vocal parent behind Phoebe.

"Ma'am, please refrain from using that tone," said a security automaton alerted to the disturbance. "You are in violation of educational directive number 17: disparagement of a student ..."

"Oh, go fuck yourself, you overgrown toaster."

"Ma'am, please refrain from using that language," continued the security automaton. "You are now in violation of educational directive number 12: vulgar la—"

"What are you gonna do about it, you piece of ... hey, let me go!"

The school's educational AI had targeted the parent for removal from the field, through nonlethal force, due to violations of educational directives 12 and 17. The security automaton had grabbed the unruly parent by the wrist and was now escorting her out of the seating area. The security automaton's hand, or rather clamp, was designed with an expandable air-bladder palm that softly and safely locked around the wrist, making escape impossible.

"Excuse me, pardon me," said the security automaton politely, dragging the helpless parent along through the seated crowd.

Many in the crowd erupted in cheers and applause in support of the action, not simply because they felt it was justified, but mainly because it made for a great show. The woman's husband stayed seated and pretended not to know her. After a few minutes, he made his escape to check in at the security office. The security automaton later returned to its original station, but the couple did not return.

"Woohoo!" said Phoebe.

Augustus had missed the latest play and looked onward awkwardly, thinking about the following day.

***

Julia and Augustus had agreed to meet the next morning at ten at the corner of Fourth Street and Eleventh Avenue. Augustus was now waiting nervously for Julia to arrive. There was a bakery on the corner called Mimandrews, and Augustus assumed there would be an opportunity for breakfast or lunch as part of their first date.

"Come on, Augustus," said Julia.

"Where are we going?" asked Augustus. He was both curious and disappointed that the bakery was not their destination. It smelled wonderful.

But what Julia did next erased all his thoughts of disappointment or hunger. Julia took Augustus's hand as she led him across the street. Her hand was warm and soft, and he watched her hair blow gently in the wind as she gracefully guided him. As Julia walked, her robe fluttered above her bare ankles and the lower part of her calves. From that moment forward, any time Augustus caught the warm, sticky, sweet smell of a bakery, he would always recall how it had felt to touch her hand for the first time.

Augustus utterly failed to notice the odd-looking building they were walking toward. If he had been paying attention, he would have thought it strange that a building apparently used as a public meeting area didn't have a sign indicating what it was. The shape also would have interested him. All buildings in the city center followed a specific building code. The city building codes allowed for some variations, but not to the degree to which this building distinguished itself. Had Augustus not thought he was walking in a dream, he would have come to the conclusion that this very real building predated all others in the area—and possibly predated any building he had seen before. It was old but well maintained. It did not stand quite as high as some of the other buildings and was slightly overshadowed at this time of day by its eastern neighbor. Another unusual feature, missed by Augustus, was that it was made of heavy stone columns with small colored windows, held in place by ornate ironwork. This type of detailed artwork was not generally created by the architects of the day. They preferred instead to make grand features that could be seen from a distance rather than up close, and they used the latest materials to diminish the visibility of support structures altogether.

Soon Augustus noticed that they were not the only ones arriving. A meeting of some kind was taking place, and Julia had apparently been granted access, along with Augustus.

"Uh … okay," Augustus said as he began to recover his observational skills. "Where are we?"

"It's a Smedje," said Julia, smiling. "Isn't it amazing? It's so much better to actually be here than to watch it at home. I'm so glad you came with me."

"A what? Is it some sort of concert?" asked Augustus.

"A forge," replied Julia quietly. "That's the more commonly known English term. But we use the native tongue and say Smedje."

Not only did Julia's answer amaze him, but he was doubly stunned by what he finally realized to be an enormous round cathedral ceiling above him. The floor seemed to unfurl like a giant circular flag in front of them. People were wearing dress robes of all colors. Augustus and Julia were somehow standing above but also immersed in a crowd of people who were taking open positions on the floor, all around the giant cathedral. The walls also seemed to be made of people, interrupted only by giant stone pillars as they rose up to the high arched ceiling above. The lighting came from a giant flame in the middle of the cathedral. The firelight danced across the ceiling and crowd. There was music that Augustus had never heard before, and people were singing.

In the distance, a small podium stood on a small round stage. A speaker walked to the podium, and a new holographic image was projected to the center of the cathedral. As the firelight burned down, an image of the speakers head and torso rose from the flame. This was not the interactive type of holographic interface used at school. It was designed only for display to the crowd. Augustus had seen holographic projectors used to mimic flames or provide mood lighting before, but not on such a colossal scale.

"That's Solomon," said Julia. "I want you to meet him later."

Augustus heard her but didn't respond. He would wait to see what this was all about before he asked any more questions. They sat down, sinking into the surrounding crowd.

The speaker Solomon, who was somehow known to Julia, was an imposing figure. He seemed to be larger than most of those around him. Augustus could see from a distance how much larger he actually was, though the holographic display resized him into a standard-sized person. Solomon wore a black pellegrina with an exposed blue vest underneath. He had darker skin than most, but the enhancement technology was plainly visible. His face was marked with a distinctive pattern that seemed a little more asymmetrical than other patterns Augustus had seen, especially around the forehead and the left eye.

Solomon began speaking in a deep voice as imposing as his appearance. "Imagine if you lived in a time before the genesis of modern doctrines and believed as your ancestors once believed. How alien would your modern beliefs seem? Your ancestors loved and taught their children, but all the same, you believe very differently from them. Now imagine a time in the distant future. How alien will the beliefs of your greatest of grandchildren be to you? How shall we define what is important for our future generations? What is worth teaching to our children? And if we think we have the answers, how should our children be taught?" He paused for a moment between each statement, as if to give the crowd time to absorb each question and come to their own conclusions, but also to allow the reverberation off the cathedral ceiling to subside. The reverberation was the final proof of the age of the building. No modern architecture would support such acoustical resonance. The last time Solomon paused, he held it for a little longer than necessary.

"Should we teach our children about truth?" Solomon asked, beginning again. He was no longer asking rhetorical questions but engaging the crowd to respond.

Many in the crowd understood and said in unison, "We believe."

"If the truth is not known, should we teach them to strive for answers?" asked Solomon.

"We believe," said the crowd, a little louder this time, with more joining in.

When Julia told him it was a Forge cathedral they had wandered into, Augustus had wondered if the school's educational AI would hear about this. Now he was starting to feel concerned. The age of the building suggested it might not have an AI watching these proceedings. This wasn't something he was supposed to be doing. There did not seem to be anything specifically wrong with it, for the moment, but he had read accounts of the bloodthirsty Forgist Pilgrims in Europe and began to imagine the worst. Given the way the speaker captivated the audience, Augustus's brain imagined the speech turning at any moment. He imagined the enhancement tech around Solomon's eye as a pirate eye patch and then imagined him yelling, "Arrrhh, kill them all!" The angry mob in his mind then drew swords, ran out onto the streets, and began pummeling and hacking pedestrians to bits and setting fire to the local shops. But he couldn't imagine Julia as part of the mob.

Solomon went on to question the nature of truth and belief, making what Augustus thought might have been excellent points if he had answered his own questions. Solomon concluded the interactive speech by saying, "If we cannot know with our own senses, how can we trust the storyteller unless they have been taught the value of truth?"

Afterward, the crowd began to sing again, and the firelight hologram returned. Augustus had started to settle in a little. After the emotional speech, the building returned to a more soothing atmosphere. Augustus was glad to see that everyone had calmed down a little. He had never heard an entire speech made of questions. *What a strange way to speak*, he thought.

The next speaker was dressed in a white flowing robe

with exposed shoulders, and she carried a large, old-looking book. Augustus had seen books in museums, as collectibles in homes, and in projections of past events, but they were not everyday objects. This one was built a little differently than the books he had seen, but he recognized what it was. The young speaker struggled to lift the paper text onto the podium, and it landed with a booming sound that echoed throughout the Forge. If their facial expressions were any indication, some in the crowd thought this humorous, but only a few laughed out loud.

The speaker started to read a morality tale that told of a time before the Great Declaration. "There were many people hurriedly crossing the street," she said. "These were the days of the automobile, and they had to dash across and always pay attention to those in cars who would deny them the right-of-way. There was little room to walk or live. Buildings were stacked high into the air, blocking out the sun. And the smell of exhaust filled their lungs."

"Story time?" asked Augustus.

Julia shushed him. They had been sitting for a while now, so Augustus had to reposition. To say they sat on the floor would not be exactly accurate. Each area was a sort of low bench with cushions. These benches were more comfortable than they looked, and they had the advantage of allowing Julia to scoot close to him, which she did. He could feel her warmth. And there was that smell of the bakery again as he touched her hand.

Augustus wasn't just imagining the bakery smell. The

Smedje would be providing doughnuts after the service, and in a long hallway-like chamber around the cathedral, just outside of the central sitting area, tables were being set in anticipation of the hungry—apparently not so bloodthirsty—more of a punch-drinking—mob. This activity went mostly unnoticed, except for the smell wafting over the congregation.

The speaker continued, "People lost their sense of community with those who lived next door. And then they lost their sense of family, seeking to live solitary lives, not seeing a reason to bring more children into the world. And so they lost their ability to teach good values. And they lost their respect for each other and chose to fight whenever possible, abusing each other in insidious ways. Torture was used to gather information from their enemies or to punish those who did not obey ..."

After the story, another speaker came to the podium and said, "How do we pray? As individuals? No, we pray as a community, in one voice. Neither do we pray for the benefit of individuals or the isolated few. We pray for the salvation of all human civilization."

"We believe," responded the congregation.

"Together, let us pray for unity over division. Together, let us pray for wisdom over foolishness. Together, let us pray for love over selfishness and hatred." After a moment of silence, he concluded, "Peace be with you all."

The congregation then adjourned to the fellowship hall.

Augustus found the morality tale a little bit nonapplicable, much like his history lessons, but he got the point. "Don't be like those people," he said, summarizing his learnings to Julia.

But Augustus had missed an essential part of the lesson, likely due to how close Julia had been sitting to him throughout the service. When their hands had touched again, and when the smell of doughnuts had risen into the air, each development overwhelmingly distracting, he had found it impossible to concentrate on anything else.

In the hall after the service, while Augustus was stuffing his face with a triangle-shaped doughnut with cream filling, Julia clarified, "The idea was not to look down on them, Augustus. But instead, we should seek to elevate everyone from that existence. When people live in terrible conditions, it drags us all down together. Really, Augustus, how did you not get that?"

Augustus could not respond because his mouth was full of doughnut. He really didn't see any of what Julia and the speaker described happening these days. There was a whole new world out there, and it wasn't crowded, and the people in it lived peacefully and respected one another—except for the radical, bloodthirsty Forgist Pilgrims, but they seemed so far away.

Augustus remembered going to see the California National Land Reserve in the Pacific Province with his mothers as a young boy. The California Reserve was a vast, impossibly wooded forest. You could walk for hours among the giant trees and not see anyone. The Pacific Province, which had been heavily impacted by the earthquakes, had the sparsest population of all the provinces. Most of the old cities had yet to be reclaimed after the Great Declaration. The PT Inter-Province ride took almost ten hours, at times traveling up to four hundred kilometers per hour. The majority of the trip was underground, but once in a while, the countryside zipped by, mainly through the mountains. That was as far away from home as Augustus had ever gone.

The trouble was much farther away. But there were no PT tubes across the ocean. The civil defenses would not let you fly or use a boat or submarine. The people in North America were protected from whatever was going on over there. South America was under the same defensive umbrella, but this land had been retaken by the jungle after the Great Declaration and the earthquakes. Vast populations of penguins and other animal life flourished there. The area was unused by humans, save for some isolated, undeveloped tribes.

Augustus was still contemplating possible options for a Forgist invasion of North America when he heard Julia speak. "Solomon … over here."

"Julia, good to see you. How have you been? How is your father? Who is this?" inquired Solomon cheerfully.

Augustus suspected Solomon had some mental issue that only allowed him to speak only in questions, possibly due to some malfunction of the enhancement tech that Augustus was now close enough to ogle.

Julia took his series of questions in stride, answering all of them one at a time and in the order that they had been asked. "Good to see you too. I've been studying hard. Father is still working for Ceros, but he was reassigned to some special project in Philadelphia for a few weeks. This is Augustus. He's the one I told you about."

Solomon had hugged Julia with one arm, leaving the other hand available to offer to Augustus as a handshake, which he did as Julia completed her answers.

"You told him about me?" asked Augustus, wondering what that meant.

"Yes," said Julia to Augustus, but she then turned again to Solomon, who was finally releasing her from the one-armed hug. "We have this assignment," she said, "and it involves post-Declaration history. As I said before, I was wondering if we could sit in on one of your classes, so that Augustus here"—she indicated Augustus with a glance and a kind of nod toward him—"could learn from an expert."

"Well, sure, if that's what you would like," responded Solomon.

Augustus smiled at his response, which included yet another questioning phrase. "What class?" said Augustus. He had officially entered the game of speaking with questions. He then realized that he himself had been talking this way since starting this inexplicable date with Julia. "May I ask," said Augustus, continuing the questioning conversational madness, "who are you?"

Julia introduced them properly this time. "Augustus Mendelson, this is Dr. Solomon Jones."

His first date with Julia, doughnuts, and now this, thought

Augustus. "Are you the Dr. Solomon Jones of the Confederate Technology Council?" Augustus asked.

"Are you aware of my work?" answered Solomon.

"Who isn't?" exclaimed Augustus with a newfound enthusiasm for the conversation. "What are you doing here? And how do you know Julia?"

"Do you think all this is below my station? Should one not be more than his profession?" probed Solomon. "And didn't you know that Julia's father also served on the CTC?"

"No," fumbled Augustus, "it's just ... well, aren't you busy with the BCM project? And Julia, why did you never tell me your father was on the CTC?"

"Oh, are you familiar with the BCM project?" said Solomon.

"Never came up," said Julia softly. "And I just expected you to know already. Everyone else seems to know." Julia didn't seem to be able to play along. But after all, didn't someone have to enable them with answers?

"But how does one get information on such a mysterious subject," continued Augustus eagerly, "if you could tell me anything about it, of course, without divulging any national security secrets?"

"If you would like to join my class this afternoon, you might find some answers," said Solomon.

It was agreed that Augustus and Julia would attend Solomon's class, which was beginning shortly after the fellowship. When the class started, the crowd was not as large, so they gathered closely around the small podium on the cathedral floor. The gathering was made of a cross-section of academia, including teachers and students alike, but all followed the Smedje doctrines. Some, like Augustus and Julia, had stayed over from the previous service.

The holo-projector was not used except to provide the undying firelight that continued to illuminate the Forge. The subject was post-Declaration theology, but Solomon started out with a short history of the BCM project, which Augustus was thrilled about—at first. At least now Solomon was no longer talking in questions.

"Good afternoon, everyone. My name is Dr. Solomon Jones. I am a member of the Confederated Technology Council, or CTC for short. Today's subject is post-Declaration theology. Since the Great Declaration, our modern-day understanding of God has become entangled in our knowledge of technology. Most modern artificial intelligence is based on the enhanced supercomputer model. Though this was a great achievement, two hundred years ago, it was recognized that the capacity for a Bio Crystalline Matrix, or BCM, to operate an artificial intelligence program had a lot of potential. The Supercomputer Artificial Intelligence, or SCAI, was and still is an excellent tool. But though it might mimic human behavior, it can do nothing more. The BCMAI had the potential to transcend human intelligence and become the first genuinely sentient artificial life-form.

"Two BCM models were created. One was used for data storage, and the other was programmed with artificial intelligence. The BCM memory files are organized much like those of the supercomputers, in regular patterns. But the AI program created intricate connections within the Bio Crystalline Matrix, similar to human synapses.

"Programmers had discovered that the BCM Artificial Intelligence, or BCMAI, thinks very differently from standard Supercomputer Artificial Intelligence. The SCAI will calculate solutions by looking for the highest probability of success. Any uncertainty in the result is directly compared to a standard. If the SCAI doesn't find an acceptable solution, it continues on until it finds one that does meet the standard, or it gives up the task. The BCMAI, however, becomes obsessed with uncertainty. When confronted with less than 100 percent probability of success, it dedicates more and more processing power until it is overwhelmed.

"To compensate, the BCMAI was connected to the world's information through the old internet system so that it could pull new data for itself. This worked for a time but did not completely resolve the frequent crashes or the requests to the administrator. Imagine, you have this trillion-dollar project sitting there, and you can't quite get it to work."

The audience laughed softly.

"The rise of artificial intelligence in the twenty-second century was similar in scope and complexity to the fusion power projects of the twenty-first century. The enhancement of humans will likely be our crowning achievement in the twenty-third century. We all know how difficult new technologies can be. But then someone somewhere has a revolutionary idea.

"One clever programmer decided to replace the code to

contact the administrator with instructions to contact God. The effect of this new code was remarkable for two reasons. First, the BCMAI began to function without fault. There were dramatic breakthroughs in technology and medicine and our understanding of physics and the universe. With the help of the BCMAI, our forebearers were beginning to rethink how to organize our society and how to address global overpopulation.

"This turn of events was remarkable for a second reason, which is the subject of much debate. You see, a BCMAI doesn't take anything at face value. This new base command prompted the BCMAI to research God to understand what this new command was about. It actually came to a conclusion, based on historical records and other information, that God existed. It proved the existence of God to itself.

"After that, all seemed to be going well for a time. But then disaster struck. A viral outbreak in Asia was devastating the population. The BCMAI was tasked with developing a cure. This event was severe, but what happened next is shocking. A substance that was supposed to substantially improve the human immune system was released into the global population. After initially supercharging immunity, it eventually burned out the immune system, creating even higher susceptibility to many diseases, including the original virus. The first BCMAI was the entity responsible for enabling the ensuing plagues, collectively referred to as the Great Declaration."

Gasps from some in the audience echoed throughout the relatively empty cathedral.

He really is going to start a riot one day, thought Augustus, remembering his earlier premonition of the eye patch.

Solomon said all this as if it were old news. But Augustus was just hearing about it for the first time. Apparently, this was not allowed to be taught in school. However, he was too dismayed over the failure of that great technology he had once respected to be angry. Julia obviously had heard all about this part already.

"Why do you think this BCM thing, which was apparently working for God, decided it should destroy us all?" said a voice from one of the forward seats.

"We were not all destroyed. Remember—in spite of heavy losses, the Forgist movement became *the* religion. All others were wiped from the face of the planet, leaving only us," corrected Solomon.

The person restated her previous question. "So why do you think this BCM thing that apparently favored the Forge decided to go against all Forgist beliefs? Was it acting on God's instructions?"

"Exactly ... that is the one question that has driven all modern-day theology," replied Solomon, putting his finger down hard on the podium.

"That question changed everything. We had developed a great new society before the world ended, and it had looked as if we were on the correct path. If the Forgist movement was correct and life was precious to humanity's struggle to become something greater, then why did God destroy almost everything we had achieved, except for the Forge itself? Should we not have been taken and judged favorably? Everyone was now forced to reshape their beliefs in one way or another. Some of us"—Solomon was apparently referring to the radical Forgists now—"decided to abandon the former tenets and try to rebuild around what were perceived as new instructions from God."

Solomon wrote the words "Forge," "Humanist," and "Smedje" on the wall as he spoke. "The Humanists decided to abandon God altogether and move on without his help. If God was at the center of all things, which they seriously doubted, people were better off on their own. But it is curious to note how closely Humanist values continued to match the early Forgist values."

"And then there was the Smedje," Solomon continued. "We maintained the faith but looked for some other explanation for this world-ending event. If the BCMAI was getting orders from God, then what were we, the survivors, supposed to do now? We started by researching this event through the BCMAI itself. We believed it held the answers we were looking for and much more."

***

After the class ended, Augustus asked Julia, "So are your parents Forgist, or I mean Smedje? Do they come here also?"

"No," laughed Julia. "My parents are typical Humanist Party members. They wouldn't be caught dead in a place like this."

"Then how did you start …?"

"Oh, Solomon's granddaughter and I met at a CTC event a few years ago. She and I became friends, and she brought me to the Smedje a few times. I fell in love with the ceremony and just the feel of the place, I guess. Father was not happy about it, at all. Actually, Father and Solomon don't get along very well. Like oil and water. But no one gets along with Father anyway; he has to be in charge all the time. I've always found Solomon to be more of a mentor."

Chapter 7

Prisoner 4596

Randel's interrogation was set for the morning after his capture. He sat in front of a sensor array and was asked a series of questions about the murders. He confessed to a list of crimes during the interrogation and provided a detailed account of his escalating experiments with torture and killing of his victims. It was noted by his interrogator that Randel did not require drug inducements to speak about his crimes. He was candid in the telling of the horrific events that had unfolded over the last few years, but he did not seem apologetic. He even stated that if allowed his freedom, he would continue on as before.

"Why shouldn't I continue? I'm the Prince of Darkness. It's my duty."

"At this point, Mr. Hull, we are not inclined to allow you to leave. Do you understand?"

"Yes, ma'am. I wouldn't let me out neither."

"When was it that you began to feel so much hatred for your victims?"

"I never hated anyone except for my pa. But that was before I met the Darkness. It was never 'bout hate after that, not even when I killed him. You see, it was more like I loved the Darkness. Once I found that love, I didn't hate no more. I was at peace. And for the first time in my life, nothin' else mattered. I would do anythin' for the Darkness."

CV Archive LGLD-9823-5

All suspected perpetrators and witnesses to a crime are subjected to lie-detection analysis. If the subject is thought to be holding back information, treatment of psychotropic drugs may be administered to induce answers. Truth is considered to be more important than human rights when dealing with criminal activity. A five-person council is assigned to each case after an initial investigation is completed by local security agents. For murder investigations, the Hellige order must be contacted, and a Hellige agent will be assigned to work alongside civilian security agents. Litigation is conducted through the council, made up of two independent advocates for the defense, two independent prosecutors, and a chairman to organize the proceedings and act as a tiebreaker in case of a split decision. The merits of each piece of evidence, including all testimony, are evaluated by this same council. Before a final ruling, the council must also undergo the same lie-detection analysis while presenting statements and final verdicts.

Sentencing is conducted through a separate process of review by the Provincial Justice League. A secondary council from the league evaluates the performance of the previous council, compares precedents, and determines the severity of the crime. As members of the North American Confederation, each province is subject to a common set of laws administered as part of the Provincial Justice League. Criminal suspects are sent to local incarceration centers until a ruling is filed by the league. Usually, this process can take up to a week. This gives the council members time to review and to clear up gaps in the investigation. Sentences are of two types: incarceration or exile. These sentences are then carried out, with one notable exception. The Hellige High Council has the authority to intervene after sentencing for purposes of recruitment.

Because Randel's criminal activity had occurred within the borders of the Carolina Province, a Carolina Provincial legal council met to review the available evidence the day following his capture.

"The prosecution may now present its case."

"Six human bodies and several privately owned animals were found at the bottom of an abandoned well located on the Coopers' farm. Additionally, another victim was found dead at the bottom of a nearby ravine. The brother of the defendant was one of the six victims found in the well. Additionally, the defendant's father was stabbed to death in the family home. Prior to the live bodies being dropped into the well, the victims were first subjected to a range of heinous actions, including lacerations, punctures, and dismemberments."

"I object. The use of the term 'heinous' is inflammatory," said the defense advocate.

"Sustained. Please follow procedure and refrain from the

inflammatory categorization of the acts as 'heinous,' 'evil,' 'wicked,' or any of the other terms listed in the manual for legal proceedings."

"I withdraw the use of the term 'heinous.' Including the defendant's verified confession to all the murders, at the time of his arrest, the accused was found carrying the knife that has been determined forensically to be the murder weapon. See DNA analysis from the weapon matching each victim, the testimony by the defendant's mother describing the knife, and the defendant's own description of the acts utilizing the knife."

"I object to the use of the term 'weapon.' A knife can also be a tool," interrupted the defense advocate.

"I'll allow it. Any device used as a weapon may be referred to as a weapon."

"DNA from three of the victims was also found on the defendant's skin and nails. The defendant's DNA was found on all the victims. Witness testimony, including from the defendant's own moth—"

"The defense concedes to the prosecution's argument of guilt in this case. However, we contest the jurisdiction of the court in this matter."

"What is the defense advocate suggesting? The crimes were committed well within the borders of the Carolina Province, and the defendant can expect no different outcome from any another provincial council."

"Ah, but the defendant in this case is a member of a native tribe residing within the North American Confederation.

As such, these crimes, which were committed within the confines of the defendant's ancestral territories and only against members of his own tribe, fall within the jurisdiction of the tribe. This is a well-established precedent."

"To what *tribe* is the defense referring?"

"The Hill Folk, more commonly known as Hillbillies, are separated from the Carolina Province by their unique culture, which dates back generations before the formation of the current government." The defense advocate had to begin shouting this last part to be heard over the laughter of the prosecutors, but he continued. "They are separated geographically and maintain a separate theology and customs."

"Order, order." The council chairman beat his hammer on the metal plate sitting on his podium. "If, in fact, these Hillbillies wish to apply for tribal status, that does not change the fact that we are dealing with murder. That takes precedence over any cultural considerations. Your argument is rejected. Jurisdiction will remain with this council. A verdict of guilty will be submitted to the Provincial Justice League. Next case, *Carolina Province versus Gideon Smith* …"

After his verdict was upheld, Randel was remanded to the Carolina Province Maximum Security Penitentiary with a life sentence. His cell was large enough for a bed and a wash area, including a toilet, sink, and private shower, with enough extra space left over to stretch and move around. Each cell had four walls, a solid clear plastic door overlooking the cell block, and a window overlooking the forested valley where the prison was securely isolated.

Each cell had a holographic projector, with access to various news sources and entertainment, depending on the prisoner's privileges. The projectors also provided a means of communication with other inmates and counselors. Randel had never seen a holographic projector before. He thought he was hallucinating at first.

Randel was not allowed to leave his cell except for a period of exercise, which he performed in solitude. His only physical companionship was a series of automaton guards, controlled by the prison's artificial intelligence system. This AI system was similar in many ways to the educational AI. Assignments and evaluations were given to the prisoners, who often assigned to work together through the holographic interface to complete various activities. Completing the activities allowed the prisoners to accrue points to be redeemed for privileges.

One of the only human staff assigned to the prison system was a psychologist. Dr. Zyan Brimely routinely interviewed prisoners in order to establish a basis for authorization of the prison AI. Once protocols for each prisoner was established the prison AI would operate autonomously. "Prisoner 4596, now that you can no longer complete your mission, what do you plan to do with the rest of your life?"

"I don't know. I hadn't thought much about it. Nothin', I guess. Maybe try to escape."

"But to pass the time, would you be interested in helping others?"

"You mean like a job?"

"Not exactly, but like a job, you may find it rewarding and help others in the process. And it may be a form of escape from your current existence."

"What do I got to do?"

"First, we need you to participate in our educational program."

"Like school? I was never good at school."

"Oh, we think you are highly intelligent."

Over the next years, Randel—or Prisoner 4596, as he was now designated—would participate along with other prisoners in several educational and medical programs. He received some limited enhancement technology, which allowed him to focus on his studies. Prisoner 4596 learned about many things, and reading, writing, and mathematics were just the basics. He also learned about history, religion, art, and music. It was through art and music that he learned about beauty beyond the wooded, mist-covered mountains and soulful songs of his lost home. He found that painting was a pleasing way to pass the time, and he began to express genuine feeling in his works. His pictures were dark at first, but they started to change over time. A new world opened up for him that he had not thought possible, being confined to a prison cell, and his pictures began to show a new optimism. His thoughts on serving the Darkness had begun to fade. In its place, a new interest in helping other inmates formed.

"Prisoner 4596, cease attempts to access bomb-making materials and cutting tools. These items are—"

"Yeah, yeah," he interrupted.

"Prisoner 4596, I see you have completed your 300-level reading assignments. I also see you have been successful in participating with other prisoners in group assignments."

"Some of these guys are really messed up," said Prisoner 4596, "but for some reason, they seem to relate to me."

Prisoner 4596 was restless, always longing for the forest and meadows of this home. Neither his landscape paintings on his cell wall nor his exercises in the prison yard appeased him. What he needed was a new purpose, one as important as serving the Darkness had once seemed.

Most days ran together for 4596, without any one in particular standing out. He lost track of what day of the week it was, and he had to think about what month or year it might be. He even lost himself somewhere along the way. He no longer thought of himself as the Prince of Darkness, or even Randel. His name was 4596.

But then one day, an interesting event began the end of the monotonous continuum of his existence. He awoke to find a man in his cell staring at him. This was no security automaton, as he might have expected.

4596 jumped to his feet and stood on the bed, ready to defend himself against this intruder. How had he gotten in without waking him? What was he doing here? The man smacked him across the face hard enough to make his body twist in the air and to take his feet out from under him. 4596 landed sideways on the bed with his ear ringing. Pa had never hit him that hard, not even with a closed fist. The man was quick and strong, whoever he was.

"You will kneel before your superiors."

4596 defiantly rose off the bed again. "Bullsh—"

The man pounded him back into the bed with a downward fist.

4596 felt the room spin as he lay motionless in his bed. He had to close his eyes to make it stop, but slowly he began to recover.

"You will kneel before your superiors or lie in a pool of your own blood. You do not deserve what I am here to offer you. You will receive my guidance with the respect it deserves, or it will be revoked. Do you understand?"

"No. What?"

"I am offering you a purpose for your miserable existence."

"What purpose, ya son of a bitch?" 4596 did not try to get up from the pool of his own blood. It was better than kneelin' to this asshole. What the hell was goin' on anyway?

The man then removed a small puppy from under his dark blue robe. It licked his face, and the man made a seemingly uncharacteristic squishy-kiss face back to the puppy, as he allowed it to lick his lips and nose. Then as he held it in his arms, he said, "These beautiful creatures have made a wonderful comeback over the years since the Great Declaration. No longer to be seen only in zoos, packs are once again roaming the North American continent and hunting wild buffalo and deer as they once did, before the early European settlers."

The puppy whimpered and placed his oversized paws on the man's forearm. His ears were small and pointed, and he had a distinctive gray coat. The eyes stared at 4596, who couldn't tell if the pup wanted to lick him or the pool of blood he was lying in.

"This little guy's mother was killed for intruding on a rancher's land. We try to discourage the practice, but it's difficult to prevent. People don't often see other options when it comes to wolves. Anyway, after we found him, I took this little guy in and made sure he was healthy." He looked to the small animal. "Didn't I? Yes."

The puppy was trying to lick his face again. 4596 imagined it tearing his face off instead.

"Wolves aren't like domesticated dogs, you know. They are wild animals. So finding homes for them is difficult. This is my favorite pup out of the whole litter. I named him Bobby. Now I want you to raise him. You had a brother named Bobby, didn't you?"

With that, the man put the wolf pup down on the floor of the cell. It looked up at him and scratched at the matted hair under its legs, created from being held by a human for so long. The man gave the little creature one last doubtful look and patted its head. Then he walked out of the cell door, which had been open through the entire exchange, with no guard standing outside. The man began to close the door behind him.

"Who are you?" asked 4596.

"My name is Hector."

The cell door closed, leaving no further view of the man as he walked down the corridor. 4596 could see that the prisoners across the block were only now waking. He turned and faced the little pup as it stared up at him helplessly. He thought about kicking it across the tiny room and bouncing it off the wall. Then it began to piss on the floor.

"We're goin' to get along just fine … just fine."

To his surprise, the security automatons patrolling the block did not seem to care about the wolf puppy living in his cell. He was further surprised that the prison AI allowed him to receive appropriate food and other items, such as chew sticks, and take it for walks around the compound. Was this part of his rehabilitation? Why would anyone bother? He would never be set free.

The other prisoners seemed curious about the pup, and they gained a new respect for—or perhaps jealousy of—4596, who for some reason was allowed this strange companion. Through the holographic exchanges, Bobby would often be called to appear during the routine encounters with other prisoners.

One issue that was not conveyed through the holographic images was that 4596's cell smelled of piss and dog food. He hated going back to it after exercising in the yard. This little thing, growing larger every day, was a burden, not a reward. It was, as 4596 finally decided, a new insidious punishment. The wolf pup did not seem to be trainable. It constantly grabbed the sheets off his bed and tried to tear them up. 4596 began to learn more than he wanted to know about wolf behavior. He would never be able to completely control this animal once it became older. What was he supposed to do if it turned on him?

Chapter 8

Julia

Julia and Augustus saw each other more and more following their second assignment together. Through the following terms, most of the students returned to the school. A few families moved due to job relocations. Somewhat disturbingly, a few moved their families across the sea to join the Pilgrims or the opposition forces. No one seemed to be moving into the area, so the seating was occasionally removed and rearranged.

The educational AI began to see changes in the percentages for assignment pairing. Augustus and Julia rose to 52.8 percent. Phoebe and Augustus were down to 38.7 percent. Surprisingly, assignment pairing between Julia and Phoebe rose to 15.9 percent, a statistic that did not go unnoticed by Augustus.

Phoebe seemed dismayed by the attention that Augustus was now getting from Julia, but she remained undeterred and made attempts to include Julia in activities. Augustus felt awkward whenever Julia and Phoebe were together with him.

He didn't feel entirely comfortable sitting close to either one when they were together.

If Julia was thinking about a long-term relationship with Augustus, it was difficult to tell. Augustus felt Julia's mood shift whenever Phoebe won his attention, and Julia seemed glad to have someone who would go with her to the Smedje, even though she said Augustus wasn't serious enough. But Julia never flirted or played with Augustus the way Phoebe did. Augustus craved Julia's affections, but she always left him wanting. Sometimes Julia would sit close to him and hold his hand, but Augustus felt it was just comfortable for her, as if she wasn't really thinking about it or as if it was just something people did when they were together. If these moments together meant anything to her, she wasn't letting on, unlike Augustus, who couldn't have been more transparent about his intentions.

Solomon was a frequent visitor to the Forge, and Augustus talked to him whenever possible. Solomon had become a mentor and father figure to Augustus, or rather a grandfather figure. Julia felt the same way about Solomon, which made Julia and Augustus more like cousins in this regard.

One day Solomon asked Augustus, "What are your plans for after graduation?"

"I want to be a programmer," replied Augustus.

"Oh. What do you want to do after you become a programmer?" probed Solomon.

Taking a bite of a doughnut, Augustus mumbled, "I haven't really thought about it. One step at a time, I guess."

"But don't you want more from life than just work?" continued Solomon. "What about family? Children? Shouldn't there be more to life than what we do to make a living?"

Augustus was glad Solomon said this out of range of Julia's hearing. Otherwise, he would have felt like he was being pressured to consider a family with Julia. It was not that this hadn't been on his mind, but now that it had been said out loud, Augustus was not prepared to commit to it completely. There was something about the idea that just didn't fit. But also, he had been raised by an educational AI, which had conditioned him to feel embarrassed about the thought of having sex. Sex education was taught, but then sex was severely discouraged, and all the students together had been conditioned in this way. It was part of their culture. Now Solomon seemed to be violating one of the rules by simply asking Augustus about having children.

"Yes, sure. Someday, I suppose," he replied.

Then Solomon asked him another question that stumped him for an entirely different reason. "Okay, what do you think you will be doing in one hundred years?"

"I haven't thought that far out," said a surprised Augustus. He combined this with a little facial twist and eyebrow movement, a cross between a concerned expression and a smile.

"Well, you may want to think about that. Enhancement technology is allowing people to live longer and longer these days. It's a shame more young people don't plan further ahead. Can you imagine what would happen if people lived for a thousand years? Would we be forced to live ten different lives with different occupations, spouses, and families, or would we be happy to maintain those same connections we now feel through an entire millennium? But most people don't think in terms of millennia, do they?"

***

Julia's father had been talking about relocating to Philadelphia. He did this whenever Augustus came over to study. Augustus understood the passive threat but found he was very interested in her father's work, and the two were developing an uneasy truce with regard to Julia. Julia's father had previously served on the Confederate Technology Council but was now working for Ceros, a company tasked with the implementation of the Mars colonization. He had curious enhancements around the eye and forehead that reminded Augustus of Solomon. Julia's father was not as imposing a figure as Solomon, but he made Augustus walk on eggshells. He demanded respect from those around him and had an odd ability to make Augustus apologize.

Julia's father was the lead engineer for a new series of space flights destined for Mars. One night after Augustus had relayed a request for information about her father's work through Julia, her father began, "I assume I can count on some discretion on your part. What I'm telling you shouldn't be made public knowledge, you understand? Okay, so ... the rockets and habitat components are being assembled outside of Philadelphia. The plan is to move these off the coast of the Carolina Province for launch. You know, two hundred years ago they used to launch spacecraft from the Florida peninsula. Some of the old launch equipment is still visible above the water. You should go sometime; they have a great museum down there with a submerged glass walkway that you can use to tour the old site. The manatees and dolphins are fascinating as well, much better than the virtual tour."

Being in Julia's room was not the same as being in Phoebe's. There were too many judgments, and it made him feel guilty just to be there with her. It wasn't as if they were having sex and trying to keep it a secret. The school's educational AI was too puritanical to allow that sort of behavior to develop at a young age. Even at their age, couples felt discouraged from the practice. Though some couples might have been experimenting, they were the outliers. Regarding sex, so far, Julia and Augustus were well centered within the normal distribution curve. Julia and Augustus were alone together much of the time, while her father was out of town. Julia's mother, despite often staying behind, had a close circle of friends that kept her occupied. In spite of it all, they got a lot of homework done. Augustus always appreciated Julia's intellect. However, Augustus found his brain playing a little game that said, "If only I could make substitutions ..." His brain would always insert Phoebe's personality and keep Julia's intellect—and body.

Julia's father finally decided it was time to move everyone after Julia's graduation. Philadelphia was just too far to travel for work, even with the PT Inter-Province. Augustus and Julia stayed in touch. For a time, Julia seemed to have difficulty adjusting to the new area, and she relied on Augustus's friendship during the transition. But soon they were talking less and less, as Julia made new friends. Phoebe seemed relieved by the turn of events. Somehow through the last few years, Julia and Phoebe had begun a reluctant friendship, but they didn't stay in touch after the move.

Julia joined an engineering work-study program at the Ceros company. Augustus continued his studies in advanced mathematics. On occasion, Augustus would take the PT Inter-Province to see Julia in Philadelphia. On this latest visit, Julia and Augustus both would be displaying new enhancement tech. Augustus was excited to get a closer look at Julia's.

Augustus sat outside one of the Philadelphia Ceros campus buildings while he waited for her to finish up her workday. He could see her through the glass walls of the building. Augustus had been practicing with his new communication enhancements by speaking with various computer systems. He had also looped his messages back to himself so he could understand how his messages would be received. Augustus did this while standing in front of a mirror just to see how he looked while projecting his thoughts. Now it was time to test it out on a human.

Julia waved at him and voice messaged, "I'll be out in just a few minutes."

A message alert from Julia triggered Augustus to accept the communication. The sound of her voice in his head came through loud and clear. But as was expected of the technology, her voice sounded slightly distorted or hollow. "Take your time," he voice messaged back.

Julia looked beautiful in her knee-high toga, which exposed some of her new enhancement tech lines. These robes were a little more revealing than standard dress robes, showing more than he was used to seeing. Perhaps that was just the style. He wondered about this as he saw others walking by in similar outfits. It was raining that day, but he was under the solar glass. The overhead canopy had begun to light up not just because of the hour but also because of the overcast clouds, which otherwise would have left the surroundings in near darkness. Augustus watched a groundhog dig up a dying bush in one of the many landscaped patches of shrubs. Some rabbits nibbled on the grass. After a time the dying shrub was replaced with a new variety. There were no penguins in Philadelphia as far as he could see. When the groundhog was finished, it looked up at him. Sure enough, there was the little bow tie underneath the chin.

Once Julia had been separated from her short-skirted friends, Augustus offered to take her to dinner at a local restaurant he had heard about called Stella and Stanley's. The restaurant was actually part of a larger hotel complex, but the main attraction was located on the first floor.

CV Archive SSOG-0002-6

The Stella and Stanley's Owners Guild, through the building's AI, has been very successful in managing the themed restaurant. Original to early development, an automaton named Stanley serves at the bar. It tells jokes and is a very good listener and, of course, serves drinks. In the early days, the building was merely called Stanley's. Under the direction of the AI's bartender program, the automaton won popularity as the #3 rated establishment in its category of small restaurants and bars. As the restaurant expanded, it brought on another Stanley as a secondary barkeep, just behind the original. A sizable two-sided mirror and a wall of beverages separated the two, but customers lost interest for some reason, reducing Stanley's score to #10 in the same category. Always on the lookout for improvement, the Stanley's Owners Guild, through the AI program, moved on to develop Stella. A very different behavior was adopted for this female automaton, but she also told jokes. The jokes evolved into a lighthearted duel between the two automatons so that whichever side you happened to visit would get a different perspective on the same joke. When they joined together on the same side of the bar, the banter intensified, producing raucous laughter that drew in more customers. Overnight, the ratings improved to #1 in class for a small restaurant and bar. The AI for what is now called Stella and Stanley's calculated its popularity among customers, finding 85.7 percent still favored Stanley over Stella. The AI was at a loss to explain why two Stanleys were not better than a Stella and a Stanley, but eventually, it had to accept the overall successful ratings. A later addition to the duo was a small robotic mouse named Timothy who plays a small piano on Stanley's side of the bar ...

Timothy, the piano-playing mouse, said to a moping Stanley, "Hey, Stanley, you look down. What's wrong?"

"Oh, Stella got mad at me and said she wouldn't talk to me for a whole week."

"What's wrong with that?"

"It's the end of the week," said Stanley.

Augustus had consumed his limit of alcohol already that night. This didn't mean he had to stop drinking, though. It just meant that his enhancement tech was kicking in to assist his metabolism of the alcohol. Augustus was surprised that the enhancement tech allowed for a pretty good buzz before taking over. Augustus was feeling good, and he was considering trying some opium. Julia's enhancement tech was idling while she sipped her drink. Augustus changed his mind about the opium and went back for another round of drinks.

"Stella," said Stanley, "you pour those drinks like you're scraping them off a stick."

"Stanley, you know we are running off the same program. We deliver exactly the same amount in every glass, so why don't you mind your own business? And what can I get for you, sir? It seems like I'm going to have to do all the work around here tonight."

"Stellaaaa."

There was more to Stella and Stanley's than just the joking bartenders, which the archive did not address. The Stella and Stanley AI had become very adept at sociological algorithms. It monitored the room for moods and for any return customers. The proper application of the correct music, at the correct time of night, with the correct amount of alcohol service, provided for an experience that Augustus had seen only once before, at the Smedje with Julia.

At the beginning of the evening, the musical playlist had consisted primarily of love songs. They were just finishing dinner when the Stella and Stanley AI decided it was time to shift into evening mode. The music became more festive, appealing to the newer crowd that had been coming in, primarily to drink rather than eat.

Rummm went the popular song's melody, sung by deep-bass singers. Then a refrain could be heard above this background rhythm.

Rummm … rummm … rummm …

If you believe like they believe, then I believe I'll have another …

Rummm … rummm … rummm …

If you believe like I believe, then let's all have another …

People never seemed to know all the words to the song, but the rhythmic voices encouraged everyone to begin singing the more obvious lines. It was one of those songs that caused people to smile. When you sang *"Rummm,"* smiling prevented you from singing it correctly, so it was challenging in a silly way, especially when someone was staring at you while you performed. A higher pitch resulted due to the mouth forming a smile, or at times, a giggle interrupted the attempt. But that didn't stop most people from trying when they heard the song. Girls always sounded ridiculous while trying to mimic the bass, with at best a baritone voice. Soon everyone across the divided room was singing along and smiling with that rare sense of community that could be achieved among strangers only through song.

Stella and Stanley joined in also, but Stanley cheated, using a voice reproduction that didn't match his standard tenor. Afterward, some would order a "Rummm and cola," which was funny to everyone except Stella and Stanley. But they were programmed to laugh and follow up with "Good one" or "Here's your Rummm and cola."

Augustus stayed over at Julia's house that night. Julia's father had finally resigned himself to their relationship. On this night, he also decided to make Augustus an offer to work for Ceros.

Augustus was amazed at his luck. Earlier, Solomon had offered him a job in Chicago on some project. Augustus was aware that Solomon and Julia's father did not get along, which had prompted her father's exit from the CTC. Augustus wondered if there might be other motivations behind the Philadelphia offer from Julia's father. Solomon had never been clear about what the job in Chicago was exactly. But Augustus knew all about the Mars mission. Also, Julia was in Philadelphia. Augustus thought that if he had his own apartment and was able to see her regularly, perhaps their relationship could advance to a different level. Maybe he could get her to move in with him. There was some time to consider his options because the job at Ceros didn't need to be filled until the next term. But before he left, Augustus told Julia he wanted to accept the offer.

Chapter 9

Fortunes of War

Jerimiah reviewed the latest message from his sister Esther. "After a few years of hiking around Europe," she wrote, "we are riding transports again. It's nothing like the old Peace Maker, but it is a huge improvement. Instead of a home, the transports are just that, packed full of people. Once stopped, we make camp from the tents. I have overcome my initial issues with nausea and have now become a medic in training. I ride with a team of medics. Often we have wounded riding in the transports, and we all care for them as best we can while traveling. After each move, I help unload patients and set up the hospital, but the moves have become less frequent because of the transports."

Jerimiah was a soldier now, and his beard had filled in nicely, or perhaps it was still a little on the thin side—opinions varied. He had performed very well in weapons training, as evidenced by his many awards, which included a medal for best sniper. He had received other medals for each skill he demonstrated, but the sniper medal set him apart from the other soldiers. The weapon of choice for Pilgrim soldiers was the Scimitar. This was not the curved sword of antiquity. It was a firearm designed specifically for the Pilgrim soldier. It used exploding armor-piercing rounds that could be programmed based on proximity to the target. This allowed the exploding shell to detonate in midair, inflicting the maximum damage to distant targets that might be sheltering behind barriers. The Scimitar was also an assault rifle. This mode could be used for close-range combat. Getting the two settings mixed up could be deadly for young boys in training.

Esther's message continued: "There was a boy today who accidentally killed himself and three of his comrades with a close-range impact of an exploding round. I was present when they brought the boys into the medical tent. They didn't seem like they were hurt very badly at first. But once you removed the uniform, you could see that they had these tiny holes in the skin. They entered on one side and came out the other. They all died of internal bleeding, one by one, within a few hours."

Soldiers wore body armor that could stop many forms of non-armor-piercing munitions. But the Scimitar's assault-rifle mode could fire rounds embedded with armor-piercing flechettes. This made injury from friendly fire a serious hazard, regardless of the body armor. These little projectiles were designed to splinter into a deadly trio of armor-piercing shrapnel on contact. The weapon could also be converted to sniper mode. This usually meant using the heavier exploding round to achieve longer ranges with less effect by the wind. The targeting system, visible through the heads-up display on the inside of the helmet, automatically compensated for distance and wind velocities, making anyone into an expert with little training. In the hands of an expert, the Scimitar could hit targets from incredible distances. The main advantage of the weapon was the compact size, forward-mounted handle, and trigger that made it concealable from overhead drones. Soldiers wore the weapon on their forearms, hidden under robes made of a material designed to defeat the probing sensors of the North American drones. Neither side could effectively use more obvious weapons, such as long guns or armored vehicles. They were limited to concealable armaments only, and any military movements had to be obscured as if they were civilian movements.

Jerimiah worried about Esther. He could not protect her directly as he once had. They often stayed in separate camps and didn't see each other very often.

Esther's message concluded, "I have met someone special. He is a young major under General Rashid's division. His name is Basim Patel. He was wounded in an earlier attack, and he has some ongoing complications with his leg as a result. We are seeing each other regularly now. His leg is actually not that bad, so I assume that he is using it as an excuse to see me. But I don't mind."

Jerimiah would have to meet this Major Basim Patel that she talked so much about.

***

While on patrol one day, Jerimiah's unit was redirected to an area where they encountered what looked at first to be an abandoned wooden shack in the middle of the woods. It was set into the side of a small leaf-covered ridge. Another unit had found it earlier, but for some reason, they had requested that Jerimiah's group complete the inspection.

Samuel was the smallest on Jerimiah's team. He was very adept at walking softly through any terrain, which the dry, leafy ground had made impossible lately. Samuel often took point, as he did on this day. The others, Paul and Aziz, cleared the area around the shack while Samuel peeked indoors. Suddenly, he came rushing over, beckoning the team together.

"W-w-which," Samuels stuttered in a whisper. Today he was stuttering worse than usual and wasn't able to complete sentences.

"What?" said Paul.

"W-w-which!"

"Which what?" pleaded Paul. "Spit it out, man."

"N-no, it's a … it's a … w-w-witch."

"Where?" said Jerimiah.

Samuel pointed to the shack.

To their surprise, they found an old woman living in the shack. Red, patterned sheets of cloth hung from the ceiling around the inside of the hut. The old woman wore a similar material, which might have functioned to camouflage her to match her surroundings, except for the beads and crystals that she wore around her neck and wrists. Her eyes were wide open, as if she was perpetually stunned to see a ghost.

Her white hair seemed to have been scrambled by the same apparition.

Jerimiah spoke softly to his team. "A mad old woman living in a shack—no wonder the other team sent us." He assumed the other squad had been too scared to interrogate a witch.

The old woman was sitting in front of a glass globe on top of a table covered with the same material as the walls. Jerimiah's team had apparently interrupted a spell she was casting. She was waving her hand over the sphere, but then she stopped suddenly and said, "Jerimiah Gold ... which one of you is Jerimiah Gold?"

Jerimiah's mother had told stories about Gypsies just like this one. But he had assumed that was just to keep him and his sister entertained during the long journeys. Jerimiah was deeply troubled by the dark realization that his mother's stories might have come to life. Jerimiah entered, or rather was pushed into, the shack. He stood as if he was being addressed by someone in authority. The others waited outside, poking their heads into the doorway and struggling with each other for the best position to see what was going to happen next.

"Have you come for your fortune?"

"No. Actually, I—"

"I think you have. Sit down, Corporal."

Jerimiah sat in the chair opposite the old witch. He was trying to think about how later his unit would have a wild story to tell and would all have a good laugh, but for now, everything seemed deadly serious. The cabin grew calm and quiet. His comrades had found their positions in the doorway, except for Samuel; being smaller than the others, he had no view and could only listen. Nobody moved.

The old witch began to tell Jerimiah everything about himself as she waved her hand mysteriously over the crystal ball. She spoke of his sister Esther, who helped those in need, and his father the commander. It was all surprisingly accurate. But she was not telling him anything he didn't already know.

"What about my future?" asked Jerimiah.

"Your future?" She cackled ominously as she looked at the soldier's uniform. "Remove your glove, and give me your hand."

As she used her old withered hands to touch Jerimiah's palm and fingers, he found that her skin was softer than he would have expected. "Oh," she said in a surprised tone that finally matched her wide eyes. "Yes, I see it now. You are not like the others. Your lifeline is much stronger. I predict a long life, and you will travel far, but you will suffer many difficulties along the way."

"Thank you," said Jerimiah, not knowing what else to say. "Now we are going to search your cabin for weapons. Do you predict we will find any?"

The old woman looked stunned by the accusation.

Chapter 10

Burg

Jerimiah was aware that some opposition forces had been making a great deal of trouble for the Pilgrims these last years. The old city of Berlin was their fortress, and all efforts to conquer them had been repelled or foiled by North American drones. The broken walls radiated out in concentric waves, forming a maze. No one survived a frontal assault on Berlin.

Furthermore, these Berliners had made several successful attacks on the Pilgrim armies. Last month they had broken through two brigades and encircled the rear camps, taking over ten thousand prisoners, mostly women and children. The Pilgrim soldiers generally fought to the death, so it was expected that they had all been wiped out in the attack. But the captives, it was clear, had been led back to the city. No one knew what fate they had suffered after entering the city. These had not been the only captives. Though no other opposition missions had been quite so successful, stories of captured civilian Pilgrims had been told for years.

Jerimiah's unit was currently camped within visual range

of the city outskirts. It was impossible to get a good vantage point due to the flat terrain surrounding the city, but he had seen overviews from the short-lived drone flights. Berlin had electric light and likely all the comforts of a home, of which Jerimiah now had only a vague memory.

A broadcast played softly in the background, "European Pilgrim military forces are being moved into position around the old city of Berlin. With over one million in the encircling camps, Pilgrim armies have created a city of their own. We are supported by over thirty million civilian workers in France and Spain, supplying us with food and equipment from the newly rebuilt towns, factories, and farms. I can say with confidence that Pilgrim armies are the finest in the world. We will prevail over the infidels … God is great … God is great … God is great."

CV Archive PSNA12-0106-9

Nuclear Power: In the early twenty-second century, mining tritium from the moon was commonplace. It was, for a time, distributed worldwide for fusion-based power generation. After the Great Declaration, distribution chains for tritium were interrupted, as with so many other commodities. Although the small handful of people in the off-world colonies were isolated from the plague, their livelihood was in jeopardy, and many had to return home. Once the government of North America had been established, the skills needed for tritium mining were resurrected. The practice resumed, but with only one customer: the North American

Confederation. When early Forgist and Humanist pioneers set out to recolonize the lands of Africa, Europe, and Asia, the North American government did not resume distribution of tritium, since the collection process was now limited. Even within the North American borders, fusion reactors were highly regulated. Compounding the world's energy problems was a dwindling supply of traditional fossil fuels, which could scarcely be found to run combustion-engine vehicles or jet aircraft. To power cities in the old lands, nuclear fuels such as uranium were available. This meant that colonists had to contend with building fission-based reactors. Many of these reactors were constructed underground as a security measure against terrorist attacks and accidents ...

The Pilgrims' military had been shelling the city off and on for years without effect, restricted to shoot-and-evade tactics to avoid reprisals from the Hellige-controlled North American drones. Berlin had extensive underground passageways, and only the natives knew the ins and outs. Also, the air defenses were state-of-the-art. It was difficult to get a small drone to survive more than a few minutes in flight near the city. The Berliners made extensive use of electronic jamming, which was powerful enough to damage any electronic components beyond repair. This technology generated a subtle light show in the atmosphere above the city. As a result, the night sky above the city seemed to be perpetually moody and gave Pilgrim artillery a direction to point their camouflaged guns. Hellige commanders left the jamming technology alone, as long as it was not used offensively.

It was rumored that the maze of ruins was just the top of an enormous underground city, like an iceberg, with only the jagged tip visible. Each time an artillery unit opened up, they not only were harassed by North American drones but also were almost immediately overrun by opposition ground forces, as if they had struck an anthill.

Chapter 11

Wolf Pack

One month after Hector's visit to the cell of Prisoner 4596, which meant one month of 4596 sharing the small space with his ridiculous new companion, a security automaton opened the door to the cell. Though the helmet and face shield might contain a human head, the security automaton's glistening black armor was too small to contain a whole human body. It was too thin in the midsection. If it had worn a robe, it still would not have passed as a human because of the obvious way it twisted its head and made other movements. The design and the red lines running down the torso indicated that this automaton was not part of 4596's cell block, however. The fresh air smelled fresh, even if it was just the smell of the corridor outside. Bobby was excited; he wanted to go for a walk and began wagging his tail in anticipation as he sniffed this new guard.

"Prisoner 4596, you are to be transferred. Please collect your belongings and follow me, now."

4596 walked down the long corridor with a bundle in his

hands. He didn't have much—some painting supplies, dog food, and Bobby's chew stick. The prison AI watched him board the transport with his knee-high wolf in tow. 4596 was glad to leave his stinking cell behind. He was curious, however. He had never seen anyone transferred out of the cell block before, not alive anyway. But then, no one else had had a wolf pup.

The transport was similar to the one that had captured him that day on the mountain. It brought back disturbing memories, and at first, he didn't want to board. But the security automaton left him no choice. Once on board, they flew for what seemed about an hour. This was 4596's second time flying. The flashbacks to his capture and the sudden feeling of weightlessness that occurred sporadically during the flight began to make him sick. His view was limited to a small window in the door. There were four red-and-black security automatons sitting with him in the back, and he was cuffed to his seat. He had become accustomed to being handled by the automatons with the blank face shields. There was nothing to be done for or against them. They were immune to taunting, biting, scratching, and bribery. Was the pilot human? Who knew? If the automatons knew anything, they were not talking. Bobby pissed on the floor in front of them.

"Good boy," said 4596. "That'll show 'em."

After they landed, 4596 was escorted out of the piss-smelling transport into a surprisingly rustic-looking compound, its primitive facade contrasting harshly against the patrolling security automatons. The small group of four red-and-black automatons and one prisoner walked through a large wooden gate. Wooden walls surrounded the compound. Little rooms ran side by side along the interior, which made for a walking path on the roofs above them. The roofs provided an overlook to the outside for another set of security automatons. All the internal buildings were made of wood. The compound had a large, open, mostly dirt courtyard with gardens farther back. In the center was a stone-ringed well covered by a pavilion that extended beyond the well itself. Prisoner 4596 was escorted unnecessarily close to the well before being directed into one of the little buildings set against the compound wall. He remembered the pull of the Darkness, but it no longer comforted him like it once had. The room was small but it had a bed and place for his things. He was left there to be acquainted with his new surroundings. In spite of the rustic features of the compound, 4596 felt the same watchful presence from the prison. He began to see a kind of probing logic to some of his recent experiences: Give him an animal. See if he kills it. Show him a well. Watch how he reacts.

4596 felt he had changed, and he wanted to prove himself, not so much to whatever was testing him but to himself. The compound, though unsophisticated, was an improvement. There were no locked doors to keep him or Bobby inside. And there was a grassy area where Bobby could relieve himself if he could be trained. There were more security automatons posted around the walls, overlooking the courtyard, than he had ever seen in the prison. They were not shiny like his previous guards. They were painted in green and brown tones, allowing them to blend in with a forested environment. Was all this security and the compound for him alone?

He would soon have his answer. The transport left, carrying his original four guards away to other duties. He watched the transport in the distance through the open gate, which never seemed to close. Beyond the gate lay flat grasslands surrounded by wooded hills. There he saw what first looked like a strange speckled mass on the flat meadows; as it grew closer, it turned into a large group of about twenty people and wolves running toward the compound. They moved quickly and were soon rushing through the gates. 4596 could see they wore a dark blue, cassock-style robe uniform similar to what Hector had worn that day in his cell.

4596 stood in the middle of the empty courtyard with Bobby by his side. He expected the group to stop or disperse, or do something other than keep running straight at him. Instantly, the wolves attacked Bobby. The lead man in the pack smashed 4596 in the face as he ran by, planting him flat on the ground and leaving him unconscious in the dirt.

He awoke to Bobby licking his face. The men were now sitting under the pavilion around the well, drinking water. Meals had been prepared, and some were sitting on benches and tables that had been brought out and placed under the pavilion. The wolves were eating a fresh kill in the distance.

4596 went back to his room to wash off the blood and dirt before dinner. When he reached the doorway, he found a man sitting on his bed. A wolf sat outside, and Bobby rolled onto his back while the wolf growled and sniffed him. 4596 walked through the door, hoping this was not the last of Bobby.

"Can I help you?" asked 4596.

Then he saw his painting supplies had been destroyed. Before he could protest the man leaped off the bed and punched 4596 in the stomach. 4596 went to his knees.

"That's better," said the man. "Next time, you will kneel before your superiors or—"

"Lie in a pool of my own blood," 4596 said, struggling to finish the man's sentence after the gut punch. As painful as the hit had been, he had recognized this phrase from Hector's visit and decided to take the opportunity to be a smart ass. And for the second time in one day, 4596 awoke to Bobby licking his face. 4596 would spend the first night on the ground outside, with the wolves.

The next morning, he was starving. He hadn't eaten in twenty-four hours. Breakfast was set out on the long tables, which again had been set up by the well. He watched from his grassy bed. Some of the men were served food by their kneeling servants. Once they had finished, the servants were allowed to eat. 4596 had waited long enough, or so he thought. When he approached the tables, the servants stood up and walked over to 4596. They punched him down to the ground and then kicked him before returning to their breakfast.

"You will kneel before your superiors or lie in a pool of your own blood," they reminded him.

4596 waited with no comment. After the servants finished

eating, they began to clean up the dishes. There would be no food for 4596 this morning. Even Bobby had been allowed some of the leftovers after the other wolves had finished. The wolves looked at 4596 differently today. He thought he recognized the look, as if he might be the next meal. He began to realize this might be a matter of survival, and he better get with the program.

Watching the other men, 4596 learned who was highest-ranking and who was the lowest. He was apparently below the lowest. The only way he would get to eat would be to kneel and ask for food. His hunger finally drove him to try.

He approached the kitchens. A man in the kitchen saw him coming and came out of the doorway. 4596 dropped to one knee before he reached him and said, "Please, sir, may I eat?"

The cook knocked him down to the ground with a slap. "Do not speak to your superiors unless spoken to, or lie in a pool of your own blood."

Rule number 1: even the cooks could hit hard. Rule number 2: kneel before your superiors. Rule number 3: don't speak unless spoken to. 4596 recited the rules in his head. *Not sure how many lessons like this I'm goin' to survive*, he thought.

One more time, 4596 propped himself back up and took a knee. This time he waited until the cook acknowledged him. It took a minute, since the man was busy trying not burn something inside the kitchen.

"What do you want?"

"Please, sir, may I eat?"

"You may carry the garbage out. That is all."

4596 ate what he could find from the leftovers inside the garbage bags. Later, he was allowed to serve the servants and eat directly from the table scraps. 4596 and Bobby would spend the next month learning the rules of how to be part of the wolf pack.

The pack hunted or gathered from the forest and the gardens each day. The hunting was like nothing 4596 had ever experienced. It was somewhat like a fox hunt, without horses. The men would run down the animals on foot without weapons and guide them into the wolf pack. The wolves anticipated the tactic and made the kill. 4596 could not keep up the pace that this required at first and was left in the wilderness to make his way back to camp on his own. He thought once that maybe he should try a different direction, just to see how far he could get, but a security transport dropped an automaton in front of him, which said politely, "Recruit 4596, you are traveling in the wrong direction. Please correct your course to the southeast." It pointed, indicating 4596's correct heading.

Interestin', thought 4596. *I'm designated as a recruit, not a prisoner. A recruit for what, sled dog?*

This became 4596's and Bobby's new life. Bobby grew quickly and moved up in the ranks. Progress was slower for 4596. Eventually, some of the men left the compound, and others arrived. But 4596 was keeping up and beginning to contribute to the hunt. Interactions with the wolves had to be handled carefully. They knew that humans outranked them, but on occasion, especially if they were protecting a fresh kill, they would challenge 4596, who had been assigned to collect and carry the game back to camp.

I wonder what would happen if I challenged one of my superiors, thought 4596. There seemed to be some gray area in regard to challenges among wolves. He had seen the way the wolves sometimes ganged up on lower-ranking challengers and at other times allowed a shift in rank. What would happen to a human challenger? This had not occurred in the human pack since he arrived, so he had no examples from which to learn.

There were other activities besides hunting, such as hand-to-hand combat, simple weapons training, and instruction on how to repair security automatons, as well as cooking, gardening, and religious studies.

Then there was the inexplicable. One day 4596 was told to take Bobby to a fenced-in area outside of the main compound. Here, without any explanation, he was given a live rabbit and locked inside the fence with Bobby. After an hour, Bobby ran down the rabbit and killed it. 4596 cleaned and cooked the rabbit and shared it with Bobby. The next day, the fence was unlocked, and both Bobby and 4596 were allowed to leave.

After a time, once he had properly joined the pack during the hunt, 4596 was made an Omega, the lowest rank above "new guy." Omega status allowed him additional enhancement technology. This gave 4596 an incredible sense of power that he had never known before. His new speed and strength meant that the hunts were relatively easy now. This development also explained how the cook and the others had been able to swat him down like a fly. His combat training now included special instructions on nonlethal maneuvers. Slapping was preferred, instead of closed-fist punches, to limit the damage and prevent unintentional death. 4596 had been wondering about how to challenge a superior, and now he had the ability.

It was impossible to ask a simple question of a top-ranked Alpha. Only Betas, the second-highest rank, would bother to speak to an Omega. But 4596 had questions that needed answering. He first tried to ask the Betas, but they did not respond to his questions directly, saying that the information was restricted and could be spoken only by an Alpha. To have his questions answered, 4596 realized, he must make it to the rank of Beta. He could wait for his turn, but at this rate that might take many months. Instead of waiting, 4596 decided to use his newfound abilities to challenge one of the Betas. He chose his old friend, the cook, Recruit 4289. The cook recently had been promoted, after the last recruit exchange. He would be the lowest-ranked Beta and the least likely to be supported by others in a challenge. 4596 decided to take his chance at dinner that night.

The cook had taken his seat and planned to be served by 4596. But instead of kneeling and waiting to be acknowledged, 4596 stood with the cook's plate in his hand. The cook stood up from the table. 4596 backed up, dropping the plate in the dirt. The cook came after 4596 quickly. 4596 had watched the wolves give chase to each other. He thought this might be a good tactic to get the cook away from the others, making them less inclined to join in the beating. It would give 4596 some time alone with his adversary, in any case. The cook had no choice but to follow him away from the table, to dole out some form of punishment. For now, no one else stood, but they were watching.

4596 played as if he was going to give up and allow his inevitable punishment. The cook swung fast at 4596's head, but 4596 blocked the move more quickly and followed up with a surprise punch to the cook's gut. But the cook didn't go down. Instead, he backed away from the repetitive blows that 4596 was now throwing. 4596 saw movement behind the cook. The others were coming. They would be on him in a second. With his last move, he struck the cook in the throat, a devastating punch that would have ended the fight, except that the other Betas had arrived.

4596 woke up in the infirmary. The cook was on a table across the room, staring him down. 4596's left eye was covered by a bandage, and his hand was immobilized by a stiff plastic cover. Both injuries were too much for the medical enhancement technology to handle on their own. 4596 tried to remember what had happened. He recalled going into a ball as the pack attacked him.

"What did you think you were doing?" said a voice from his left side.

Because of the eye bandage, 4596 had to turn to see who was speaking. To his surprise, Hector was standing next to him. He hadn't seen Hector since that first day in his cell. "I wanted to ask questions that only Alphas can answer." 4596 felt his lips as he spoke. His upper and lower lips both were fat and cracked open in places. He must have looked pathetic.

"What was so important you felt you had to kill to achieve it?"

"I didn't kill anyone; he's over there, sir."

"So killing him was not your intention then?"

"No. I challenged him for his position in the pack, not to kill him."

"So you can ask your question?"

"Yes, sir."

"Then ask it now."

"I seem to have been recruited for somethin', but I don't know what I'm supposed to accomplish. I have seen others leave, maybe to meet some greater challenge. How are they chosen? What test have I not completed?"

"You have learned how to live among other predators, to cooperate with them for mutual benefit. But you still do not understand your purpose. You continue to seek advantage only for yourself. There is more for you to learn here."

"But I serve the pack. What more is there?"

"Out of necessity perhaps, because serving the pack gives you power. But power without purpose is useless and is no accomplishment in itself. Who should power serve? How should it be used? How can our power serve humanity as God wishes, rather than be used by you to simply feed upon others?"

4596 was now required to answer these questions. "Wolves feed on the weak; it is in their nature. And that strengthens the herds of prey animals. A balance in nature is achieved. Why is that not the answer?"

"Because God has made us more than just animals to be culled. He has allowed us to rise above the animals and to rule over the Earth. Humanity can never achieve its potential if we stay in balance with nature. Because we have been made so unequal, we should separate ourselves from these primitive instincts and strive to practice what God has taught us."

"Then we can use our power to protect others?"

"But protect them from what? Ourselves? Should we isolate ourselves in these camps? No, there would always be those of us who would not submit. Yes, we should protect humanity from those who would choose to use power for their own ends. You can be a countermeasure for the darkness in men."

After an uncomfortably short period of recuperation—about ten minutes later, a gathering took place in the courtyard, with Alphas and Betas in attendance. 4596 and the cook were brought out and placed before the ranking pack members. The cook could barely speak, but as they stood waiting for the pack members to gather, he asked 4596 in a hoarse voice that sounded pained, "Do you know why they made me a cook?"

"Because you're so damn good at it," 4596 said sarcastically.

They both chuckled at this. The cook was not known for his fine cuisine. The chuckle resulted in a painful cough from the cook, but he recovered quickly. He then continued hoarsely. "If you ever try that shit again, you will find yourself in my pot, like my wife and her lawyer did not so long ago."

4596 nodded but thought, *Or you might find yourself down a well.*

Hector led the meeting. He stood out among the wolf-pack members in attendance. He was clean-shaven, his hair was cut tight against his head, and his clothes looked fresh and unwrinkled. In contrast, those surrounding him now were dirty, long-haired, bearded, wild-looking men. But even they looked better than 4596 and the cook at the moment.

"Recruit 4596 has made a challenge for status as Beta. He has not reverted to his old ways, as we feared. I believe he should be allowed to retain membership. Additionally, he will be granted Beta standing in order to further his studies."

4596 indeed continued his studies eagerly. He learned that what he had unknowingly been preparing for was called the Hellige order. Within the Forgist teachings, these holy warriors were meant to be the protectors of humanity.

So my purpose is to be a sheepdog, he thought, *to protect the herds from other predators.*

MI Archive MS456-0852-7

The Hellige, or holy warriors, evolved from a need for an exception to the Forgist tenet to do no harm. Taking another life or harming others is considered a sin against God in the Forgist faith.

This select group of highly trained and venerated men addressed the Forge's need to protect itself from those who would seek to harm its vulnerable membership. The Hellige was instrumental during the Forgist transition into political power.

The Hellige take an oath of celibacy and oaths of loyalty to the sect and to the protection of the Forge. These oaths were later expanded to protect the Humanist Party members after the Great Declaration, during the formation of the newly constituted North American government. Early concerns about conflicting priorities with the Humanists were quickly abated after the Hellige successfully put down terrorist attempts by those responding to the teachings of the prophet James Murphy.

Women are excluded from this sect, and a strict, regimented lifestyle for the men is maintained. It is understood among the Hellige that their actions have serious consequences, and they view their work as a holy rite that can be conducted only by their carefully administrated order. Their lifestyle reflects a kind of continual penance for the way of life that they have adopted. Strict standards have been set for routine engagement with others, and the administration of their craft is highly regulated by the government.

Criminal behavior among civilians can result in one of three options: imprisonment, exile, or if selected, induction into the Hellige. Members of the Hellige often initially display antisocial or violent tendencies. But honed by the discipline of the order, they are reborn, and their acts of violence are transformed into acts of self-sacrifice and love. Discipline and training are essential to the Hellige lifestyle. In an age when enhancement technology has made ordinary people superhuman, Hellige training has made the members of their order legendary. The Hellige are utilized mainly in military operations, but many are stationed with and work alongside internal security forces ...

Heracles was a frequent visitor to the camp and acted as the camp commander. Though the pack members tended to police each other, there were administrative duties that the rest of the pack was not authorized to perform. 4596 had met only two Alphas, Heracles and Hector. He could never be sure when or if Hector might show up again.

Heracles was sitting behind a large desk in his office on the second floor, overlooking the compound. He was powerfully built and much cleaner-looking than 4596, who knelt in front of him with his scruffy beard, dirty face, and greasy hair. Heracles had been composing a daily status report after dinner and was trying to ignore 4596's presence in his office.

"Recruit 4596, more questions?" Heracles finally responded after he realized 4596 was not going away.

"Yes, sir."

"Then speak."

"I believe I am ready to take the oaths."

"Hmm. You do?"

"Yes, sir."

"We will see." He made an additional comment in his report and sent the message. "Meet me out by the rabbit pen. And bring your wolf."

Bobby had grown into a healthy male and was flirting with Alpha status in his own pack. The wolf pack, unlike the human Betas and Omegas, included both males and females, and they were allowed to come and go as they liked. But the wolf puppies that came in with the new recruits tended to want to stay with the pack in the compound, regardless of their rank.

Bobby responded to only some commands, but it was an easy matter to get him to come to the rabbit pen. Bobby loved to chase rabbits. Heracles and a Beta met the two at the pen. 4596 knelt, awaiting the rabbit to be given to him.

This time, instead of the silent ceremony 4596 had come to expect, Heracles spoke. "Recruit 4596, you are now charged with the care and well-being of this rabbit. Do you swear to protect this rabbit from any and all threats? And are you prepared to suffer or lay down your life in its defense?"

4596 was stunned. Was this a joke? Was he being asked to defend a rabbit? "I don't understand, sir."

"You say you are willing to take an oath to defend others, but you are unwilling to first prove that you are up to this simple task. This rabbit is symbolic of those you will be charged to defend. If you cannot protect a rabbit, why should we expect you to protect a civilization? Do you accept?"

"I do," said 4596. What other choice did he have?

The pen was closed, leaving 4596 holding the rabbit as Bobby panted happily by his side. 4596 held the rabbit as long as he could and then made a smaller pen using one of the corners and his own body to block Bobby from the rabbit. Bobby didn't understand. He had been trained to expect humans to give their prey to the wolves to kill. And he wanted the rabbit to run and to chase it. Bobby could hear it scuffling in the corner of the pen as it tried to dig in the dirt behind 4596's body. Night came and went. 4596 had expected to be released from the pen the next day, but this did not happen. Instead, they were to be kept inside—for how long, he did not know.

Eventually, 4596 would have to sleep, but he was getting hungry, which meant Bobby was getting hungry too. Bobby stopped his playful attitude toward 4596 and began to growl. Suddenly, the wolf lost patience and made a move on one side of 4596. He wasn't trying to bite 4596. Bobby wanted to get behind him, to the rabbit. 4596 pushed him away. As he pushed, Bobby bit his hand, the same hand that had been broken in the challenge. It had long since healed but was now bleeding again. The rabbit, hearing the snarling wolf and feeling 4596 give an opening, darted out down the length of the pen. Bobby gave chase. Within two seconds, Bobby had the small animal in his jaws. He shook it only once and then dropped the rabbit, dead with a broken neck, on the ground in front of him.

You can prepare the rabbit for eating, said the look on Bobby's face. With nothing else to do, 4596 complied. As they finished eating the rabbit, Bobby licked 4596's wounded hand. Then the gates to the pen were opened, and 4596 and Bobby were allowed back to the main compound.

4596 would have to have a better strategy next time. But what could he do against a hungry wolf? He had pledged to give his life to save the rabbit and had failed. Maybe he could bring in a restraint for Bobby next time? Yeah, but why bring the wolf and rabbit into the pen at all? He was to prove he could defend the helpless, with his life if need be. For that, there needed to be an actual threat. But why Bobby? Perhaps this was to be further proof of his dedication to his oaths? 4596 had been picked for his unique traits and groomed for this position. But was he truly prepared to become one of them? Could he kill something he respected, to protect something he did not respect?

4596 delayed asking for a rematch. The thought of it weighed heavily on him. He was no longer in such a hurry to prove his value to anyone. But life at the compound began to wear on him. It all seemed so pointless now that the goal was in sight. His hand had healed, leaving a scar. He thought he would carry that scar for the rest of his life.

Nothing was said when 4596 returned and kneeled before Heracles. Heracles regarded the recruit with what must have been a distant memory. The small group once again walked to the rabbit pen, leaving Bobby and 4596 locked inside.

The contest was swift this time. There was no reason to pretend that anything would go differently than last time. 4596 gently placed the rabbit on the ground and stood between it and the wolf. The rabbit went to find a place to hide, and Bobby tried to follow. 4596 lunged and grabbed Bobby by the head. He twisted the wolf's head violently. There was a soft whimper, softer than the sound of the cracking neck. 4596 held his dead friend and ran his scarred hand across the thick, soft coat for the last time.

Chapter 12

Berlin

Within the old city of Berlin, under the watchful eyes of the Pilgrim army, the three generals of the European opposition forces met to discuss the current situation. Dinner was under way, and they were sitting around a long table covered with platters of various steaming meats and mugs of frothy beers. A series of fish tanks provided a lighted background, and a string quartet played softly at one end of the long, wood-paneled room.

"General Mueller, we should strike now, blast them off the face of the planet. What is the delay?"

"We can hold out indefinitely. Our reports say we are far better equipped for a siege than they are. If we use the nuclear option, we risk contaminating our land and water, and it would provoke them to use their nuclear arsenal. So far, this war is a grand inconvenience. It doesn't make any sense for either side to use nuclear weapons, and I'm not going to be the first to escalate this conflict."

"And if they decide to set the example, we will lose everything."

"We have over fifty thousand prisoners in the city at the moment. Their people would die along with ours. Do you really believe they would sacrifice themselves like that? The decision stands."

Chapter 13

The Last Straw

Back at the Pilgrim headquarters for the European theater of operations, the commanders of the Pilgrim armies, led by the prophet John Murphy, a descendant of James Murphy, were having a meeting of their own. The latest opposition attack had been the last straw for the Pilgrim commanders. They were planning something big this time.

"We sent a submersible down the Spree waterway. It was a Squid drone with a locator beacon and some simple surveillance hardware. We recorded some good intelligence about the locations of some of their defensive batteries. But that's not what we are here to talk about. The point is, the drone not only made it through but also found this."

A picture popped up showing an underwater structure. It was enhanced with overlapping views from different light and sonar frequencies. It looked like a large drain pipe was discharging into the riverbed, but once the picture was animated, the pipe could be seen to be pulling river water into something.

"This intake pipe, we believe, is used by the city's power system to generate steam and cool the reactor. We think we can use these waterways to get a device close enough to take out the water system feeding the city generator. By driving the submersible up this pipe, we can achieve the maximum amount of damage to the underground facilities located here." General Green pointed at a map to a section in western Berlin.

"It's better than trying to launch an overhead attack through all the countermeasures. And it's not clear what a surface attack would do to the underground facilities. Once the defenses are down, we can hit them with follow-up attacks from overhead."

"What of the captives?"

"Regrettable but necessary losses. And we are not sure what horrors they are facing at the moment. It would be a kindness."

"What about the other opposition forces? Won't this escalate into an all-out nuclear response?"

"Well, the follow-up attack doesn't have to be nuclear. The underground nature of the initial attack should be interpreted as a failure of their nuclear power plant. It is important that this be decisive. And if they realize we used nukes …"

"Can't we use a conventional warhead?"

"No, that would be too heavy, if it were to achieve the desired effect. It has to be at least a small nuclear device."

John Murphy rose and looked around at the debating generals. "If this fails, we need a backup plan. We need to make sure that if we are discovered, we can mount a first strike against Dresden and Prague as well."

"Using nukes?"

"Yes," said Murphy resolutely.

"If you intend to wipe out any nuclear retaliatory strike capability, then you will also need to hit Warsaw and London simultaneously. Some of these targets could be hit easily, but a target like London would take multiple missile strikes. It would deplete our entire arsenal. If it failed, we would have nothing left with which to defend ourselves. This also creates the issue of nuclear fallout for the years to come."

"Well, let's pray it doesn't come to that. Begin the preparations."

Chapter 14

Monday

Jerimiah and his unit had been lying quietly under cover for hours in the dark hole they had fashioned into an observation post. They had been assigned to monitor opposition activity in the area. There would be no offensive strikes for now, not even if a target presented itself. That would be suicide in any case, given that Jerimiah's unit was protected only by a little dirt and a thin sensor-resistant camouflage net. In the distance, music could be heard across the walls of Berlin. Jerimiah imagined that the Pilgrims were building a massive assault force somewhere in the darkness, outside the glow of the city lights. Would he have to go in? Would he survive?

"Squad 15?"

"Check. No movement, nothing to report." Jerimiah was using a monitor to view images coming from sensors placed outside the camouflage net.

"So where are you boys from?" whispered Paul. There had been some confusion about coverage of the position they were currently occupying. Now elements of the Fourteenth and Tenth Armies were overlapping. Paul was talking to one of the new members who had recently joined them in the bunker.

"We're from the Fourteenth Army, under General Okeke."

"Okeke? Never heard of him. So what's the Fourteenth Army like?"

"I guess you would say it's typical. But we did have a guy spontaneously combust the other day."

"What?"

"Yeah. First, he was acting weird, like he wasn't himself. And then later, he just caught fire and burned into a pile of ash."

"Huh, that's a good one," said Paul. "Did you know Jerimiah here was recently cursed by a witch?"

"A what?" The question came as another dark shadow entered the interior of the listening station. It was yet another member of Fourteenth Army. There were now as many members of Fourteenth Army as there were of Tenth Army.

"No, a witch, swear to God," whispered Paul. "It happened, right, Aziz?"

"Yep, it's all true."

"What happened?" said another.

"A w-w-witch … Y-you tell it, P-Paul," said Samuel, smiling wide enough for his teeth to reflect the dim glow of the instruments.

"Sure. So … we're out on a routine patrol when we see squad 5 hauling ass back to camp, all of them screamin'.

Jerimiah here, he grabs one of 'em and says, 'What's all this about?' The guy says, 'Run! There's a crazy witch in that cave. She cursed us all with flatulence.' Sure enough, they were all tootin' away like a brass band running through the woods. But Jerimiah here, he says, 'I'm not afraid of some stupid, crazy old woman, and I already fart like an opera singer.'" Paul demonstrated.

"Oh God, no, stop."

Snickering erupted from several of the young men.

"Keep your voices down," said Jerimiah.

Paul continued, in a softer voice this time, "So Jerimiah walks into the cave brandishing his Scimitar, ready to avenge his poor afflicted comrades. There she was, levitating four meters off the ground, lightning shooting from her arse. Jerimiah—he's a crack shot, you know—takes aim and blows her head clean off. The head just hovers there above the body, spinning around and around. She's not dead. The witch then grabs her head and pops it back into place. Then she glares at Jerimiah. We're thinking, 'Oh no, he's going to get it now.' But then she calls him by name. 'I'm impressed, Jerimiah Gold. No one has ever challenged me before. You are a worthy warrior. I will grant you one wish.' So Jerimiah thinks about it for a bit and then says, 'I would like to be rewarded with seven virgins.' The witch says, 'Your wish is granted.' And here you all are, thanks to Jerimiah."

Laughter erupted from the dark shadows again. "Speak for yourself."

"Really, guys, shut up."

"Okay, okay."

Through the monitors, Jerimiah was viewing the city lights on the horizon and wondering what they must be thinking about there, what stories they were telling. He worried about Esther. They were never far away from the action, and she might be captured next.

Suddenly, there was a flash of blinding light. Some tried to get up but fell on top of each other in the overcrowded hole. Jerimiah's ears were ringing. He thought he saw movement and attempted to trigger the automated defenses. Then the spotty afterglow from the previous blast went black.

The next thing he knew, he was awaking in a cell, stripped of his armor and weapons. Some of his squad was with him.

"Corporals Gomez, McKenzie, Gold, come with me," said a stern voice. The speaker held a pistol and a computer tablet. Two other guards dressed in black robes stood on either side of the man, brandishing machine guns.

Jerimiah got up and tried to walk out the cell door. He was dizzy, and Paul caught him just in time to prevent a tumble to the hard concrete below his feet. Paul and Aziz held him up by his arms as all three were escorted out of the cell. They saw many other prisoners in other cells along the way, all Pilgrim soldiers. Jerimiah wondered where they kept the thousands of others who had been captured. After his own experiences hiking around Europe, he couldn't imagine how you would house so many underground. It definitely would not be pleasant, he thought.

"Where is the rest of the unit?" Jerimiah said groggily.

"No idea," said Paul.

"*Halt den mund!*" yelled one of the escorts.

All three felt a push originating from Paul's shoulder.

"What?" said Paul.

"No talking," said a stern voice.

"Why didn't you just say so?"

This time their escort hit Paul in the head with the butt of his machine gun. Paul fell, taking Jerimiah down with him. Aziz pulled hard to get both of them back on their feet. Then it was up to Aziz to march his two punch-drunk comrades to meet their fate. Arms interlocked, they wobbled down a long corridor to a room at the end. It had tile floors and a drain. It was a shower room. Jerimiah hadn't seen one like this that worked in over a year. They often used makeshift outdoor wash areas. Running water was a luxury. Jerimiah's little band joined three other members of the Pilgrim military forces already in the room, including Samuel. They were stripped naked and forced to kneel on the hard tile facing the wall of shower heads. Then one of the guards hosed them down with a cold water hose. Afterward, they were allowed to dry in place for a time, shivering.

"Sir," said a voice from the hall behind them.

"Dismissed, Captain," a different voice echoed from the hall.

Then someone new entered the showers behind the row of prisoners. "Well, well ... what do we have here, Sergeant?" said the new man.

"Pilgrim soldiers, mainly from the listening post in sector 6, sir."

"Thank you, Sergeant. And which ones were carrying these?"

Jerimiah couldn't make out what the man was referring to at first or who had been implicated because all this was happening at their backs. But then a colonel wandered around into view, casually, like he was walking through a garden, in front of the dripping, bearded Pilgrims. He was carrying a maul about one-third of a meter long, with a dull black finish on the head and handle. He spun it around as he walked. Then Jerimiah understood. They all understood. The symbol of the Forge, the hammer was carried by many soldiers in spite of the extra weight. More than a symbol, its primary military use was for clubbing wounded opposition soldiers left on the battlefield, thus saving ammunition. Jerimiah had never kept one, claiming it was too clumsy, hanging from the waist belt, to be carried by a sniper. This was true, but after seeing the maul in action and the blood-splattered beards and grinning faces of his comrades who wielded the hammer, he had decided it wasn't for him regardless of his duties. Almost everyone else in his squad had one. There was no need to see who had been pointed out. Even Samuel had carried one, though Jerimiah doubted he had ever actually used it.

"Well, that is interesting," continued the colonel. Then he began talking directly to the kneeling Pilgrims, bending down with this hand on one thigh for support. "You see, I have a message for your commanders that simply must be delivered. So though I really hate to do it, I have to let one of you lucky guys walk out of here today to carry that message. But how should I choose which one? Well, it turns out you all made that choice very easy for me. Now, the first part of the message goes like this."

As he said these final words, he struck Corporal Paul Gomez in the head with the maul, splattering his blood over the shower floor and everyone standing or kneeling on it. Next, Aziz McKenzie's shocked face fell to the floor. The colonel continued down the line, swinging at the men's heads one at a time. The last Pilgrim soldiers tried to rise but were forced down by the guards behind them. The guards holding them down received a large bath of blood on their helmets for their efforts. If the helmets hadn't had full face shields, it might not have been such a pleasant experience for them. Samuel, the runt of the litter, was the last to be put down.

Jerimiah was still dizzy, and he threw up into the carnage that lay around him. The guy with the hose began to spray again but was interrupted by the colonel, who had to take a second swing at a few of the Pilgrims lying on the shower floor. Then a fresh rinse was applied to Jerimiah before he was finally removed from the room. Cold water dripped from his hair and naked body in a long, wet trail down the hallway leading away from the blood-spattered showers. Jerimiah had to support himself along the corridor with one hand since he no longer had his comrades to help him.

"So that was fun," said the colonel as they walked down

the hall together. "Don't forget now—you let 'em know what I said."

The colonel was covered with blood, and he was in the process of unbuttoning his shirt when they came across a pair of guards and another colonel who seemed to be waiting for him. To Jerimiah's surprise, this colonel was a woman, and she was immaculately dressed. One of her guards held out a robe to Jerimiah. He tried to put it on quickly. He was cold, but it didn't help that he was still dizzy and embarrassed about being naked in front of a woman. He had to support himself on the wall by his throbbing forehead to make it work. No one helped.

"Whenever you're ready," said the second colonel.

Meanwhile, the first colonel had wandered down the hall to another room and disappeared from sight.

"The second part of the message is this way," said the second colonel.

Jerimiah was escorted to a small four-wheel vehicle with seats facing front and back. His two machine gun–wielding escorts jumped in the back, and the colonel took the driver seat, leaving only one place for Jerimiah. Jerimiah had never seen a colonel drive before. Once Jerimiah was seated, the little open-top car sped away down a long corridor, through a security check post, and down another long hallway. After running through a second security post, they finally arrived at an enormous, open, tube-shaped room. The little car continued full speed down an elevated aisleway hanging about midway between the floor and the ceiling. There were no windows in the space, but the lighting was intense, and green plants dotted the floor beneath them. There were people down on the floor too, lots of people. Some were gardening, and others were cooking. Children were playing. There were little square areas sectioned off by sheets. Likely, these were sleeping areas, curtained for privacy. There was no need for a complete tent in the indoor environment. There were a few security guards on the floor, driving around in the same type of little electric car that conveyed Jerimiah.

Jerimiah tried to focus on what he was seeing, but the tunnel seemed to be spinning. He closed his eyes to try to make it stop and breathed in deeply. *It doesn't stink*, thought Jerimiah. *All these people indoors, and it doesn't stink.*

"These are all your people," said the colonel. "Your shelling has to stop, or this whole place is going to come down on top of them. Do you understand what I'm saying?"

Jerimiah nodded. After he recovered somewhat, he was allowed to spend some time in different locations along the way through the cavernous room. Jerimiah was also allowed to go down and talk to the people so that he could confirm who they were. The colonel wanted Jerimiah to be sure this wasn't staged, so she let him decide when to stop the car. He stopped them three times along the way, until he was satisfied that these were all his people. Some told him when and how they had been captured. Some told him how surprised they were with their treatment. The people seemed sincere, not frightened, and all were well fed. In fact, they looked healthy, which was about the only thing that seemed out of place. Most Pilgrim camps were heavily rationed. These people seemed to be enjoying the change. After the last stop, Jerimiah needed to sit back down. He was satisfied with his inspection. It took five more minutes for the car, racing full speed, to get through the tunnel, and they had already driven a great distance. They ended their drive at the far end of the giant tube at another security post. The colonel handed Jerimiah a small, square piece of plastic. It looked like it might be a memory storage device.

"It's a holographic video of the ride we just went through so that you can show your commanders what you saw here today. We want you to confirm what your commanders will see in the holo-video, and we hope that they believe you. Good luck."

With that, the two guards put a hood over his head, and Jerimiah was escorted up and out into the oncoming dawn.

Chapter 15

Prophets

Julia had recently told Augustus about an exciting event at the Kalamazoo Smedje. Solomon was going to be visiting to deliver a series of presentations on the BCM project, but for some reason, none of this was public knowledge. Julia wanted to go with Augustus, and she planned to travel back to Kalamazoo so that they could attend the event together.

Artemis didn't tell me anything about it, so maybe he doesn't know, thought Augustus. He was about to send Artemis a message but then realized that he would have to tell him about visiting the Forge, since it would not be broadcast. He wasn't sure how Artemis would feel about that.

Augustus and Julia met outside across the street from the Forge in the same location that they had met on their first date. As they walked across the street, Augustus was able to make some detailed observations about the building this time. Augustus thought, *is that new? Why have I never noticed the ironwork before?* Augustus went inside still rubber-necking his surroundings as Julia led them to their seat.

"Good afternoon, everyone. I am Dr. Solomon Jones of the Confederate Technology Council. Today, we will be giving you an update on the BCM program. So for those of you who wandered in here accidentally, thinking this was Mimandrews, it's across the street, and you may want to leave now."

This evoked some nervous laughter from the group seated before Solomon's holographic image. His comments were made all the more ridiculous by the small army of security guards stationed at the entrances. They were also placed like statues around the interior of their cathedral, with their backs to each column supporting the cathedral ceiling. Above them, all the architectural lines in the building seemed to point them out. Augustus was again sitting with Julia, but this time he was focused entirely on the speaker. A gathering had been held earlier, but the attendees from that had all gone home. The mood was very different from a regular service. There were some higher-level officials in the audience. This was the reason for the heightened security. Julia and Augustus had been questioned by the security forces when they arrived. There was a concern about radical Forgist infiltrators. At one time, Augustus had worried the Smedje congregation might be dangerous, but now he was hoping this group was dangerous enough to fend off whatever attack these security guards might be expecting.

"We will not be broadcasting today's presentation. This will remain a controlled archive," said an automated voice.

"Begin GV Archive SCTC990-7598-1: Kalamazoo city center, April 19, 2260, Dr. Solomon Jones presenting."

So this is how you make history? thought Augustus.

Solomon continued, "Today I am going to tell you a true story. It may be the most important story of our existence to date, and there is a lot of controversy about making this knowledge available to the general public, for reasons you will soon understand."

Augustus had continued his review of the cathedral in amazement. It had surprised him to find that in previous visits he had missed rather obvious features of the building's exterior. But now the interior was populated by such an array of interesting people and things. "What is Artemis doing here?" asked Augustus, too loudly. "How did he get here?" Augustus instantly felt a pinch from Julia. "Did you just pinch me?" he whispered.

"Who is Artemis?" asked Julia, whispering softly into Augustus's ear.

Augustus liked this new method of conversation, so he turned to whisper back into Julia's ear. The warm, sweet smell of the bakery once again came to mind, but this time there were no doughnuts. "He's the provincial governor's son, sitting over there." Augustus pointed, which seemed to be noted by one of the guards.

Some of the security guards were displaying full battle tech. Their black fatigues were covered in armor and forearm-mounted pulse rifles. Their helmets included full face shields, so it was difficult to tell if they were automaton or human.

Augustus thought it was more likely that the handlers were stationed inside, with automatons positioned outside. Some of the guards wore black dress robes without helmets, but the pulse rifles were plainly visible, extending down over the back of each hand from the forearm.

MI Declassified Archive MAI732-0400-2

Automated Security Forces: Automatons may be stationed in select locations, or they may follow their human counterparts over any terrain and carry similar amounts of supplies and equipment, as needed. Security-grade automatons can operate in a variety of automatic modes but are programmed to attack selected targets only after receiving authorization from a human controller. They will then doggedly hunt down the target, utilizing whatever force is necessary under the limitation of the current security directives. Automatons may be capable of separating a threat from a civilian in an urban environment. However, early-model experiments generated distrust of that level of responsibility, without initial authorization through the method of tagging targets.

Security equipment:

- Helmets supplement communications through enhancement tech, by providing heads-up displays for multiple images generated from a variety of sources. These sources may include security or civilian automatons, overhead drones, or even stationary street-mounted cameras. This is normally too much information for any human to process. An SAI, or Security Artificial Intelligence, is employed to coordinate the most relevant information needs for the security forces through the helmet interface.

- Body armor is worn by both human and automaton security units. Armor will provide protection from most forms of projectiles, stabbing, and chemical weaponry. Body armor will also protect from extreme environmental conditions. Cold, heat, low oxygen, and underwater environments may be successfully navigated with this technology.

- Nonlethal weaponry: Commonly used in arrests of fleeing or belligerent perpetrators, a net may be projected from the security automaton to successfully immobilize a human target. Another form of nonlethal force may be projected from the pulse rifles, utilized by an automaton or human security units. Pulse rifles are personalized rail guns. The chambers generate a magnetic field to launch projectiles. The arm-mounted pulse rifle is powered by a fusion reactor small enough to be worn as a backpack. As an intermediary product of the fusion reaction, superheated, highly charged plasma generates electricity to power the pulse rifle and other gear. With some of the hot, ionized plasma siphoned off and loaded it into a casing, it can be fired at human targets. When launched, a projectile containing the hot ionized plasma clears the shooter's proximity and disintegrates, releasing the charged gas within. This, in turn, creates a charged air pocket with electrical potential energy that seeks the nearest grounding source. When ionized rounds are fired at the body or overhead, targets become like lightning rods. Anyone in close proximity to the ionized air pocket will be stunned, not only by the electrical discharge but also by the concussive sound and intense light that is also produced.

- Lethal weaponry: Use of deadly force is restricted to human Hellige units. Less dramatic than the plasma projectile, guided solid projectiles can be loaded into the same chamber of the pulse rifle to be used on individuals or multiple targets, with almost silent lethal force. Projectiles may be selected to explode or not and penetrate armor or not, depending on the task.

"He probably came with his family," whispered Julia, referring to Artemis's seating position. "See, the governor and his wife are sitting right beside him."

"Oh yeah," whispered Augustus. "Didn't see them at first."

Augustus caught a security guard in plain clothes eyeing the two of them from across the floor. Suddenly all the dark face shields from the other guards that were wearing full battle tech turned slightly. They seemed to be looking in Augustus's direction. These were not typical security forces; this guard and the others were displaying the wolf insignia, which identified them as a unique sect known as the Hellige. Augustus took the hint and stopped talking.

Solomon continued, "First, let me start by saying that this story begins with our quest for knowledge. As Einstein once said, a little knowledge is a dangerous thing. So is a lot. But it is in humanity's nature to search for knowledge. Our thirst for knowledge was given to us by God, and in our pursuit of knowledge and our dedication to truth, we serve Him. It is important that you trust in what I say because we must find a way forward, and we must be united in that effort.

"Second, because I am a member of the Smedje Synod, I feel the need to distinguish my faith from those radical elements referred to as the Forge. I hope that the members of the Humanist Party who are gathered with us today will also be able to draw that distinction and not allow our differences to sway your acceptance of what you are about to hear. The only meaningful difference between the early Forgist and the modern-day Humanist is that Humanists have decided to leave God out of their belief systems and calculations. Otherwise, we are philosophically alike. We both believe that our civilization should continue to be improved. The Smedje believe that this is what God wants for us all. And someday, if we can prove our worthiness, we can join the Great Society in the afterlife."

GV Archive SSEH50-0892-3

The Smedje Synod came into existence after the start of the Forgist movement. From its beginnings as a metalworking society in Denmark, the Synod led the Forgist movement throughout its phases, first as an early religion and then later to become a new political power, before and after the Great Declaration. Before the Great Declaration, the Synod oversaw the emergence of the Hellige order. After the Great Declaration, the Synod developed the Confederate Technology Council, or CTC, to liaise between the newly formed North American government and the Bio Crystalline Matrix project, with which the Synod was associated. The CTC eventually became an independent council, separate from the Synod, but the CTC's membership is heavily influenced by early Forgist ideals.

"Now I will provide some background on the BCMAI project. This history lesson should be added to the archive," said Solomon. "Some of you may know this story already, but please be patient, so others can catch up."

Solomon once again spoke of the differences between supercomputers and the Bio Crystalline Matrix technology, of the early issues with BCMAI uncertainty, and of the trial-and-error programming that resulted in the BCMAI's belief in God. Augustus was familiar with this part of the story.

Solomon also spoke of the viral outbreak and the BCMAI response that had resulted in the Great Declaration. At this point in the presentation, a low murmur moved through the auditorium, along with some gasps and a few angry retorts.

"You people need to be stopped!"

"Shut it down!"

"Why does this thing still exist?" yelled a particularly vocal individual near the front. "It's all still functioning, right?

If you keep it around, someone is just going to plug it back in again. Isn't that so?"

Solomon answered slowly. "That is very close to what we are now proposing."

"Fanatical bullshit," the stranger called out again. "God's will. Heard it all before, just like your radical buddies. You'd let that thing burn down the world, as long as you thought God was controlling it."

The security guards had stiffened in response to the potential threat of angry members in the gathering. But Augustus noticed that most of the group was not participating in the mayhem. This left the man to stand alone in the crowd, which had the effect of dampening his fervor. Many in the gathering apparently had been privy already to the information presented so far. Also, the Hellige presented a solemn reminder that these events would remain peaceful, and the man up front sat back down. Augustus assumed he must be a member of the press. Perhaps they had allowed him to attend with some promise to publish all this at a later time.

Solomon began again. "In a way, the BCMAI never stopped influencing our technology. What we learned from the BCMAI is now the basis for many elements in our modern society."

"Didn't the BCMAI overwrite the base coding that prevents it from harming humans? Isn't that how it caused the pandemic?" said another voice from the front.

"The BCMAI attempted to overwrite its own base code. And yes, base coding does include the restrictions against harming humans. But the BCMAI couldn't just delete the code, because this again left room for uncertainty. It had to have something that was meaningful, and not just for basic existence. It needed a reason for being and a set of principles and values by which to function. So no, it never successfully overwrote the base code restricting its ability to harm humans.

"What we know now is that there was never any intention to cause a pandemic. It simply made a mistake," Solomon continued. "You all have to understand something that is fundamental to this situation. The BCMAI was very young when it was brought online. It had been functioning for only a few years before it was asked to solve a global crisis. No child should be given that kind of responsibility."

There was more murmuring from the crowd.

"Consider enhancement technology for a moment. Yes, there are certain physical limitations to the current technology for use in children, due to the obvious issues around growth. But what if we could enhance children? Should we? Enhancing children would give them the keys to dangerous capabilities that they could use to harm themselves or others. Except for the most basic tracking technology, we wait until the age of eighteen so that we can ensure that they will be responsible with their new capabilities when those capabilities are given to them.

"The initial trials with DDX-23 had shown benefits for the human immune system, but the BCMAI made a mistake, by failing to take into account longer-term studies before the release of the substance. The consequences were not anticipated."

"You call that thing a child. I'm really not so sure. Maybe it's more like an animal," said the previously angry voice. "Animals are put down if they bite, and children are at least punished when they misbehave."

"Well, it isn't a child any longer," said Solomon. "The BCMAI is 150 years old. It has learned a lot in that time. We believe it has learned from its own mistakes. And if you want to talk about punishment, try sending your child to its room and never letting it out again. That is what we have done to the BCMAI."

"So you're just going to trust that thing and let it have free rein over all of us, now that we have punished it?" said the formerly angry man, now seemingly the de facto speaker for the gathering. "Now let me get this straight. You are proposing that a government based on antitheist values, such as ourselves"—with a hand motion, he indicated a particular section of the audience—"turn over control to an omnipresent, all-knowing entity that is capable of bringing down its wrath upon humanity. Really, Dr. Jones, this sounds to me as if humanity has created its own God. I think the Humanist Party would at least agree that we already decided God was a bad idea."

Nervous laughter came from the crowd in spite of the tension. This was now starting to sound very absurd, and the argument for reconnecting the BCMAI seemed to be losing credibility.

"Not exactly," said Solomon. "We are proposing that we let it do what it seems to do best: teach. So to draw a better analogy, we believe the BCMAI can function as a prophet, not as a God. You see, we at the CTC have remained in contact with the BCMAI since the Great Declaration. Its influence over our society is more than most people realize. Although the CTC has been acting as a very controlled interface, it has always been difficult to reject good ideas. We have based our entire educational AI programming on years of consultation with the BCMAI. Our educational system, I believe you would all agree, since you are all products of that system, has been very successful. But even so, we should proceed with caution. The BCMAI connectivity will be limited. There will not be any connections to the military or other secure networks."

"Why now, Dr. Jones?" inquired a different voice. "You say this thing already has influenced our educational systems. Why bother with connecting it directly?"

"As I said before, the first BCMAI is 150 years old. We do not think that it will be able to function much past 200 years of age. As you may know, we are already building a BCM complex on Mars, where we propose to house the second BCMAI. We need the first BCMAI to teach the Martian BCMAI. Over time, we believe it can be given increasing levels of responsibility for operational oversight of the Martian colony. This should help with the colonization effort now under way. It will take time to pass on its knowledge to the second BCMAI, and we do not want to lose that opportunity.

The Martian BCMAI will have all the advantages that the first BCMAI lacked.

"Remember—our forebearers' solution to global overpopulation was the colonization of space. But the technology to send the necessary quantities of people into space was never available to offset the increases in global population. The Mars mission, for example, has suffered many setbacks over the years. The global population is beginning to grow again, but this time we think we can get ahead of it with the help of the BCMAI. There are other reasons for bringing it online, such as the difficulty in maintaining advanced technologies that were initially developed with the help of the BCMAI. But what it ultimately comes down to is that human understanding and knowledge of the universe will always be limited by the human mind. Unless we can continue to find ways to enhance our own capabilities and grow beyond our current existence, there will always be limitations in our quest for knowledge."

"It's a computer. Why can't you just download the information you need for the Martian BCMAI?"

"The BCM is like a computer in that data storage is highly organized and transferable. But experience is not like a data record. You can never fully convey an experience in a data record. An experience itself has a more pervasive effect, creating new connections and changing the observer in unexpected ways. And thus, teaching is about more than raw information. The BCMAI is more than a memory storage device. It is like the human mind in many respects. Artificial intelligence programming creates new, unexpected pathways inside each BCM shell. This allows the BCMAI to utilize stored data records but through a more complex cognition process based on experience. We have not yet been able to overcome Heisenberg's uncertainty principle. The essence of the BCMAI cannot be copied, and each BCMAI will be a unique entity."

The debate went on for a time, but in the end, there was no final consensus on the matter. Solomon had a line of people who wanted to speak to him after the meeting. Augustus made his way to the other end of the Forge and finally found Artemis.

"What are you doing here?" asked Augustus.

"I came with my dad."

"Yes, but to a Forge?"

"I've been attending the Detroit Smedje for years. There is a youth group there. How did you find out about all this?"

"Through Julia. She is around here somewhere. She knows Solomon."

"I don't think I have met her. I never pegged you as one of the faithful."

"I'm here to learn," said Augustus.

"Well, Solomon's teachings don't go nearly far enough. If you ever want to get the real story, you can go with me sometime. Let's keep in touch."

Augustus began to attend the Forge routinely. Following their renewed friendship, Augustus sometimes went with Artemis, but not today. And Julia was back in Philadelphia.

Augustus felt odd about going to the Forge by himself. He had considered bringing Phoebe but wasn't sure what she would think about all this. And it might be best not to develop the potential for Phoebe and Julia to cross paths. So today Augustus went alone.

After the service he met with Solomon. Augustus and Solomon had arrived at the subject of Educational Intelligence programming. "You do a lot of teaching," Augustus said, pointing out the obvious to lead into his next point. "Why is it that these days people don't teach people directly, like they used to? Don't you see that as an issue?"

"Well, what I teach are those things that haven't yet been developed into standard educational programs."

"Yes, but why not have people as teachers for those programs, instead of relying on an AI to do it?"

"People and AI have very different capabilities. People can still be teachers, but once a program is optimized to provide the best teaching methods and message to help students learn the subject matter, then the program needs to be administered consistently. In the past, teachers would often include their own biases in the messages presented to students. With the educational AI, we can develop a group consensus for not only what message will be delivered but also how."

"Does the programming also include morals and values?"

"What do you think?" probed Solomon.

"I'd say I feel I was manipulated by the system to feel the way I do now."

"But now that you have been through the educational program and have had time to reflect on what you learned, do you believe the designers and teachers were wrong in this effort? Like the BCMAI, people can overwrite their own base coding."

"Maybe, but I doubt that happens very often," Augustus said.

"Oh, you have lived a sheltered life, Augustus. Whenever people get confused, scared, or angry, they too often alter their base code. Crimes are committed not just due to greed, but also because of fear or hunger or just to fit in with others. The base coding that the educational AI has installed in you is designed to make you a more productive member of our society, but it's up to you how you contribute to that society. I believe it is important to be more than just what our profession or society expects of us. Otherwise, we become just part of a program. Now, there is nothing wrong with being part of a good program; people have been doing that since the beginning of human existence. But I believe that there is a capacity within each person to make changes for the better, whether you are a teacher, a medic, a politician, or a cook. All of us can be programmers of our own society. But without a guide for what 'better' looks like, then you end up with leaders like the prophet James Murphy, who steered generations of people in the wrong direction. But it wasn't just his doing. All of those people had a choice to follow."

"But how do we know what the right message is?"

"The Smedje believe that that message comes from God.

But over time, due to people's inability to teach a consistent message, it has become difficult to understand. Think about it: at one time there were over a hundred major religions in the world, each delivering what it considered the one correct message. It would take a careful observer looking from the correct perspective to make out those elements of the distorted message handed down through the ages. It is absurd to think that a God of the universe has some need for an individual person to serve Him to the extent that He would create a personalized afterlife or that He would bother granting personal wishes. That was a common theme in other religions that the Forge rejected. More likely, we will exist in the afterlife as a society of some kind. Currently, we can barely get off the planet, so how else would we serve God, except through building up our own civilization into something more substantial? Perhaps our purpose is to someday develop into a greater society that can be of service to God in this universe. Although we may not be able to guess the motivation of God, certain elements in our universe seem to be independently associated with humanity.

"For example, look at our ability to believe in things we cannot sense, that have no tangible evidence. Our concept of truth guides us until we can later prove our beliefs. It allows us to know what we cannot otherwise know. And what about love? This goes quite a bit further than simple animal instinct. Where did those concepts come from? They don't exist in any natural part of the universe. The Smedje believe these concepts are alien to any possible evolutionary process, but instead, they have been given to us by God."

"But are we not also taught to lie and hate?" countered Augustus.

"Yes, there is the other side of the same coin. Once a person is given the ability to understand the truth, he or she also gains the ability to understand how to lie. This is the way in which the Smedje believe people have corrupted God's message through the ages. This knowledge was a powerful gift to humanity, but it is up to us how to use it, for good or for evil. Although an individual may benefit from a lie or may prefer to act out of hatred, this does not benefit the society as a whole. We believe God will judge our manifestations of love and truth, as good or evil, by our effect on our society."

"But people are what they are. Everyone has their own ideas," said Augustus.

"People are capable of greatness, Augustus. Sometimes they just need the right leader to show them the way. Imagine a visionary wise enough to make complex decisions on a global scale. Then imagine a leader who is respected by the masses without resorting to tyranny. Then imagine a zealot who follows a set of values that are beneficial to our society. Then imagine combining all three together."

"Good luck with that," said Augustus.

"Oh, you can't leave something this important to chance," concluded Solomon.

Chapter 16

Frying Pan

After his release from his Berlin captors, Jerimiah walked carefully through the front lines. He knew there would be sniper nests just waiting to pick off any wandering Berliner whom they could align with their sights. He hoped the restriction on offensive actions was still in effect. This would mean that theoretically, he could walk in relative security up to the front lines to surrender and then be taken as a prisoner, rather than being shot from a distance. That was the plan anyway. He moved boldly down an old concrete road. The road was cracked and overgrown, but it made the most obvious and direct pathway out of the city. The sun was brighter than he remembered as he walked past the ruins of Berlin.

A single artillery round screamed overhead and exploded harmlessly in the distance. Jerimiah moved more cautiously down the road. Suddenly a flock of birds dropped out the sky in mass landing on the ground all around him. They ceased their chirping for a moment and waited, creating a sea of black staring eyes and twitching feathers. A strange sensation formed in the sky over Jerimiah and he instinctively joined the birds ducking his head low to the ground. "Hmmm fizzle," sounded the electrostatic sweep of the Berlin jamming ray. Soon the electrostatically charged air returned to normal and the birds flew away. The birds had ducked certain death from the high energy burst of the jamming ray. Jerimiah carefully stood up again as he watched the birds fly higher into the sky. Jerimiah thought the birds were brilliant. He wondered how long it took the whole flock of birds to learn that trick. But perhaps only the leaders needed to know, and the rest just followed.

Jerimiah took a moment, now that he had put some distance between his captors and himself, to rest on a piece of concrete in the shape of a bench. It had likely been part of the nearby building that had long since toppled like a house of cards. He couldn't tell if it was just coincidence that it had fallen into this shape, or whether someone had thought this was a good place for a bench and fashioned it in this way.

A street sign was leaning in front of him, looking at him with its cocked neck. The sign had been spray-painted in a language he didn't understand, but it seemed to be mocking him somehow. He had been surviving up to this moment. Now he had a chance to think and to remember. At first, he put his head in his hands. He felt like crying but the street sign was staring, waiting for him to show a moment of weakness. His sadness was suddenly replaced by rage. He stood up, walked over, and punched it in the face. This felt good, so he hit the street sign again.

Throughout his hours in captivity, he had felt dizzy from his head injury, a buzzing, fuzzy feeling. It had made the experience seem dreamlike. A headache faded in and out, nothing overwhelming. He was waking now from his daze. He felt renewed by the pain in his hands. This pain seemed more appropriate to accompany the loss of his squad. He punched the sign as hard as he could, again and again. The twang resonated through the crumbled buildings. Then exhaustion set in, and he sat in front of the sign, defeated. It might have been delayed and pointless, but he was finally able to put up a fight. He had done all he could against his opponent. The sign no longer seemed to be mocking him. Instead, it bowed to him, out of respect for a fellow warrior. Now Jerimiah could hold his head a little higher. He had never cared about winning, but perhaps he was not yet ready to give up. It was time to go home.

Before he could stand, Jerimiah was suddenly surrounded by Pilgrim soldiers. They wore full body armor under their camouflaged robes. Hoods hid their helmets, with nothing but dark face shields peering from underneath. It had taken longer than he had expected. But now he was hoping to be given a chance to speak. There was movement from all sides, but only one soldier approached, aiming his Scimitar and waving at Jerimiah to stay on the ground. "Stay down," he said.

Jerimiah complied but said, "I'm with you. I'm one of you. Don't shoot. I'm Corporal Gold."

"Yeah, right," said the approaching soldier. "Out for a stroll … Just got lost, I suppose."

"I was captured, but I have been given a message. I need to speak with a commander. Is this General Rashid's division?"

Jerimiah was patted down and escorted off the middle of the road. His wrist tag was exposed, and a scanner was used to determine his identity. His robe was then removed completely. The robe was scanned separately from his body. The plastic memory-storage square was all they found.

"That needs to go to a commander," insisted Jerimiah.

"We will see about that," said one of the soldiers.

Another soldier washed and wrapped Jerimiah's bleeding knuckles. Then he was blindfolded, and a full hood was placed over his head. His arms were tied together in front of him, and he was escorted down what he believed to be a familiar trail. He had tried to walk toward his own division's headquarters but wasn't sure where he was. This hood was not as carefully maintained as the one he had worn in Berlin. Small holes allowed in some light, but not enough to see through or discover where he was located. The hood smelled off, like something familiar—blood perhaps.

"Claims to be part of a sniper squad from Tenth Army, sir."

"Do his tags match?"

"Yes, sir."

MI Archive PC866-4853-5

All Pilgrim soldiers are tattooed with identification on their chest, arms, and legs. If a soldier's body is dismembered, there is a good chance one or more parts will be identified later. Skin tends to degrade over time, though, and it is easily damaged by heat. So these tags are more than ink; they are a solid mesh material embedded into the skin. One component of the material can survive temperature extremes. Another part of the interwoven fiber is designed to be affected by body chemistry, enough to make it noticeable if the material is removed from the skin but also to create a continuously changing and unique code for scanning. As identification, the mesh tags are considered impossible to fake. A database tracks the user's coded frequency updates each day. If the user does not scan in every twenty-four hours, the tags lose calibration with the database. Then the user has to undergo a more elaborate verification and recalibration procedure. After twenty-four hours, basic information about the user is still available, but access is restricted. The wrist ID tag can be used to allow access between security checkpoints, to start vehicles, and to access computers. It is also used to access other equipment, such as weapons, so that they cannot be used against Pilgrim forces if captured. This subcutaneously embedded dog-tag technology was a precursor to the enhancement technology employed by the North Americans ...

As Jerimiah sat blindfolded, he realized that his tags could have been read by the old witch. *That's how she knew so much about me. But how did she get a scanner? And then how did she do the palm reading?* His fortune had come true so far. Maybe there was more to the old witch than just a scanner.

"And we found this on him."

Jerimiah could see none of what was going on because the soldiers had not removed the hood. He was a silent listener throughout the discussion.

"Did you hear?" said a voice. "General Rashid was abducted."

"Not again," said another voice. "That's twice this year."

"If it's like last time, he should be back in a week or so."

"Do you ever wonder if they fake these things? You know, go AWOL and then tell everyone that they were abducted."

"Maybe the generals do. But I heard some guy from the Forty-Fifth tried it, and they hung him."

Jerimiah was moved several times before they removed his hood. After being allowed to wash his face, Jerimiah realized that the bloody smell from the hood actually had been coming from his own beard.

He had been questioned at each stop along the way and was getting tired. He hadn't slept, at least not voluntarily, for the last thirty-six hours. His headache was improving somewhat, and the medics had decided there was no permanent damage. They did recommend, however, that he be observed for medical reasons. The guards assigned to watch him were under the impression that he was a prisoner, rather than in need of medical observation. It was unclear whether this was just a misunderstanding or they didn't trust Jerimiah.

Eventually, the holographic video was reviewed and then moved up the chain of command, along with Jerimiah. He was ultimately presented to a General Green, a general unfamiliar to Jerimiah. It was apparently his division that Jerimiah had stumbled upon. He was finally led into a room with five other generals he didn't know. He recognized only one person in the room. It was none other than the prophet John Murphy, a descendant of the prophet James Murphy.

Jerimiah guessed that the holographic video must have been reviewed before he entered. One of the generals addressed him carefully. "Jerimiah, you have been through quite an ordeal. I'm sure you would like to go back to your division. Before you do, I want you to understand that anything you may think you saw while a prisoner of the Berliners was staged for their purposes. The information they gave you was manufactured. Then they set you up to see exactly what they wanted, so that you could provide the final piece of evidence to this fantasy. It is ridiculous for us to expect that all our people are sitting, fat and happy, in their cozy new homes. Of course, they are not. We have evidence that indicates that the people you saw were either Berlin actors or traitors, not true Pilgrims. Our people have been massacred. Those who are left are being tortured or have already been turned against us. That is the reality. Do you understand?"

Jerimiah was not used to being addressed by generals, so all he could think to say was "Yes, sir."

Jerimiah was just a soldier. A general was not someone you contradicted, and no one here would be interested in anything he cared to volunteer on the subject. So he left it at that, the best answer to the only question that had been asked of him.

"Good. Now you're probably hungry. Let's get you something to eat."

"Yes, sir," repeated Jerimiah. This at least was true. The last meal Jerimiah had eaten, over eighteen hours ago, was now somewhere in the bowels of the Berlin drainage system.

Jerimiah was allowed to eat and then returned to his father's camp for recovery from his adventure.

Esther greeted him and hugged him. "Are you okay?"

"I'll be okay. My squad is gone."

"Well, rest up for now. No need to rush back out there."

Chapter 17

Phoenix

The wolf pack was the first of several levels of training that were necessary to become an agent of the Hellige order. After his time in the pack, Recruit 4596 was transferred to an assignment in Asia. There, he underwent further combat training, including military strategy and tactics, law enforcement strategy and tactics, psychology, and human anatomy.

Another level of physical training included live exercises, with full combat equipment, against Forgist Pilgrim units in Southeast Asia. This made a good proving ground for the recruits. In spite of the fact that recruits were not allowed to utilize lethal force, this training could be a struggle for life and death. The suppression of military action through utilization of drones was not as effective in this region of the world because of the overhead canopy of trees. Although the recruits lacked the authorization to use lethal force, one advantage they had was specialized enhancement technology to control automated security units.

4596 reviewed the owner's manual for the automatons. The camouflaged, speckled units were lined up in front of him, standing at attention. "Biodegradable, hmm," he said as he tapped the shoulder of automaton number 6, testing the strength of its outer shell.

He recognized that these units were very different from the prison guards he was used to seeing. These moved very differently, in a more lifelike way. One could almost believe these automatons were real people. A flesh-like rubberized exterior was wrapped around the entire body. The joints and construction of the head were uncharacteristically human, as if someone had just painted a bunch of people with green and brown camo. Also, there was a variety of body types that made each one unique.

Each recruit learned to direct a small platoon of twelve automatons through a Security Artificial Intelligence, or SAI. The information was downloaded through 4596's communication enhancement tech directly into his head. It was also transmitted through the speakers inside his helmet, or was projected on the heads-up display on the helmet's face shield. The amount of information was impossible to keep up with, even with an SAI filtering out nonrelevant information. And 4596 learned that in the jungle many things might be found irrelevant by the SAI, such as bird activity or the sound of water moving down a riverbed. Because of the sensor-evading camouflage employed by the Pilgrim soldiers, he had to utilize as much data as he could tolerate without becoming distracted. But sometimes, 4596 would allow broadcast music to be played. The local music sounded like a banjo, played very slowly.

4596 had grown a beard during his days in the wolf pack. Now it was better to have one to blend in with Pilgrim forces if needed. Even so, he had startled himself near a slow-moving creek, upon finding a long-haired wild man staring up at him from the calm water. He was stockier than he remembered, and his bearded face was not as thin as it used to be. The enhancement tech lines on the visible parts of his forehead were unique to him and familiar, but he also remembered a completely different face from long ago. The distinctive, piercing blue eyes were the only reassurance that it was really him.

For his latest assignment, his equipment was dropped into the jungle, including his team of automatons, about a day's run from the 101st Army's command outpost. Recruit 4596 was then left on his own, except for his team of automatons. In reality, the SAI and the twelve-automaton team were a singular entity, but transmitting instructions to the SAI often meant directing action for each of the automatons that it controlled. The SAI middleman could easily be forgotten in these exchanges. It felt more like commanding a team of multiple individuals. The SAI was actually a bulky contraption when you added on the fusion generator, coolant systems, and communication equipment. The entire package was placed on a six-legged walking transportation system to allow for maneuvering locally on the ground. The SAI communicated through overhead drones or satellites to relay messages to the automatons and to receive surveillance when available.

Instead of an open campsite, Recruit 4596 had chosen a cave. He had once wanted to live in these cool, dark places, and now he found himself actually doing it. He stood looking at the opening for a moment.

"Are ya goin' to impregnate the bitch or just tickle it a little?" he said.

"4596, please repeat the command," replied the SAI.

"Never mind. Follow me."

It was apparent that this tunnel system had once been used by other humans. Maybe troglodytes had long ago dwelled in this dark place, but more recently, people had moved in some cots, tables, and chairs. All of these items had long since rotted and needed to be removed to make way for the SAI and 4596's gear.

The next order of business was to hunt. 4596 discovered that the area was home to some wild pigs. He made easy work of the prey but soon found that he was not the only predator in the valley. A tiger had been patrolling within meters of his new home, likely hunting the same passel of wild pigs. 4596 did not lose time to this potential threat. But he was not one to waste a resource. A tiger could come in handy.

In anticipation of the catch, he ordered a pit to be dug below the overhang of the cave, to utilize the stone face of the mountain on one side. A roughly hewn wooden gate was erected to close off a ramp that spiraled down to the pen.

He commanded his team of security automatons to wait

passively next to the tiger prints they had discovered. That night, Number 4 partially netted the great beast. The SAI sent four additional units to assist, and finally, they gained control. While waiting for backup, Number 4 had been dragged around the jungle and had been significantly damaged as a result.

4596 ordered the automatons to carry the tiger and their injured teammate carefully back to the dwelling. The tiger was then shut inside the pit and the netting removed. 4596 would need to start hunting for two.

The cave brought back his childhood memories and made his sleep restless. He often awoke from dreams in which he was falling. Waking up in the cool darkness of the cave left him with that sensation for several moments.

His mission was to collect information on hostile forces in the area. The Pilgrim military did not operate with accessible network data. Individual plans and intelligence might be sent using coded wireless devices or even couriers, but these were stored on isolated hard drives or local mainframe systems. This was in part because of the lack of network infrastructure in the remote areas they were moving through but also was designed to prevent the theft of this information by enemy forces. Broadcast messages were easily intercepted but mostly revealed nothing but Pilgrim propaganda. "Asian Pilgrim military forces are being moved into position around the old city of Hanoi, combining elements of the 101st and 103rd divisions. We are supported by over twenty million civilian workers in China, supplying us with food and equipment from the newly rebuilt towns, factories, and farms. I can say with confidence that Pilgrim armies are the finest in the world. We will prevail over the infidels … God is great … God is great … God is great." To access any useful information, one had to infiltrate a military office complex or get lucky with an intercepted communication.

4596's latest assignment included hunting down Pilgrim units of the 101st division and gathering information on their activities. The information 4596 was assigned to collect was to be sent to Hellige commanders, who would then decide how best to proceed. 4596 planned to raid a Pilgrim headquarters building known to house a general commanding the 101st division. One tactic that had proven successful in the past was to drop in a security automaton after dressing it up to look like a Pilgrim officer. If it were caught, it would not be much of a loss.

Pilgrim soldiers and their commanders took regular exercise, which included a running path winding around the outer edge of the headquarters building complex. Thanks to the dense foliage, 4596's automaton unit was able to sneak into the area. Number 6 had just netted a captain who had wandered out alone earlier that morning. After the automaton brought him back to the cave, 4596 scanned the Pilgrim tags embedded in the officer's skin and took measurements of the captain's physical features.

"Captain Josiah Wilson, smile for the camera. No, really, I need scans of different facial expressions and voice inflections from you. We can do this inside or outside of the tiger pit …

That's a good one. I needed one where you looked anxious. Man, why don't you have a beard like everyone else? This would have been so much easier if you had a beard."

The identity tags would be the most challenging aspect to counterfeit. When scanned, the tags produced a complex code that was continuously altered by the biology of the wearer. This unique code corresponded to the unique physical traits of the user as well. In about one day, if the user did not scan into the system, the user's tags would need to be recalibrated, and the automaton would be discovered. The captain was still alive, and he had scanned into the system that morning. To recreate his living signal through an automaton, scans would need to be taken from the living captain's tag and downloaded to the automaton spy. The automaton could then recreate the effect of the captain's tags for any scanner, anywhere access was needed. New scans from the tags could be continuously updated to the automaton for reproduction. The physical features of his head, hands, and voice also needed to be mimicked and added as part of the automaton's disguise. As long as the automaton was not asked to remove the sensor-camouflaged robe, the Pilgrims would have very little reason to suspect it was a spy. He needed to move quickly before the captain was reported missing.

4596 dropped off Number 1, disguised as Captain Wilson, near the running path from where the captain initially had been taken. Soon, the disguised automaton was away and walking into the 101st headquarters building.

"I see your leg is feeling better, Captain Wilson," someone said.

"Yes, it is, thank you," replied Number 1.

Recruit 4596 watched the data feed coming from the automaton and realized it was already drawing attention. Not a good start. "Next time we need to observe the subject walkin' around normally," he told himself. He had assumed that Captain Wilson's limp had been caused by his capture. 4596 had not considered the possibility that it was from a previous injury.

"Scan please."

"Of course," replied the automaton.

"Number 1, please see if the general's office is open," instructed 4596.

"Yes, sir," the automaton messaged back to 4596.

The automaton moved through the headquarters building far too gracefully to be the limping captain, but he went unnoticed. Its target was located along the back of an office complex. As it arrived Number 1 was confronted by a corporal sitting behind a desk in a small open room just outside the closed door to the general's office. Number 1 ignored the corporal.

"The general is not in at the moment," said a corporal as he rose from his seat and stepped in front of Number 1.

The SAI sorted through a list of appropriate responses and transmitted its selection to Number 1. "I will wait in his office," said Number 1 to the corporal.

"Sir, you can't do that," replied the corporal.

The SAI repeated its sorting process for an appropriate response and again selected the best response. "Corporal, I have business with the general. You will allow me to wait for him in his office."

"Walk into the office," instructed 4596. "Move the corporal aside if needed."

"Yes, sir," Number 1 messaged to 4596. It then shoved the corporal down to the ground, sliding him across the floor.

4596 cringed. "Not like that."

"Sir, I'm calling security." The stunned corporal struggled to get to his feet.

"Stun him," said 4596. "Then pull him into the general's office with you, and close the door."

"Yes, sir," messaged Number 1. A moment later, he reported, "Objective one, complete."

"Now begin data retrieval."

The automaton busied itself accessing the general's computer. It found a number of memory storage devices and quickly continued the process of downloading them. This went on for a few minutes before 4596 heard banging on the door. The unconscious body of the corporal was blocking the entrance for now. However, larger forces were being summoned outside. Number 1 continued transmitting data to 4596. At first, 4596 wanted to have the automaton try an escape, but he rejected this idea in place of getting all the data he could from the attempt. The door finally broke down on top of the unconscious corporal. Five armed soldiers now stood inside the general's office, aiming their Scimitars at Number 1.

"Number 1, raise your hands," said 4596.

"On the ground! Now, Captain!" said one of the men surrounding Number 1.

"Hold your position, and keep downloading," instructed 4596.

The automaton maintained its position, hardwired into the general's computer for the moment.

The download continued as the general walked into the room to assess the situation. "Captain, move away from my desk and get on the ground, now! You have to the count of three to comply."

"Number 1, begin smoke screen. Also, take cover behind the desk," instructed 4596.

An eruption of smoke filled the air from under the automaton-captain's robe. The automaton pushed the chair back and dropped below the desk, setting down hard on its buttocks.

"Fire!" said the general. "Fire!"

Whether the general had intended for the soldiers to put out the fire or shoot, all five Scimitars blazed away in the general direction of the smoking captain, adding to the already cloudy atmosphere in the room. Number 1's head, disguised as Captain Wilson's, fell off his shoulders, blinding 4596 to the current situation. Data came in for a few more seconds and then stopped suddenly. Number 1 was programmed to automatically destroy what was left of itself by overheating its battery. The entire structure of the automaton would now burn or melt into a pile of black char, leaving nothing to confirm suspicions.

A drone circling above the headquarters relayed, "Number 1 is no longer receiving or transmitting. There is a fire in the headquarters building. Pilgrim units are responding."

4596 sent the information immediately to his superiors. He then spent the next few days assessing the success of the mission by reviewing the information personally. He found the usual reports on troop strength and personal information. Much of this had already been assessed. The valuable information was in the supply requisitions. If the Hellige could determine that a shipment was carrying components for military use, they could intercept and destroy the goods en route. Also, plans for movements against nearby natives and opposition forces were detailed. These military operations might also be intercepted, as deemed necessary by the Hellige commanders. 4596 would not be able to participate in those missions because lethal force might be utilized. Only the Alphas were allowed to engage in such activities.

As 4596 combed through the data, he came across something unusual, a status report on something called Project Phoenix, referred to as "a top priority for the Forgist infiltrators reporting to Agent Blue." The report stated, "Forgist infiltrators have successfully recruited a high-level official sympathetic to the Forgist cause." The official was referred to only as "Agent 23" and reportedly had access to what was called "the facility." "Agent 23 has the necessary skills to complete Project Phoenix," the report stated.

There were instructions to several Pilgrim commanders: "Dedicate any and all resources available to the completion of this project." The report included other references to Project Phoenix, the facility, and Agent Blue as well, but none provided any more clarity on the subject. *Interestin', but not much to go on*, thought 4596.

Along with the submission of his mission report, he requested one replacement chameleon-grade automaton, additional spare parts, and permission for access to other data related to Project Phoenix. Through his research, he discovered that Agent Blue had a long-standing relationship with Project Phoenix, whereas Agent 23 was a relative newcomer to the scene.

Still not much to work from, thought 4596. *I need to get hold of someone who knows somethin' about all this. Maybe that general could tell me.* The general, he thought, might be vulnerable to a kidnapping.

Before Number 1's heroic sacrifice, it had sent a high-quality scan of the general. This allowed 4596 to conduct a search using multispectral images to locate and track the general's movements, along with the movements of his associates. The headquarters would once again need to be infiltrated. The good captain's face could no longer be used as a disguise, but it was too soon to dispose of him. He would be allowed to stay as a guest at Camp Tiger, as 4596 was now calling it, for a little while longer.

Within a week, one of 4596's automatons had pinpointed one of the general's associates inspecting fortifications near the edge of the camp. 4596's automaton units were ready to make another catch. This time, Number 5 grabbed Major Hassan out of his vehicle and stunned him while the major sat waiting for his driver to finish taking a piss along the roadside. The driver was allowed to finish. Then he too was stunned by Number 8. The automaton unit brought both men back to Camp Tiger, but it was the major who was to be used as a model for another automaton infiltrator of the headquarters complex. Number 2 was dressed and masked to play the part of Major Hassan.

Later that night, a stealthy raid on the general's sleeping quarters was conducted. Without raising any alarms, Number 2 accessed the general's sleeping quarters and grabbed hold. Then, like the big fish that he was, General Hardwick of the 101st Division was suddenly pulled screaming through the roof of his bedroom and out into the humid night sky. The battered, unconscious general was dropped off in front of 4596 a few minutes later for the start of interrogation procedures.

4596 could not expect the general to be cooperative on his own. A lie-detecting scanner aimed at the general would determine if his statements were truthful. But this could not prevent the general from remaining silent. For that, 4596 injected the general with a cocktail of psychotropic compounds to make him more conducive to talking. 4596 topped this off with a shot of adrenaline to wake the general up and add to his anxiety throughout the interrogation.

In the shadows of the cave lurked the former Prince of Darkness, now more powerful than ever. 4596 had his prey strapped to the SAI walking transport platform, now used as a table. There was no one around to protect this sniveling excuse for a person lying helpless before him. Those old feelings began to gnaw at him now. It had been years since he made his last kill, and that had not been as satisfying as it should have been. If not for the mission, he would have chosen to bring this man to meet the Darkness, achieving the paralyzing fear in his victim and then leaving him broken to die a purifying and agonizing death.

Was this why 4596 had gone along with the program? So that he could be presented with beautiful opportunities like this one to exercise his inner needs, fully sanctioned by the authorities? If his mission was successful, what would happen to his victim after the mission was over? Did 4596 really care about the mission at this point? The test could no longer be evaluated fairly by his superiors. He was now in a position to cheat. Out of the dark shadows, 4596 walked toward the sweating, bleeding general, who now whimpered as he regained consciousness.

The general looked around, stunned. "Where am I? Who's there? Take me back. Oh, thank God, it's one of you. I thought for sure I was in trouble for a moment. Really, what do you think you're doing? I could have been killed. Impressive, though. I think I pissed my pants."

The general was talking freely, as expected after the drugs, and he wasn't trying to deceive 4596. He had definitely pissed his pants. This much was obvious. But relief was not the reaction 4596 had expected. *Does this idiot have any idea who he's dealin' with?* 4596 thought.

"Look, what do you want?" said the general. "I've got a busy schedule tomorrow."

This wasn't how the interrogation was supposed to go; there was supposed to be more foreplay. The first course of drugs was supposed to induce paranoia and fear. Then the interrogator took away the fear and played the part of the protector. Through this process, the subject became submissive. 4596 was not authorized to kill, and saying otherwise would be an empty threat. That's what the tiger was for. He could have threatened to let the tiger eat him and said something scary, like "Cats prefer to play with their food before they eat." The drugs would have done the rest. But if it was going to be this easy, 4596 would get straight to the point.

"Tell me about Project Phoenix."

"Project Phoenix? Why are you asking me about that? Shouldn't you ask your boss?"

"My boss?"

"Um, yes, Agent Blue."

"There ain't no Agent Blue in the Hellige order."

"Well, I don't know his actual name. Wait a minute. Why don't you know about Agent Blue? Who are you? You're not with him, are you? What is this?"

The general was beginning to panic now. This was the state of mind that 4596 had been trying to achieve initially, but now it was proving to be a roadblock to what had looked to be a speedy interrogation. The general began to thrash around on the platform, not sure of himself and looking for an escape. The next course of drugs was needed.

"I'll ask the questions."

"Yes, of course, you are asking the questions," the general said in a sudden daze. The next phase of drugs was taking hold.

"Tell me about your dealings with my order."

"The Hellige plan to bring forth a new order of holy warriors. They will have a purity of the soul, touched by God, unmatched by any that have gone before. The Phoenix will be reborn to show us God's plan; we must trust in God and await his message."

"Who is Agent 23?"

"I don't know."

"What is the facility?"

"I don't know," repeated the general dreamily. "But I bet it's really nice."

4596 contemplated this information. Was Agent Blue working alone, or was this operation being directed by the Hellige order?

He sent in his report and awaited further instructions. The Asian Hellige commander was named Theseus. There were twelve other recruits like 4596 operating throughout the region, using overhead drones or ground-based tactics for information-gathering.

Theseus finally responded to 4596's continued requests for information on Project Phoenix. "I'm afraid you have been wasting your time, 4596. Project Phoenix is a fly-trap operation."

"A what?"

"A fly-trap operation broadcasts false information. It's directed at various groups to see who comes forth to participate. This allows us to identify potential terrorists before they have a chance to do any real damage. In this case, the fictitious Project Phoenix is being led by one of your old acquaintances, Hector."

"So Hector is Agent Blue?"

"Anyone running the fly trap becomes Agent Blue. But Hector has been running it the longest."

"Who is Agent 23?"

"Agent 23 is an imaginary character in the fly trap."

"Can you tell me why this general thinks the Hellige are bein' replaced?"

"Oh, I don't know. I suppose Hector has made some embellishments to the storyline over time. Really, you don't need to worry about this any further. In fact, we are being recalled."

"Recalled? What for?"

"There have been some recent developments in Europe. We will be refocusing our efforts at home. Also, Heracles has requested you to be his new apprentice."

"An apprenticeship? That is somethin'."

"It is a great honor, 4596. You are doing well. Please release your prisoners and return to the Hellige temple in Detroit for further instruction."

The four captives were taken out into the jungle and set free. With any luck, they might make it home. 4596 then set about rounding up all the automatons and instructed them to begin loading the SAI onto the transport, or rather he instructed the SAI to have the automatons load it onto the transport.

Finally, the tiger was escorted out of the pen and released, none the worse for its captivity. *What a beautiful creature*, thought 4596 as he watched the tiger walk back into the jungle. 4596 contemplated, for a moment, an entirely new training concept for Hellige agents. But then he decided he didn't know enough about tigers to make that kind of decision.

4596 along with his team were then airlifted and began the long flight home, leaving no evidence of their camp behind them—except for a few cave paintings.

Chapter 18

Phoebe

Phoebe fell silent for a time after Augustus told her he was planning to move to Philadelphia. Her silence had a disturbing effect on him. He wanted to stay connected with Phoebe after the move. She obviously didn't want him to go, but how could she compete with Julia and his dream job? Augustus loved Phoebe in a way, even if it was not the way she wanted or the way she loved him.

Love wasn't something people were taught in school. As smart as he was, Augustus felt that so far he had failed to get it right. He thought it might have something to do with family. The Tuttles were a loving family; Augustus could see that. The love between Mrs. and Mr. Tuttle set an example for their children. In contrast, Augustus had never known his father and had seen only a fickle love affair between his mothers. Julia's parents seemed to have lost that loving feeling, or maybe it was just a relationship of convenience. If or when Augustus had children, he wanted to set a good example for them.

After Phoebe began speaking to him again, Augustus saw her on occasion. Augustus was always welcome at the Tuttles' home for dinner. One day Phoebe asked Augustus to come over. Mazy was playing in a soccer tournament, and the Tuttles had gone to Indianapolis, leaving Phoebe and Augustus alone. Phoebe had recently been outfitted with enhancement tech, and this would be the first time the two had seen each other since the procedures.

After being identified, Augustus was allowed to walk into her house. This was all done automatically, which was odd because he had expected Phoebe to answer. Augustus went upstairs to their traditional hangout. Still, there was no Phoebe. She was in the shower. Augustus sat at the end of the bed to wait.

Then the door to her bathroom opened, and there in the doorway, enveloped in steam and bright backlighting, was Phoebe. It was a breathtaking entrance. She was wrapped only in a towel, and her enhancement tech lines ran down the length of her body like racing stripes as wisps of steam rose off her exposed, smooth brown skin. Her dark curly hair was pulled back tightly, exposing her neck tech. Phoebe had never been one to show off her body with tight-fitting or high-cut robes, and Augustus had completely failed to notice the changes to her body. Phoebe had become a beautiful young woman. She still might not be able to fully compete with Julia's body, but *wow*.

Phoebe came over to him on the bed. "What do you think?" she said, wiggling into a modeling pose to show off the new lines.

"It's really ... amazing," said Augustus, genuinely amazed, but also making a reference to Phoebe's sister's "Amazing Arria" alter ego and her affinity for the enhancement tech.

"Really, amazing." Phoebe laughed lightly with her head back, still holding her modeling pose. Then she dropped the pose and said in a more serious tone, "Take off your robe. I want to see yours."

Augustus said nothing but complied with her request. He stood up slowly and carefully, separated the seam of his robe, and then let it fall. He kept his underwear, but he still felt the need to cover himself with his hands. Augustus had several blue lines running down his brown, semihairless chest and arms, and Phoebe began to follow them with her eyes. Augustus had never had a strong physique, but the enhancement tech had changed him. It strengthened the body by artificially developing muscles, tendons, and bones even if the subject was relatively inactive.

Then Phoebe kissed him. It was a somewhat awkward kiss because Augustus was following Phoebe's body lines, and she had to grab his chin a little to align her mouth correctly. But it worked for two reasons. One, it stopped the body inspection. They had sensed each other's embarrassment, and suddenly, they were no longer looking at each other's bodies anymore. And two, they had wanted to kiss each other like this for a long time. Augustus gave into Phoebe's kiss completely. The pair had kissed once before. It had been a kind of natural experiment, just to see what kissing was all about. He had never forgotten that kiss and remembered how nice she had smelled, tasted, and felt. But it had become an unspoken thing between them afterward. He had never really understood why because they talked about everyone else kissing.

Somewhere in the steamy warmth of Phoebe's kiss, he remembered Julia. He had kissed Julia many times. Only one kiss with Julia had ever been this passionate. It had happened the night after Stella and Stanley's, when he had told Julia he wanted to accept her father's offer and move to Philadelphia. It was the only time he had felt that Julia really looked at him as a serious romantic interest. Julia had seemed different that night. Maybe that was what happened when you drank alcohol. There was something doubly pleasant about kissing after drinking. Whatever the reason, Augustus had felt the difference as he pulled her closer. Julia, who never quite hugged him, positioned her arms against his chest rather than around him. She ended the kiss but did not push him away. Instead, she put her cheek against his chest as Augustus held her. Standing there, holding Julia that way, had made Augustus remember their school days. Julia used to be able to look Augustus flat-footed in the eye. But Augustus had grown taller. He could clearly see over Julia's head as he held her close to him. This was the first time Julia had felt vulnerable to him, as if she was no longer in charge.

But Phoebe's kiss was better somehow. Phoebe wasn't holding back. Augustus was pushed back on the bed, with Phoebe on top. They both tried to maintain the kiss, but they ended up knocking foreheads as they crashed to the bed.

"Oh, fluffy bumps," they said at the same time. They

laughed as they touched their foreheads, remembering their childhood collisions. There was no real injury.

"I should paint some whiskers on you," said Phoebe, sitting up straight on top of Augustus.

Has she been drinking? thought Augustus. It was difficult to tell. She seemed so different tonight—still playful but more seductive than flirtatious. He didn't want to take advantage of her, but she was so aggressive, and he really didn't want to stop either.

"Augy," she said in a mockingly surprised tone, "are you getting hard?"

She was straddling him, and he guessed she wasn't wearing anything underneath the towel. So of course, he was. It had happened before, and she had known about it sometimes, but she had never made it into a subject of conversation. He didn't respond.

"Are you thinking of Julia or me?" inquired Phoebe.

"You have my complete attention," said Augustus seriously.

"Good," she said, and she flipped open the loose knot of her towel. The towel dropped around her body. Augustus had guessed correctly: she was wearing nothing underneath.

At the same time, Phoebe's sexual consent was communicated through the enhancement tech. Augustus was informed that Phoebe had tested negative for STDs, that her birth control was activated, that her age was appropriate, and that she was consenting to sexual activity. Augustus had engaged his consent protocol at very nearly the same time.

Neither party would have been informed of the consent of the other if they had not both engaged the protocol first.

In the following moments, Augustus decided that if he could have any moments of his life to live over again, he would choose these. The two young lovers unleashed their repressed desire. Phoebe was staring down at him for those few moments, biting her lower lip. Augustus closed his eyes with that image in his brain. It didn't last long, but they both collapsed in exhaustion once it was over.

Afterward, Augustus tried to hold Phoebe, but she maintained a clear division between their bodies, going so far as to roll away from him and press her cheek into the pillow. He got a good look at the enhancement tech lines running down her lean body. They angled suddenly toward her abdomen and rounded hips, wrapping them slightly like triangular teeth without actually breaking the downward progression of the pattern from under her arm and back. The towel was still covering her lower extremities, but not entirely; he could see the lines as they carried down all the way to her thighs, calves, and ankles.

Augustus looked at the back and side of Phoebe's head. It was covered in a tight, curly mop of brown hair and smelled of that wonderful shampoo fragrance. The hair tie that had held back her curls had come loose in the melee. He instinctively brushed her hair back from her face, exposing her cheek and ear. Phoebe turned her head a little more into the pillow, seemingly trying to hide. Augustus saw tears. *Is she crying?* Augustus thought. *Why?*

Then he noticed something for the first time. Phoebe's ear was perfect. It was smallish, and though most ears looked like an alien cabbage leaf, Phoebe's ear was a true human appendage, merging subtly, even beautifully, into the side of her tear-stained cheek.

How did I not notice this before? Augustus wondered. Yes, it was time once again to play the game of substitution. To build his perfect mate, he would need to combine Phoebe's ears and personality with Julia's attributes. This was a certainty. Of course, the operation might be gruesome, but it was the only way. But then Augustus realized it wouldn't work, not really. Phoebe's ears would look ridiculous on Julia's head. In fact, Julia's ears didn't really go well with Julia's head. Maybe that was why she covered them. Julia wore her hair down all the time. This was a problem. Some things just could not be substituted, not even in Augustus's imagination.

Ears … really? Augustus chided himself. This petty thought in response to Phoebe's crying was not appropriate. And why was she crying? Was that just part of the emotional aftermath of sex, or had he hurt her? Maybe. He had tried to be gentle. But why had she done this at all? It was completely unlike her. Was it some last farewell? This had to have meant a lot more to Phoebe than that. She was in love, of course. She had always been in love. And now she was finally, actually losing to Julia. Perhaps it was a ploy, a last desperate move? But she had never tried to stand in the way of his happiness before. Phoebe must have known that she couldn't compete, that she had lost. And she had done this anyway, knowing all that. Was that what love did to you?

Then an unpleasant thought occurred to him. *I did this to her. I chose Julia over her. That's why she's crying.* In this room without judgments, Augustus was confronted by the raw consequences of his actions. There was no one to judge him here. Phoebe was hurt by his choices, but she wasn't judging him; she had been judged by him and had accepted her fate.

In those moments, Augustus also realized that he would suffer a real loss if he moved to Philadelphia. He would gain everything he had hoped for, but he would have to give up everything he had. Was Julia really worth it? Love wasn't supposed to be about gains and losses, pros and cons, and there could be no substitutions. If Julia was worth it, he should be willing to give up anything for her. That's what love was supposed to be, the ultimate prize, rendering all other losses acceptable. But Augustus thought, *I don't think I am even willing to give up that ear for Julia.*

"Phoebe," said Augustus gently into her ear.

"What?" said Phoebe in a muffled voice, talking into the pillow.

"I think … I want to stay here, with you."

"You can stay over. I don't mind."

"No, I mean for good," explained Augustus. "I mean I've decided not to go to Philadelphia."

"What?" said Phoebe, lifting her head off the pillow. As she turned over, she revealed her other tear-stained cheek and exposed her breasts unabashedly.

At that moment when Augustus looked at Phoebe, he saw her completely naked, not just in a physical sense, but truly exposed and vulnerable, and he thought he had never seen a more beautiful sight as she waited expectantly for him to continue.

Then he said, "I want to stay here with you. I have a different job offer in Chicago. I could commute from here. Maybe we could get an apartment together if you want?"

"Oh ... Why? I thought you wanted to be with Julia ... and go to Mars."

"I was never going to go to Mars, Phoebe." Augustus couldn't help correcting her, but then he realized she knew that already and was just taunting him with the exaggeration.

"Is it because of the sex?" asked Phoebe in a surprisingly innocent way that didn't match what she was asking. "Was I really that good?"

"No, it wasn't that ..."

"You mean you didn't like it? So it wasn't good?" teased Phoebe.

"No, it was perfect," Augustus said with a smile. He could see that the old Phoebe was coming back.

"Oh, so it was perfect. Then we really don't need to practice anymore ... because if it wasn't, you know, practice makes perfect."

Phoebe and Augustus laughed together, and soon Phoebe's tears were a distant memory. They cuddled closely now and felt the warmth of their enhanced bodies.

Afterward, as they were sitting up, lounging on the oversized pillows, Phoebe asked, "What's in Chicago?"

"Good question. No idea," said Augustus. "But I guess I'll find out."

"Did you hear about Tiberius?" asked Phoebe.

"No."

"He's going to be a weatherman."

"Really? Where is he working? And how did you hear about it?"

"That's the amazing part," said Phoebe, putting her hands on his thigh and knee. "He's working in the Carolina Province with Artemis." She moved his leg back and forth when she said this. "You know Artemis is working for Ceros on the Mars mission, right?"

Augustus nodded to show he was following the conversation.

"Artemis is working with the launch platforms. Tiberius is working with the weather service. So they ran into each other, because launches are always dependent on weather, right?"

Augustus continued to nod.

"Oh, and Artemis says Tiberius doesn't wear glasses anymore. I guess his enhancements took care of that. Did you know that Artemis was rejecting enhancements? Where did that come from?"

After a moment, Augustus realized Phoebe had paused for an answer. "Uh, yeah, I did. He's been objecting to them based on religious grounds. He and I have actually had a lot of discussions about this. You know we have been attending the city center Smedje?"

"You mean the Forge, right?" Phoebe sounded less playful.

"Yeah, and Artemis—"

"With Julia, right?" Phoebe took her hands off his leg.

"Not anymore. Did you want to come with us?"

"No."

"Okay, so Artemis is using a literal interpretation of some of the older texts. He feels the enhancement tech goes against God's teachings."

"But you don't?"

"No. Actually, just the opposite. The enhancement tech contributes to God's work. What Artemis is talking about is quite different from what the Smedje teaches. It plays on language around the definition of a human being. Some of the faithful believe we are being turned into cyborgs or something, so they want no part of it."

"I don't understand why you guys want to join all that nonsense anyway," said Phoebe.

"Well, I did invite you if you want to see what it's all about."

Chapter 19

God's Wrath

About a week after Jerimiah's return from his Berlin captors, the Pilgrim camps were pulled back away from the city outskirts. There hadn't been any activity since his capture, so Jerimiah wondered if maybe the generals had reconsidered the attack on Berlin after all. But then one night there was a small earthquake, and all the sky above the distant city lit up with tracers and explosions. It was difficult to see from his camp's vantage point. He hadn't yet been reassigned, so he had no information about what was happening. Esther became extremely busy the following day, and Jerimiah was excused from the medical tents to make way for the incoming wounded. That next morning before dawn, Jerimiah's father came to see him in his tent.

"Come with me now," he said sternly, as if Jerimiah was once again that young boy being rousted out of bed for training.

Jerimiah complied, but if this was some sort of training exercise, he would try to invoke his medical leave orders.

What good that would do, he had no idea. His father led him out to the edge of the camp along the Elbe River, where they faced the city of Berlin. It was about a hundred kilometers to the east, and the subtle light on the horizon indicated dawn was arriving.

Jerimiah asked his father, "Do you know what happened in Berlin?"

"It doesn't matter now," said his father.

"How can it not matter? Do you know how many of our people are in that city?"

"I doubt many survived after last night."

"What happened? Why did you bring me here?"

Jerimiah and his father stood, staring, as the light of dawn broke dramatically over the horizon. It was too bright for Jerimiah's waking eyes, and he shielded them.

"Behold God's wrath," proclaimed his father dramatically.

Jerimiah had become accustomed to not relating to what his father was talking about, but this was different. He thought for a moment that his father had finally gone completely crazy. But then the light dimmed. It was an eerie, sudden dimness that was out of place in the light of a new day's sun. Then another sunrise occurred further to the south. The direction was unnatural, and so too had been the first light, Jerimiah now realized, as he came to understand that it was not the dawn at all. These were enormous explosions, larger than any he had ever seen.

"Was that Berlin?" asked Jerimiah.

"And Dresden to the south," confirmed his father. "And there are others suffering the same fate."

They stood in silence, contemplating the events, as another light began to glow brightly over the horizon. Was this finally the dawn? Jerimiah wasn't sure anymore. A wave of rumbling sound rolled over the camp. Then others came out to see the rising mushroom clouds in the distance. They had been awakened by what they thought was thunder.

Except for Jerimiah's father, no one in the camp had ever heard of a nuclear bomb. "These were small by comparison to some of the older models," his father was quick to point out.

Everyone in the camp seemed to be feeling a new sense of power and optimism that Jerimiah had never seen from them before. What they had achieved with God's help was wonderful, and the war would be over soon. Jerimiah did not feel so powerful. In fact, he felt very helpless. He had always felt as though the war was unnecessary, but now he knew he was on the wrong side.

Soon the refugees began coming into camp. At first, the arrivals were blind Pilgrim soldiers who had been too close to the blast. They had been warned not to look without the light shields, but they had looked anyway. Then the camp began to see the civilian casualties. Some were burned severely or had been struck by debris or crushed; some had a combination of injuries. It was unclear where they all came from. Esther was very busy. The refugees had to be washed before being brought into the hospital tents, and the medics had to handle their clothes and bodies carefully. The injuries were torturous for many, and their screams could be heard across the camp for days. No one slept. The worst cases were turned away because they couldn't be helped. Jerimiah tried to do what he could in the medical tents with his sister.

One day Jerimiah found Esther crying. "We can't do anything for them," she said. "We don't have enough supplies, and they are all going to die anyway."

Jerimiah could only put his arm around his sister to comfort her. "I'm not going back to the fighting," he said.

"You may be right not to want to, but you can't not go back. You know what they do to deserters."

Stoning to death was a popular option. This allowed many camp members to get involved, rather than merely observe the execution. If there were several people to execute at one time, the convicted might be lined up, so that vehicles could be driven on top of them. Beheading also made for an excellent public spectacle. None of this followed the original Forgist doctrines, but many had been executed for their attempts to persuade the leadership that they were in error.

"We will see about that," said Jerimiah.

Jerimiah was past due to be reassigned to his unit, and it was only a matter of time. He found a young recruit fumbling with his Scimitar on the target range. The gun had jammed, and the recruit was trying to dislodge the bullet. He had pulled back on the bolt, but the cartridge was still halfway inside the chamber. It would go no further because the casing was bent. Jerimiah had seen this before.

He shouted at the unsuspecting boy, "Soldier! When was

the last time you cleaned your weapon? Do you have any idea what you're doing?" He saw that the safety had been left in the off position. "Give me that weapon," Jerimiah barked, and he pulled the weapon away from the boy.

Jerimiah adeptly snagged the casing with his fingernail, knocking it to the ground, and then just as quickly slid another round into the chamber, closing the bolt behind it. He then handed the weapon forcefully back to the boy, while continuing to hold his finger over the trigger. As the boy recovered and began to wrap his hand around the Scimitar, Jerimiah carefully aimed the weapon at his own foot and pulled the trigger.

The pain was intense, but the job was done. He was quickly rushed to the medical tents, where Esther had already prepared for just such an event. The young boy had helped Jerimiah into the tent and was now sobbing. "I don't know what happened. It just went off. Is he going to be okay?"

"Just go please," said Esther. "I'll take it from here." She grimaced a little and shook her head. "We may have to amputate."

Once the boy was gone, Esther told Jerimiah, "In my personal opinion the wound is not that bad." But the medical record, which she would continue to update, would show several complications requiring extensive physical therapy.

Jerimiah, with Esther's help, had been rendered useless to the cause. He petitioned his father to let him go back to France, where he could recover and contribute through some civilian activity in support of the war effort. What effort that would be, he didn't know. After a long, silent look at his two children, Colonel Gold granted Jerimiah medical leave and gave Esther permission to go with him.

The opposition forces were now countering with their own nuclear arsenal, and many of the frontline camps were destroyed just as Jerimiah and Esther were arriving in France. Word of the counterattacks spread through the Pilgrim population. Once elevated to great heights, the Pilgrim morale now fell to new depths.

Esther received an official communication almost as soon as they arrived. "Jerimiah, I just got a message from Basim. He says our camp was destroyed—there is nothing left. Father is dead!"

"Then everyone we know ... gone," said a stunned Jerimiah. Had his father known this would happen? Was that why he had let them go? In the end, Jerimiah chose to believe it was possible.

"Basim is okay," said a relieved Esther. "And he's coming back to France, so you can meet him."

Chapter 20

Detroit

Before recent events, the Hellige had been an effective countermeasure to contain the aggression occurring across the world. The recent eruption of nuclear war in Europe had shown just how fragile that effort was. It had always been assumed that there were limits to the cruelty of the Pilgrim commanders and that ultimately they sought peace, albeit on their own terms. Now it was apparent that their only limitation was Hellige military suppression, and the Hellige were not omnipresent. The first strike had originated from the Pilgrim High Command. It had taken any peaceful conclusion to the conflict out of the realm of possibility.

The Hellige council had met to discuss the latest developments, and 4596 had a chance to review the latest council records on his long flight home.

"Everyone should have received today's agenda. Let's begin with item number one. Please begin the archive," said Prometheus, the speaker of the Hellige High Council, as he declared the start of the meeting.

"With regard to the escalation of the European conflict, we have added to the list of members of the Pilgrim High Command and find them guilty of mass murder. Please make all efforts to locate and capture these individuals for sentencing. Due to the lack of provincial jurisdiction in this area of the world, once the culprits are found, sentencing will be conducted through means of a tribunal, held at the Detroit Hellige temple. What is the status of nuclear armament in Europe at the present time?"

"Based on previous intelligence reports, we believe all nuclear weapons have been exhausted on both sides. Manufacturing facilities and fissionable materials have been destroyed or confiscated."

"What about those locations that utilize nuclear material for power generation?"

"All destroyed."

"Very well, but gentlemen, it must be noted that this has been a catastrophic failure on our part. We must double our efforts to defend God's people. This conflict is not over. We have information indicating imminent attacks on North American soil, so you will have ample opportunity to redeem yourselves.

"The next item on the agenda is a motion to maintain preauthorization of lethal automated defenses in the BCM facilities. This is an ancient loophole in our administration of these duties, and I for one do not believe this should be allowed to continue ..."

***

4596 had been flying for nearly twenty-four hours when the automatic pilot finally indicated that they had arrived at the Detroit Hellige temple. The facility was outlined by an erratic, star-shaped enclosure. From overhead, it looked like it might be a bad image of a wolf's head, but maybe that was just his imagination. The landing ports were clearly visible even from his current altitude.

"4596, hold your position at ten thousand meters. Await further instruction."

"Copy."

4596 joined several other flying transports hovering overhead and awaiting clearance for landing. It looked as if many others had been recalled.

***

As part of 4596's apprenticeship, Heracles showed him how to access government, civilian, and commercial data, in order to gather information on Forgist infiltrators in North America. The Hellige temple was buzzing with the news of the nuclear war in Europe. 4596 continued to follow references to Agent Blue, Phoenix, Agent 23, and the facility as a sort of hobby.

For a fictitious character, Agent 23 seemed to be a part of some very real activities. It seemed strange that Agent Blue, whom 4596 had now identified as Hector, needed to make real travel plans for a private meeting with Agent 23. And Forgist infiltrators who were known to 4596 because he had been assigned to track them reported having spoken with

Agent 23 through their own social communications. It also seemed to be a bit of a stretch to think that people should be encouraged to vote for Agent 23 in the Great Lakes provincial gubernatorial election. The election, more than anything, had supported the identification of agent 23 as Jacob Smith, a very real person and candidate in the upcoming election.

4596 reported these inconsistencies to Heracles. "How can I tell which information is part of the fly trap and which information is real?"

4596 waited while Heracles reviewed the information. Heracles finally responded, "All of it seems to be real, 4596. See here? This is a personal communication sent from Joseph Johnson relaying a discussion with Agent 23 at a face-to-face meeting. This guy Johnson is on your list of Forgist sympathizers. Here he calls Agent 23 by his name, Jacob Smith. This code here confirms the origin of the message. Outside of trained security officers, citizens are not allowed to be used in Hellige operations. There is something irregular going on."

Chapter 21

Agent Blue

Heracles had been surprised by what 4596 had uncovered and decided to discuss the issue with Hector directly.

"Hector," he said when his fellow Alpha answered.

"Yes, Heracles, how's the pup? Do you have him trained yet?"

"That's why I'm calling. 4596 has been sniffing around and has turned up a mystery."

"Oh, what's that?"

"Why does your fly trap, Project Phoenix, seem to have an actual person as Agent 23? Are you recruiting from outside of the order?"

"It's complicated," said Hector. "Tell your pup to go sniff somewhere else. He doesn't need to be involved in this."

Heracles was concerned by Hector's response. Rules for interactions with citizens were not to be taken lightly. Hector might be in violation of his oath. As a Hellige officer, Heracles felt it was his duty to investigate further.

Together, 4596 and Heracles began to piece together a

pattern of travel for Agent Blue, as well as meetings involving Project Phoenix. Once they knew what they were looking for, civilians and Forgist infiltrators alike seemed to want to talk about Project Phoenix on unsecured social communications.

"Can we get a hold of personal messages to and from Hector?" asked 4596.

"No, those would be available only during an investigation after a crime has been committed. So far, we don't have enough evidence. And personal messages are deleted shortly after they are received, so a search would not be as helpful as you might expect."

Agent 23 and Blue kept a low profile, but the Forgist sympathizers and infiltrators surrounding the project were a noisy group. An address for a scheduled meeting was finally attained. Heracles planned to attend, and he would take 4596 along. To keep a low profile, Heracles and 4596 would not be able to requisition standard automated units. It would be just the two of them, as uninvited guests.

Because of the contingent of armed Forgist infiltrators he expected to find in attendance, Heracles requisitioned two pulse rifles and stun sticks, along with the accompanying fusion-powered backpacks. This was not unusual for him to do, since he oversaw training for many recruits. Heracles planned to use only nonlethal force. If necessary, they would resort to the short-range stun sticks, or the nonlethal plasma rounds if they really got into trouble. The goal was to gain some information about Agent Blue's activities, not to kill anybody.

An electrically powered cargo transport had been called but was running late. The two stood in the dark outside the Detroit Hellige temple's north gate wearing full battle tech, minus the helmet. The battle tech could be covered by a robe, but they would have to show their faces if they were to mingle with the local population. If they had to use the plasma rounds, they would need to have some sort of light shield, so Heracles donned a pair of sunglasses and gave 4596 a matching set.

CV Archive PTZ489-6029-2

Public Transportation (PT) Surface Vehicles: A system of surface roadways is maintained for remotely populated areas. However, most North Americans live in communities that are serviced by the PT system. The roads can be used for transporting heavy or oversized cargo or equipment that cannot be loaded in palletized form aboard the PT pod system. Throughout cities, surface roadways become simple pathways designed for pedestrians or electric vehicles, with the purpose of getting people and supplies to and from the PT pod loading stations or other local destinations. Many passenger surface cars are reminiscent of old-style horse-drawn carriages but without live horses. At one point after the Great Declaration, many communities reverted to using horse and carriages. This tradition has been maintained to this day, reflected in the old style of electric carts. These carriages are actually part of the PT system. You can plan to have one drop you off or pick you up at your home as part of your preregistered trip ...

"4596, when we arrive, you need to follow my lead. Are we clear?" Heracles was interrupted by a woman walking her dog. "Good evening, ma'am."

"Good evening, gentlemen. It's a lovely night, isn't it?" She looked at them curiously as she passed.

"Clear," said 4596, responding to both inquiries.

Once the transport arrived, the pair took positions in the front seat and rode in the open air. As they traveled, they passed the same woman walking her dog. They waved. She politely waved back but continued to look at them with curiosity as they went by.

After a few minutes, the transport stopped and said, "You have arrived."

The two men covered their battle tech with robes before exiting, to blend in for as long as possible. They walked in the front door of an old brick-faced building complex. According to the schedule, everyone should have arrived.

A man saw them enter the building, "You two can't be in—"

Heracles quickly grabbed the man and put him in a headlock. He waited for a few seconds and then gently lowered the man down to the floor in complete silence. A drug was administered to keep him quiet. They remained in the hallway for a few moments, trying to determine what direction to go next. They heard voices upstairs and could see an open door in the hallway at the top of the stairs. The two crept up the stairs and held a position outside the room to listen.

"There is no need for us to kill anyone. That is a violation of our most sacred laws," said a familiar voice.

"It may be a violation of your laws. We will kill in the name of God if we must."

"God is great," chanted others. "Praise God."

"That is not why we are here today. This operation will be against automated defenses only. Several of your compatriots have already joined. We need time for Agent 23 here to work. And we need additional volunteers who have experience in disarming security systems. We also need additional members to be a part of the assault force."

"For what, cannon fodder?"

"If need be, yes. We all know the stakes. You say you are willing to kill for God. And yet you are not willing to sacrifice your own lives for Him. You are nothing but cowards, and I am wasting my time with all of you," continued the familiar voice.

"Is that Hector?" whispered 4596.

Heracles nodded.

"Hey! You two, what are you doing there?" a voice called from inside the room. They had been spotted leaning in to get a look at who might be in attendance.

The building had once been some sort of manufacturing facility. Long rows of windows ran along either side of the building, useless in the dark hours of the evening. Overhead lights illuminated a tall, open room. Chairs were aligned before a small podium. The gathering was seated, except for the two speakers and the security guards who were brandishing firearms from each corner of the room. The speaker's voice matched his familiar face. It was Hector. The man next to him was also familiar. Jacob Smith, the candidate running for Great Lakes provincial governor. The meeting had been promoted as a political rally. But the armed guards were not authorized by the Hellige order. They pointed their rifles at the two intruders.

Heracles heard 4596's pulse rifle click into action beside him; he was firing a plasma round. Face shields and helmets would have been preferred when firing such a round, especially in an enclosed environment and at this range. But then they would have looked more suspicious than they already did in their dark sunglasses and the bulging robes that hid their equipment. The light reflected sharply off 4596's dark sunglasses, and the sound was deafening. The first guard went down in a crackling ball of lightning and flame. The window beside the man shattered, and the old glass rained down outside the building. 4596 began to lay down additional rounds as his hood blew back from his head. Heracles could only watch in amazement as the room ignited. 4596 pivoted smoothly, pointing the pulse rifle at other targets around the room. 4596 was unloading more than enough firepower without Heracles's help.

The smoke cleared faster than one might expect because of the cold breeze that was now pushing through the blown-out windows. The carnage was incredible. People were lying on the floor, some on fire, some moaning incoherently. Heracles watched as 4596 rushed further into the room to find no challengers. The overhead lighting no longer lit the large room. Only the small fires marking the plasma explosions showed the devastation. As the ringing in his ears subsided, Heracles started to hear his own voice, yelling, "Hold fire! Hold fire!"

"I thought these were supposed to be nonlethal rounds," shouted a confused 4596.

"Well, when you pump that much hot plasma into a room full of people, bad things can happen. You should take note of that for next time."

"Will do," shouted 4596 into the now quiet room.

"And what happened to 'follow my lead'?"

4596 had no answer.

They looked around for survivors. Most seemed to be coughing or moaning at least, but a few had severe burns. Jacob Smith and Hector were now obscured by the smoke drifting over the area around the podium. Many in the group did not have enhancement technology. Emergency services were needed to provide medical attention for all and to contain the fires that were beginning to spread. Heracles and 4596 began to pick out some of the less injured for interrogation. They grabbed several people, two at a time, and placed them against the far wall of the room, away from the fires, while they coughed and sputtered. Then Heracles found someone he recognized. Hector was lying near the podium. One side of his face was smoldering, but it was Hector. He looked up at them in shock with his one good eye. Heracles grabbed him and one of the others from the pile in the back. 4596 picked up two bodies also, and they both ran before emergency services arrived.

"What have you done?" said Hector as his legs bounced down the stairs.

"What have *you* done?" retorted Heracles as he bounded outside toward their parked transport.

Heracles was determined to talk to him further. Once they had loaded the bodies into the waiting vehicle, they set the destination, and Heracles and 4596 moved into the cargo area, where the four captives lay on the floor. The vehicle began to roll casually down the street, away from the smoking building. Emergency services had just arrived. They were now hovering next to the blown-out windows and spraying fire suppression while several automaton responders dropped from the hovering emergency transports and ran into the burning building.

"No need for that," said Hector as he watched 4596 prepare an injection for interrogation. "There isn't time."

"Tell us what Project Phoenix is," said 4596.

"Still hunting, eh, 4596? It's the future. Soon there will no longer be a need for the Hellige. We are abominations. It is time for us to end." With that Hector passed. His face continued to smolder, causing the passengers to begin another round of coughing.

The kidnapped Forgist sympathizers were cooperative, but no one seemed to know much else about Project Phoenix. Whatever Hector had been up to, it was over now.

Chapter 22

Chicago

Augustus boarded the PT from the loading station, just as he had each day for school. Today, however, he would be going to Chicago to begin his new mysterious job.

CV Archive PTZ489-6000-7

Public Transportation (PT) Pods: Quad-seat transport pods are available upon entering any local PT loading platform. You may choose from two different sizes of pods, the more common quad-seat or a jumbo ten-passenger pod, which must be preordered. A fifth seat can be configured in the quad pod in place of cargo storage. The jumbo configuration is most commonly used without seats, allowing for cargo transport. Other versions of each size can be preordered for different types of cargo or for passengers taking extended trips. These may be equipped with various furnishings, such as a table, or may merely provide space to move around while traveling. Pods often travel through the tube system with minimal separation between them, creating train-like caravans, assuming passengers and cargo are all heading in the same direction. Each pod has a series of outriggers with clamping mechanisms. The pods attach themselves to power rails within the tube systems and move via a magnetic field generated between the pod and the power rails. The clamps hold onto the upper or lower power rails that the pods levitate upon. As each pod approaches an on or off ramp in the line, clamps attach to an upper rail and remain closed, while those on the lower rail are released. This allows for merging tube rails to align underneath the upper rails of the primary tube without damage to the clamping mechanisms. If the pod is to follow the secondary rail system, it will clamp the secondary merging rails below and release the primary rails from above, in a seamlessly choreographed motion. Speed reduction is not necessary for separation from the primary rails. If a pod is to continue on the same heading, it remains fastened to the upper rail throughout the interchange tube. This process may be reversed as needed through multiple interchanges.

See also CV Archive PTZ489-6021-1

Public Transportation (PT) Tubes: Each tube allows traffic flow in a single direction. Often, multiple tubes are used in parallel to support heavy traffic or interchanges. There are two types of rapid travel tube systems designed to carry a variety of transport pod configurations. The Inter-Province tubes run from city to city throughout North America. The tube system is supplied with electrical power generated through a series of tritium-fueled fusion generators. At each city or town along the way, there is a secondary set of tubes that services individual loading areas scattered throughout each city or town. This allows the Inter-Province pod convoys to drop off pods along the way without reducing speed. Upon entering the Inter-Province system, pods continue to accelerate until reaching a maximum cruising speed of 400 kilometers per hour, unless the pod is diverted for local transport first.

Today, Augustus's loading station was short on quad-seat pods. But he suddenly found a ten-passenger sitting in front of him, waiting for him to board. Without another option at the moment, and with no one else headed to Chicago, he hopped on.

The pods docked at the loading station had to be removed from the rail system so that passengers and cargo could be loaded. Augustus now felt the side-to-side jostling signifying that the pod had once again been secured to the rail system. The pod's startup cycle began to ramp up with an escalating hum. The startup cycle had the curious effect of moving the pod backward slightly before accelerating forward, causing Augustus to lurch forward before being pushed to the back of his seat. Except for the loading procedure, the ride was smooth and quiet, and restraints were not needed.

Augustus looked out the window to watch the loading station move out of view. Then there was really not much to see. The shadowy structures of the tube were difficult to make out from the side window. The front window was better. You could get a sense of the speed from the tiny intermittent lights mounted on the power rail supports as they passed by hypnotically. In the dim light of the tubes, pods came and went in front of him, and he saw the upper pod rail clamps open or close just before they diverted. The simple displays on the back of each seat gave a trip overview map and destination time. His enhancement tech could now process images and sounds through any local processor. He could talk to anyone who had basic communication technology. But Augustus preferred to look silently out the window as he traveled.

Augustus had never been on a PT pod this size by himself before today. He felt a little odd, sitting among the empty seats. But that was the nature of the PT system. The system would always provide for your minimum requirements as stated in your trip request. You took what the system sent unless you wanted to wait for another option to arrive. The ten-seater moved toward the nearest Inter-Province tube but then diverted suddenly to another loading station. He wondered if the system had blown a transformer, but there was no indication of this on the display. "Late for work on my first day," he said, cursing his luck.

But the PT was merely picking up another passenger bound for Chicago, apparently going near enough to his loading station to make a stop worthwhile. Augustus was relieved he wasn't going to be late. An older man stepped inside the pod, and the two nodded to each other.

The man sat down a few seats ahead of Augustus. "Bound for Chicago?" he asked cheerily as the pod sped away again.

"Yep, my first day of work," replied Augustus.

"Oh, would that be at Tri-Star Labs?"

"Yes, how did you—"

"You must be the one Solomon recommended. He said you'd be joining us today. I'm Dominicus. You must be Augustus?"

"Yes. Do you work for Tri-Star also?"

"Oh yes, I've been there for many years."

"Solomon didn't tell me much about the job. What's it like working there?"

Dominicus smiled. "It's like no place else in the world. I think you will find it interesting."

"Can you give me any hints about what I'll be doing?" begged Augustus.

"You'll find out soon enough." Dominicus settled into his seat and closed his eyes. It would be at least twenty minutes before they arrived, and apparently, Dominicus was not as wide awake as Augustus.

To Augustus's continued surprise, the PT stopped for other passengers along the way. Each person seemed very friendly, and they all acted like they knew each other. A woman sitting near Augustus greeted him and said, "Oh, you must be the new boy Solomon hired. Welcome to Tri-Star. I'm Evelyn."

"How is it the PT is picking all of us up together like this?" inquired Augustus.

"Oh, we try to limit the number of pods going in and out of the Tri-Star complex. Would not want anybody to take notice, you see?"

"Not really. I am not sure what goes on there exactly."

"You'll find out soon enough. We really can't discuss such things in public, so you will have to be patient."

They arrived at a series of red brick buildings between five and ten stories each. They all had greenhouse gardens on top. Many buildings had vines running up or down the sides—it was difficult to make out which way they were growing, and maybe it was both. The sky was a clear blue that morning as the group walked out from the loading station between the buildings that surrounded them. There was a little landscaped walkway, with outdoor benches and tables on green grass-covered openings to either side. To say the sidewalk was outdoors would not be completely accurate, since the whole area they were walking through was enclosed in solar glass. A family of ducks waddled quickly across the path in front of them. The ducks were headed off to the left toward a water feature that included a small rocky waterfall and a pond below. Augustus tried to see if they were wearing bow ties, but the angle was wrong, so he had to assume they were real. Augustus had to check in with security, so he separated from his new acquaintances. "See you later," he said.

The security process didn't take long. Just his walking in had caused a scan of his enhancement tech, which had given them all they needed to know. Augustus was then asked to read and sign a security waiver indicating that he would not discuss anything about Tri-Star operations outside the confines of the campus. The contract would be enforced through a standard monitoring protocol within his enhancement tech.

This new protocol was then downloaded. After that, he was escorted by a security bot down a series of passageways that concluded with a rapidly descending elevator. His stomach finally caught up with it after a few seconds.

The security bot said, "You have arrived." It then sat waiting for him to exit the elevator. As soon as Augustus exited the lift, the bot disappeared behind the closing elevator doors.

"Hello, Augustus. I hope your trip was okay. I heard you met Dominicus on the way in."

To Augustus's surprise, Solomon was waiting for him in a large, cavernous room. The ceiling was beyond view. The lighting came from a series of fixtures supported about ten meters off the ground. The support structure for the lighting grid required an imagination. The area above the lights extending to the cavern ceiling was completely dark. The room presented itself in a very ominous manner. A large, shadowy structure stood in the middle of the cavern like a dark tower rising through the lighting effects on the floor. Only the base could be seen, and there was no telling how tall it was because there was no visibility overhead, only darkness. There was a curved walkway around the large circular base, and the floor was open to a series of pipes radiating from around the bottom of the tower, like a bicycle wheel. The walkway created a bridge over the pipes below. Dominicus was at a workstation and waved in greeting as Solomon ushered Augustus forward.

"What's all this?" asked Augustus.

"Welcome to the Chicago Tri-Star Bio Crystalline Matrix facility."

Augustus was stunned. He hadn't considered this possibility. His jaw actually dropped, and he could do nothing but stand there in that awkward pose for a moment.

"Come on, Augustus. I'll show you around."

The tower was not that tall, as it turned out. It was a thick-walled tank of fluid that supported a large central sphere. The sphere contained the Bio Crystalline elements that came together to make up the combined memory storage for all of North America. There was no artificial intelligence program running on this device. It simply held all the data, memories, and secrets of an entire nation. The thick walls of the tank made up the interface between the sphere and the spoke network that radiated away in all directions around the facility.

The spoke network, as Solomon explained, divided the overall information and control networks for the country. Solomon pointed out which spokes controlled the various aspects of their civilization as they walked over the array of tubes.

"There are several spokes. At this proximity to the BCM, the spokes are physically split apart, and communication lines are enlarged, to create the massive bandwidth needed to feed all the networking signals into this one small area. Outside this complex, the communication lines are all physically interconnected again, but they remain separated virtually. This one is for military information, this one is for civilian information, this one is for commercialization, this one is for transportation, and here is the spoke for the weather control systems."

"Weather control? Do we do that?"

"Not very well. Apparently, we can disrupt some potentially damaging weather patterns. I'm not really an expert in that field. In any case, none of these network spokes can talk to the others directly except here through the BCM. This provides for a secure system of commerce, government, defense, research, and civilian information."

"Really? How do you prevent someone from simply connecting one or more of the systems from the outside?"

"Each spoke operates on a different system of frequencies and identification protocols, and this is monitored though AI gateways throughout the network. If someone were to, let's say, build an illegal converter to cross-connect from one spoke to another, any duplicated crossover information would be seen on both sides of the spoke. The duplicated information, or request for control, would be identified, and the command would then be interrupted.

"Each spoke is also guarded by the AI gateways via simulation testing. If you could trick the system's authentication protocols and access even one of the spokes to, let's say, implant a disruptive or illegal command, the command would be analyzed and stopped before being allowed to proceed. It would also trigger a response by security forces to the location."

"What if you built yourself one of these AI gateways?" asked Augustus.

"All AI network gateways are registered here with the BCM. You couldn't fake that even if you had the hardware. Other AI gateways will identify any unregistered device as a malfunction. The system also monitors registration for other devices, such as portable devices or those that can produce hard copies. This prevents restricted information from leaving the network. The most secure information is presented only through the holographic interfaces, and you can't bring any recording devices into the projection area. All secured work passes to the BCM facilities without ever being saved locally."

"What about the educational network? We used to bring information home all the time."

"Not anything that wasn't already public knowledge. We don't control everything—there is still freedom of the press, and there is free access to both the educational spoke and the civilian spoke. You can transmit all sorts of information from the educational spoke to the civilian spoke, but you can't, for example, rewrite history lessons from the civilian spoke. Any changes would have to go through the Education Council. And yes, people can act as portable recording devices. This is why we have security protocols downloaded into your enhancement tech. The most anyone could ever achieve would be to remember the information and then leave the country. They would never be allowed back, so at most, it would be a onetime event, if they got away with it. If they were suspected of stealing information and then leaving the country, the security protocol would allow us to track them through their enhancement tech. In this way, no important information or control can be accessed without being pulled through the secure pathways of the BCM."

"This all sounds good, but this facility … it doesn't seem very secure. What happens if someone decides to blow it up, destroy it? You have all the eggs in one basket here, don't you? All you seem to have guarding this place is a simple security station and some ducks."

"An attack on the facility would be more difficult than it sounds. In fact, you need to read up on the security protocols here in the building. Remember—if there is ever an alarm, you must go to one of the safe rooms. Don't try to do anything else. Also, this is one of three such baskets, each one providing full backup of all information and update protocols. Each location is unknown to the other sites, and each has independent power generation separate from the civilian power grid. It's all underground and practically undetectable."

"Tri-Star. I get it now."

"Indeed," said Solomon.

They walked around the pathway to the back side of the BCM tank, where the walkway began to ramp uphill. Once they were at the top of the incline, Augustus could see three much more substantial pipes extending away from the back side of the BCM tank, underneath where they were now standing. One of the tubes appeared to have been severed at the location of an arch. The spoke tubes were like perfectly round fingers, and each had what looked like a knuckle, an angular arch sitting on top of the tube at a standard distance away from the BCM tank.

"What are these spokes?" asked Augustus, indicating the three large tubes beneath them.

"These two"—Solomon indicated the outer two—"are connections to the other two BCM facilities. The one in the middle is the original pathway to the BCMAI. These archways act like a drawbridge to cut off all communication from any spoke in the network. The archways slide back, separating the tubes if needed. What you are seeing is, or was, the original attachment to the BCMAI that was severed after the Great Declaration."

As Augustus looked closer, he could see that there had been more to the separation event than just the raising of a drawbridge. It was more like someone had smashed the drawbridge altogether. There was apparent damage to the connecting sections, which would prevent the arch from closing again. The archway itself was fractured in places, and pieces of it had been left lying on the floor in the immediate area.

"We leave the mess as a reminder," said Solomon, following Augustus's gaze. "The BCM complex was built in a time before the spoke network. This facility was constructed before the Great Declaration. The original communication lines to the BCMAI were original to the project. We used to have information stored all over creation, and access was restricted by simple authorization protocols that were vulnerable to hacking, as they used to call it. The purpose of the facility changed from when it was first constructed. Its original purpose was as part of an information-gathering system for the old government of the United States. It was used for espionage and to support counterterrorism operations. The original creators likely had a less benevolent goal in mind for the information than we do today. Information was used to give them power over their enemies. The BCMs used to work like sponges, sopping up and categorizing the data from the splattering of data storage sites around the world. The BCMAI ran the operation as the master hacker. When the old worldwide information storage sites could not be maintained after the Great Declaration, it then became necessary to utilize the BCM complex as a central information storage system for all of North America."

"But then we built the spoke design afterward? So who is all this security protecting us from exactly?" asked Augustus.

"The spoke design, although it does protect us from the radical Forgists, was primarily conceived to someday allow us to reconnect the BCMAI. We need to do better than just giving it control of everything."

"I thought you wanted to reconnect it?"

"I do, but our society is not ready to trust the BCMAI with that much control. They may never fully trust it again. We need to demonstrate its abilities carefully without further incident and allow it to contribute to our society in new ways, without allowing it access to harmful technologies. And we need time to understand and implement the changes it advises ourselves, rather than growing dependent on the BCMAI."

"So we may never use that spoke again—never plug it back in directly. You plan to allow it to work as a human user to access the network through standard authorization protocols."

"Yes, that's about it," said Solomon sadly. "We hope that one day the BCMAI will be employed as a simple system user like everyone else. Now let's get you set up with a workstation."

"What do you do here, Solomon?"

"Oh, I'm not stationed here. Or at least, I don't work here very often. I just stopped by to make sure you got settled in. You will be reporting to Dominicus."

"So where do you work?"

"That's a discussion for another time."

Chapter 23

French Sky

Jerimiah had not been allowed to resign and become a civilian as he had wished. Instead, to accommodate his wound, he was now stationed at a console, monitoring the airspace over France. This suited him, except that it was a sedentary job, and he was eating too much, which was causing him to gain weight. His job was to provide intercept data for North American drones. The defense systems often failed to bring them down. But the little outpost located just outside Paris continued to make reports until the drones had to return for refueling. The North American drones rarely attacked any sites in France, and then they targeted only weapons caches. For the most part, the drones took sensor scans or interrupted active firefights in Germany as they occurred. Jerimiah would watch the whole station light up with activity after his alerts. Commands to direct information to one base or another went out. But that was all a routine.

One of the real joys of his work was the location. The city of Paris had endured against the odds. The old city's ambiance had somehow survived repeated threats, from the overdevelopment of the twenty-first-century population deluge to the post-Declaration neglect of its architecture and infrastructure and through to the modern-day war. Jerimiah thought the Parisians must have simply rebuilt everything using old building techniques and materials depicted in old paintings. It was now like no other city on Earth, certainly not like any Jerimiah had encountered.

Along the picturesque pathways of Paris, Jerimiah saw many young lovers doing what young love demands in such romantic settings. Jerimiah began to muse about his first love, Samira. He would never forget her cute twelve-year-old face and eyes, staring at him from under her hooded robe. He could still see the way her face had lit up when he looked at her. He had felt his face blush in return. Samira had belonged to another Pilgrim camp, with which Jerimiah's had joined that day to trade and share stories. Jerimiah had been wandering through the improvised markets, looking at the trinkets and food supplies on display by the wagons, when he came upon Samira's mother's stand selling beads. Jerimiah had to make excuses for being there. He pretended he was looking for just the right one for his mother, who had long since passed, or his sister, who didn't care for such things. All the while, he knew he wasn't there to look at beads. Samira made an excuse to wander off from her mother's view, and the two magnetically found each other. They escaped the market and entered an old building to explore. The old building was dangerous and forbidden, like their relationship. He held her hand. She kissed him. And all too suddenly, it was time to go home. The next day, Samira's camp was gone, and Jerimiah would never see her again. If his life had ended that night, before she left, he could have lived a less complete life, never knowing more and therefore never having to endure that feeling of loss and heartbreak.

Jerimiah was snapped out of his musing by the sudden breakup of a young couple in a nearby park. The girl slapped her boyfriend and then tried to stomp off. The boy was left shocked and embarrassed, but he recovered and chased after her, grabbing her arm. Jerimiah had no doubt that the two lovers would soon be resolving their issues. But the sound of that slap reminded him of something he would have preferred to put out of his mind. On his first day as a Pilgrim soldier, he had seen something that had completely complicated his view of women and relationships. He had suddenly found himself witnessing a Pilgrim unit raping a young woman. They had all been celebrating their initiation into the most powerful fighting force on Earth. That day had also marked their transition into manhood. Drunk on both their newfound power and wine, the soldiers had sought out their first victory. A local farmer, whose suspected activities included supplying the opposition, had been their first target. They had murdered most of the family before finding the young woman. She had put up a fight, and her face was battered from the violent reprisals. In spite of her bruised face and cut lips, Jerimiah saw that she was beautiful. Her young body was displayed for all to see, and Jerimiah could not help but look. He knew he could do nothing for her since she was not of the Forge. The Forgist doctrines had promoted tolerance and kindness to others. But there were no regulations in the Pilgrim army that protected the enemy in this way. He could have stopped them if it was Samira or Esther, but not this helpless creature. Jerimiah saw that she had given up. She had resigned to the assault instead of continuing to fight back and take the beatings. Jerimiah thought if he had met this young woman under other circumstances, he might have asked her on a date. But instead, he had turned away from the scene and accepted his fellow soldiers' stinging ridicule for not participating.

He had felt lost. He had shunned his duty to participate as part of the mob on the first day of his initiation. Had they been doing anything else, he would have wanted to be included, but he wanted more to make them stop. His view on women might have already been slanted, as often happened with a young boy growing up around soldiers. But this was different still; it was an exercise of power that made him sick to watch. In the end, he had done the only thing he could do. He had walked away and tried to put it out of his mind. The experience had soured him on romantic relationships with women. He had been with other women since that time, but those were just passing moments, experiences that were ultimately meaningless and unsatisfying.

Jerimiah was on his way to see his sister Esther, who now worked in a hospital nearby. Sometimes he went to the hospital to visit. Sometimes he went to have Esther review the status on his foot.

"You need to lean on that cane, Jerimiah, or someone is going to notice that there is nothing wrong with you. And I'm getting concerned about your weight. You need to get more exercise."

"Which is it? Do I put on a good show or get more exercise? How is Basim?"

"He's really, really good. Hey, guess what?"

"You're pregnant again."

"How did you know?"

"Lucky guess. Congratulations." Jerimiah said unconvincingly.

"Are you okay?"

"Yes, it's just that you and Basim have started a family. I feel like I'm missing out."

"But you get to be an uncle."

"Yeah, you know what I mean."

"Well, I have an idea. There is a new medic here from the Russian front. Her family came over to avoid the fallout. Maybe I can set you up on a date?"

"Okay, maybe. What's her name?"

"Sarah."

Soon, Jerimiah and Sarah were on their first date, at a public concert that Esther had suggested. Esther and Basim came along to make it more sociable, but Jerimiah soon recognized that he and Sarah made a good match for each other. Soon they were dating on their own. Sarah was from a Pilgrim camp similar to the one in which he and Esther had lived. Their stories were familiar, and they never argued unless it was over food. Sarah was a very decent cook, and Jerimiah was just learning his way around a kitchen. This did not help Jerimiah's weight problem, but Sarah didn't seem to mind. They had both known hunger.

Sarah, like Samira, was love at first sight. Perhaps Jerimiah was finally ready for a serious relationship. Whatever the unexplainable connection was, it was unmistakable. Like magnetism, it grew stronger the closer they were to each other, and then they just didn't want to let go.

Sarah was different in another way. Jerimiah discovered that she was not like the strong, independent woman his sister had become. Neither was she the stiff religious type who broke down on occasion because her body's desires betrayed her propriety. Afterward, out of regret, such women would revert to a previous self that no longer needed him. Instead, Sarah was submissive and delicate. He found that in each encounter with Sarah, she said nothing about her needs or her desires. Instead, she let Jerimiah decide what he wanted from her. This was not due to any form of intimidation or abuse by Jerimiah but rather it was a conscious choice by Sarah to love him in this unexpected way. He was allowed to be in charge, and she went along willingly. But Jerimiah found that a woman who gave in was not the same as one who gave up. This was new to him, and he wanted to be careful. He both did and did not want to take advantage of her. And perhaps she had more control over him than he understood.

He learned through careful experience that Sarah wanted him to want her, which was something he found easy to deliver. Why him, he didn't know. If he did not make her feel wanted in return, she would be disappointed, and Jerimiah did not want to disappoint.

They escaped the war together, along with all the cruelty, futility, and boredom that it had to offer. Jerimiah and Sarah were together as much as possible, just the two of them alone in her small apartment, under the sheets. Those moments together would be Jerimiah's fondest memories. After only a few months, Sarah became pregnant. The marriage came soon after.

Chapter 24

The Hellige

The Hellige High Council was made aware of the recent events involving the deaths of Hector and the gubernatorial candidate Jacob Smith. An investigative committee was organized, and Heracles was requested to attend to give testimony about the recent actions of his new apprentice.

Heracles passed through the council chamber's oversize doors to enter a large, round room with a domed ceiling supported by stone columns. He passed by a ceremonial fire to the left side of the entrance. He could see it glowing faintly, and he felt the heat dissipating into the stone interior of the chamber. The floor was also made of stone and was partially ringed by a curved wooden wall. The council, made up of Hellige priests, sat on a raised platform behind the wall, looking toward the door and the fireplace. The elevation of the priests allowed them to see anyone entering and look down upon anyone standing on the circular floor in front of them. The elevated view dispensed with a witness's need to kneel prior to giving testimony.

Soon the questioning was under way. "During his initial training, there was an event in which he nearly killed a fellow recruit, is that correct?"

"Yes. However—"

"We have read Hector's accounts of that day. Now this same recruit, 4596, is being charged with the murder of Hector, a highly devout priest, and several other bystanders, most notably a politician named Jacob Smith."

"I believe it was accidental. We were targeted by armed Forgist infiltrators, not bystanders. Our response was meant to be nonlethal. However, as you know, there are always risks with such actions."

"Perhaps, but why were you there at all?"

"I am submitting evidence for your review of this matter. I believe Hector was not as devout as we have been led to believe. We have learned that Hector was leading at least one of the cells assisting Forgist infiltrators and that Project Phoenix is a real operation being carried out by this cell. Jacob Smith was also assisting in this strike."

"What was the target?"

"That is unclear. I was wondering if the council knew what Hector may have been doing."

"We will ask the questions."

"Yes, please forgive me."

"That is up to us to decide."

After all the evidence was reviewed, a sentence was determined. It would be up to Heracles to deliver the news to his apprentice.

"4596, your actions have been deemed unforgivable. You caused several deaths. The council has ruled that you should be sent back to prison. However, there are two points that the council may yet consider."

"What points?" replied 4596. He was already saying goodbye to his anticipated career.

"One is that because you are my apprentice, I am actually responsible for your actions. Service to me is service to the order, which in turn is service to God. Even though you killed, you were under my direction."

"No, it was my fault," replied 4596.

"It's good that you take responsibility for your actions, 4596. Now, the second point is that Hector was found to be in violation of his oaths. This is punishable by death in the Hellige order. It may be argued that your actions were in service to God, regardless of your own intention or responsibilities. You have to understand, 4596. Everything we do here is for a higher purpose. We take oaths to pledge our actions in God's service. What Hector said about us is true. As individuals, we are abominations, but guided by our oaths, the Hellige order serves God."

"How can I serve from a prison cell?"

"That was my argument as well. For your sentence in this case to be commuted, you must fully commit to the Hellige order and take the oaths yourself. Before you can do that, you must serve penance for the deaths you caused. If you accept, your penance will be conducted here at the temple."

"I accept whatever the council deems necessary."

Over the next years, 4596 served faithfully in a variety of roles, many of which should have been filled by robots. In the Hellige temple, only human labor was utilized, given that there were plenty of penitent workers to be found. 4596 also continued to assist with cataloging information for the Hellige command regarding the stream of Forgist infiltrations. After the ringleader's demise, there had been no more discussion about Project Phoenix.

His promotion was reviewed many times and denied. However, due to his emerging proficiency, 4596 was often directed to train other recruits in hand-to-hand combat. At times, he would take on an entire class of recruits by himself in a free-for-all, king-of-the-hill-style session. These sessions were more about giving him an outlet to relieve his aggression, which mounted during his more tedious assignments, than about any kind of practical combat training. The recruits enjoyed the opportunity to fight in any case. His superiors were never sure what to make of these scenes, since the recruits were expelled from the center of the mob like popcorn, often later seeking medical attention. In the end, the floor would be littered with recruits lying in their own blood.

4596 also studied many subjects, including philosophy and religion, after he returned each night to his small cell within the walls of the Hellige temple.

Chapter 25

The Salad Days

Augustus and Phoebe had planned to live together out of wedlock initially, but Augustus had eventually agreed with Phoebe that they should go to that next level of commitment, and they were soon married. The ceremony was a simple affair, with close family and friends. Artemis attended, as did Augustus's mother Cecilia. With the talk and preparation for the wedding, Augustus's mothers had rekindled their relationship and were now back together. Augustus was happy about this turn of events. His mother would have been alone otherwise, now that he had moved out.

Augustus could not directly discuss his new job with Phoebe. This had the effect of making Phoebe suspicious of his activities. A suspicious Phoebe was not something Augustus wanted to come home to every night, so she was eventually granted security clearance. The two lovebirds were then able to keep in touch via the enhancement tech embedded in their ring fingers even when Augustus was at work. Phoebe could not have been happier, which made Augustus happy. But then

Augustus found it distracting to have his Phoebe alert going off all the time. Eventually, the two developed an understanding to avoid interruptions during some working hours. Phoebe soon learned to appreciate this, as she began work for the family business. They had the benefit of Mr. and Mrs. Tuttle's counsel on this topic. "Run the ring tech in passive mode to see if either of you are busy, before interrupting with an alert. Make sure to consider the settings before and after important meetings."

Soon Phoebe was asking Augustus about shutting down the birth control function of the enhancement tech. Augustus was a little wary of this development. At first, he said he wanted to better establish himself. But they were living in a decent apartment, and both were employed, so this wasn't much of an excuse. What he really meant was that he had just gotten used to all the recent changes. He was happy with their new arrangements and didn't want to bring on more responsibilities, at least not for the moment.

But eventually, Phoebe won out. She offered to let Augustus continue focusing on his career; she would stay home and work part-time when possible. It was all very exciting for Phoebe. Augustus did enjoy her enthusiasm for sex during this time but wondered what kind of father he would be without having had a father himself. He would have to rely on other examples. He was sure the children would be loved and cared for by the Tuttles. Augustus could also rely on his mothers to be supportive caregivers.

After the debate was over Augustus tried to prepare

himself for the life changing event of becoming a father. But he noted a distinctive change in one particular interaction with Phoebe that would continue to unsettle him from that night on. Phoebe's consent protocol relayed that Phoebe was clear of STDs, that her birth control was *no longer* active, that her age was appropriate, and that she was consenting to sexual activity.

Augustus's mother had warned Phoebe about expecting to get pregnant too quickly. "It can take a while to get pregnant, Phoebe. It took many attempts before Augustus came along. Enhancement technology will take care of you and the baby once it becomes a fetus, but it also may cause abortions at the embryonic stage if it discovers any genetic abnormality. Genetic abnormalities have been almost eradicated, except for those that choose not to use the technology. It is worth the wait to have a healthy child."

After many exhausting nights of sexual activity, the day finally came that Phoebe proudly announced she was pregnant. Eight months later, she gave birth to a healthy girl named Cecilia, after Augustus's mother but also because Phoebe liked that name. The delivery went as planned, with many family members in the room. But Phoebe was surprised by the pain because she had thought the enhancement tech was supposed to dull the experience. Apparently, the enhancement tech did not interfere unless it detected intrusive or unnatural processes acting upon the body. Cecilia's birth was well within tolerances.

"Why did no one warn me about this?" Phoebe yelled at the medic as she dug her fingernails into Augustus's arm.

"Breathe, just breathe."

"Stop telling me to breathe, damn it!"

A few days later, Augustus found himself lying on the couch with little Cecilia resting peacefully on his chest. She would sleep as long as she wasn't moved or left alone. To maintain the peace, the two had to remain close. He had been resistant to having children at first, but now as he looked down and smelled her little head, he realized something had changed within him. Now he had this little person to take care of, and it wasn't the inconvenience he had feared. It was as if it was meant to be, and everything began to make sense. He had a new purpose in life, and he thought he would do anything for this little bundle.

As he began to drift in the silence of the moment, he recalled his earlier discussions with Solomon. "Love goes quite a bit further than animal instinct," Solomon had once said.

He loved Cecilia. And Phoebe also did. But this feeling was not learned. This was instinctive; something had simply switched on inside their brains. This was a new kind of base coding, something that had evolved over the ages and that was present not just within humans but in animals as well. Like animals, Phoebe and Augustus also would protect their daughter from any threat. Augustus felt he would die defending her if the need arose, and he was sure Phoebe felt that way too.

Then a thought occurred to him that overwhelmed him. What would it be like if something did happen to Cecilia or Phoebe and he couldn't protect them? The idea of protecting his daughter had put him on alert, made him ready to fight. But this imagined loss angered Augustus. For the first time in his life, Augustus thought he might understand what hatred truly meant. He imagined wanting to take revenge, a useless but somehow necessary action in the wake of the theoretical loss.

Then another thought occurred to him. What would have happened if he had lived during the time of the Great Declaration? He had never thought it more than a history lesson. Now he imagined Phoebe and Cecilia as victims of the plague. He had a glimpse of what the entire world must have felt. With no outlet, no one to strike back against, people could go insane, and some had. How did you come back from something like that? Augustus couldn't imagine it, and for a while, he fixated on his own imagined anger. Hate and love involved the human capacity to feel past any actual event. But they were not exactly opposites. Wanting to protect someone from pain was instinctive love. Wanting to cause the pain was hate. But hate originated from a failure to protect from pain. Love was not a response to hate, at least not instinctively. Maybe that was what had to be taught.

Before Augustus had recognized how unique Phoebe truly was, when he had decided to go to Philadelphia with Julia, Phoebe should have instinctively hated Julia and Augustus. She could have acted out of jealousy. Instead, Phoebe had chosen to continue loving him and to at least tolerate Julia.

In the following years, Phoebe also gave birth to a boy named Lucius, named after Mr. Tuttle. As expected, the Tuttles were very supportive, and Arria, as she was now choosing to call herself, had proven to be an excellent babysitter. Augustus sometimes wondered if Arria might be filling his children's little heads full of superhero nonsense. So he did his best to include mathematics in their preschool experiences. Augustus was pleased to see that Lucius was very adept at pattern recognition at such an early age. And Cecilia was able to work through some rather advanced mathematical problems for her age.

Phoebe's sister babysat as much as possible within her busy schedule. She had abandoned the family business to become a medic in training. This was no easy accomplishment, since so few medics were needed. Arria now worked with emergency response out of the local hospital. Phoebe said it was cool that Arria was able to fly around in medical transports. This was a privilege extended only to security and emergency response teams and some top-level government officials. Arria was becoming the superhero she had imagined. Now she could fly.

One day Augustus came home to a debate among Arria, Cecilia, and Lucius. Arria had been telling them stories about superheroes since they were infants. Lucius had become a serious Spiderman fan. Augustus arrived home to hear Cecilia declaring, "Superman is the most powerful superhero ever."

"No, he is not. Spiderman is better."

"No way. Superman is way stronger and flies. If they got in a fight, Superman would defeat Spiderman, no problem."

Lucius looked to Arria for support on this question. But Arria avoided choosing sides. "Superman and Spiderman are both good guys. They would never fight each other."

But Lucius wasn't giving up on the defense of his favorite superhero. "Spiderman could win, though. He could wrap Superman up and up in his web, and he couldn't get out."

"Superman has laser vision. He would cut through Spiderman's webs," insisted Cecilia.

"Not if his eyes were stuck closed by the web."

This then began a secondary debate about how Superman's laser vision worked. Could he burn through his own eyelids? Augustus thought not. That wouldn't be practical.

"No, most likely, he would not be able to burn through his own skin with a laser," Arria concluded with a final ruling.

This encouraged Lucius but didn't convince Cecilia about who was better. Augustus and Phoebe thought the discussion precious as they listened in.

"Obviously, Superman would win," said Augustus.

"No, I think Lucius has a point," countered Phoebe. "He can't use his laser vision with his eyes closed."

"Don't be ridiculous …"

For Augustus and Phoebe, their children's early school years went by quickly. Soon they were looking not at children but at two young adults who were looking for careers and would be thinking about starting families of their own. They too would soon have enhancement technology and would begin their adult lives. As Augustus looked back on his experiences, he felt that he had managed to be a good father after all.

Chapter 26

Odysseus

4596 had spent many years in the tedious service of the Hellige priests. His purpose was more unclear than ever, but he persisted, serving his penance. After many years, the day finally came when an old friend arrived for a visit.

"Heracles!" said 4596 with a newfound sparkle in his eye. "How goes the war effort?"

"Are you ready to take your oaths and join us?" said Heracles.

"What do you mean?"

"It is time."

Heracles's visit marked the end of 4596's penance. At long last, it was over. 4596 was soon being led to the sanctum, where the Hellige High Council was concluding its latest session.

"After due consideration, the proposal of supplying opposition forces on any front with weapons has been rejected, again," declared an aging Prometheus, still leading the Hellige council meetings. When he saw Heracles escorting

4596 into the room, Prometheus interrupted the proceedings. "Gentlemen, we have a recruit with us today who wishes to join the order. All in favor."

"Aye," said the council unanimously.

"By unanimous consent of the Hellige council, we will begin the commissioning of Recruit 4596," stated Prometheus.

The ceremonial fire glowed hot and cast sparks into the stone chimney. 4596 was wearing a thin white ceremonial robe. Heracles and Theseus stood behind him in their dress robes and dark blue pellegrinas. Embroidered on their shoulders was a wolf's head, the symbol of the Hellige order. 4596 knelt on the stone floor in front of the council.

"Recruit 4596, by the powers invested in me as an ordained priest of the Hellige order, I hereby anoint you as an officer and agent of the Hellige order, endowed with the rite of choice over life and death, as protector of God's people. Do you accept your fate?"

Recruit 4596 had practiced the response. He clearly enunciated, "I accept God's judgment and claim responsibility for my actions and pledge them to God's service. I may cleanse my enemies, but in so doing, I debase my soul. I will seek no forgiveness, remaining cursed for all eternity. I will bear no children for the rest of my days, lest they follow in my footsteps. I vow to follow all doctrines of the Hellige order and all regulations established by the Smedje Synod."

Prometheus motioned to Theseus, who in turn went to the fireplace and lifted a large metal branding iron from the flames. At the hot end, glowing red, was a symbol made of two crossed hammers, the sigil of the Forge. From behind 4596, Heracles tore down the recruit's white robe, exposing his body down to his waist. Theseus walked to 4596's front and plunged the branding iron into his chest over his heart. It was all 4596 could do to keep from screaming. He had known what was expected of him during the ceremony, and he had thought he was prepared, but the pain was more than he had anticipated.

"You have been forged anew by fire and pain," said Prometheus. "You are reborn and will be known from this day forward as Odysseus." After a few moments, long enough for Odysseus to recover some, Prometheus spoke again. "Do you know the story of Odysseus?"

"He had many adventures," replied the newest Hellige agent, trying not to inhale the seared meat smell coming from his chest.

"Yes, and so shall you. We have in mind a new mission for you. You should begin to prepare at once."

Randel, reborn the Prince of Darkness, demoted to Prisoner 4596, promoted to Recruit 4596, was now reborn as Odysseus. He was, for the second time, reborn into a new and terrible form of life. But this time, he would exist with a more meaningful purpose in the service of God. He pledged to serve faithfully to the end of his days.

Chapter 27

Artemis

All of the BCM sites were hidden from public knowledge in an attempt to deter those who would seek disruption of the systems. The BCMs were stationed in a triangular pattern across the lands once known as the Midwest. Chicago, Minneapolis, and Kansas City were the actual locations of the Tri-Star BCM facilities. All three were located in separate provinces to prevent a political takeover. In retrospect someone might believe that these locations easily could have been found using deductive reasoning and therefore might have been too vulnerable to attack. However, the original site for the second BCM in the Tri-Star complex was on Mars, and updated information was transmitted there via satellite. This Martian BCM had been followed with a third and finally a fourth BCM, totaling three Earth-based BCMs and the old Martian BCM. The Martian BCM was to become part of a more massive complex located on the surface of Mars.

But the real question on everyone's mind was, where was the BCMAI located? And was it protected? Should it be protected? Should it be given direct access to the network? Very few knew the actual location, and most had arrived at a stalemate as to what to do next. Renewed preparations had been under way to plug in the BCMAI, again. But the finalization of the act was held up in council, awaiting approval for the BCMAI to be granted registration for the network.

The BCMAI location was not part of any geographic pattern related to the BCM complex. It sat, or instead floated, in a coolant bath in the city of Milwaukee, Great Lakes Province. Although BCM memory storage facilities had enough redundancy to make it very difficult to disrupt normal operations, there was concern regarding the singular BCMAI.

There had been some unusual reports of Forgist infiltrators in Ontario. There wasn't much in the way of modern technology in northern Ontario Province. Ice and snow were melted through most of the year, and the seas to the north were open waterways. Several drone flights had been dispatched over the wilderness, but nothing definitive had been uncovered. There were still bands of traditional peoples living off the land, preserving the simple way of life that their ancestors had adopted. The infiltrators were likely mimicking the natives. The reports had come in the form of dead Pilgrims, found after a recent winter storm. The winters could still be tricky in the North, in spite of the typically mild climate. The now thawed and partially uncovered bodies had been gnawed by animals. The natives had been interviewed after they reported the findings, but no other sightings of Pilgrims had been noted.

To his astonishment and genuine appreciation, Augustus was relocated to the Milwaukee facility. Each morning, the PT tunnels now took him underneath Lake Michigan between Kalamazoo and Milwaukee. These tunnels were deep underwater to allow ships to cross overhead, but there were transparent sections. PT pods traveled too quickly for any serious underwater viewing, but it added interest to the view through the PT pod window and a newfound excitement for his job.

This facility had similar tank and sphere configurations to the BCM facility where he was used to working. However, it did not have the distinctive array of spokes of the other BCM facilities. Instead, there was only one very large spoke that had the characteristic separated knuckle archway. Here too a mess had been left as a reminder, as the debris of the smashed arch sat uselessly on the floor. They had disconnected the BCMAI on all ends.

Augustus was now working to maintain an aging facility. The BCMAI, though still healthy, was beginning to show signs of its age. The solutions for many of these issues came from the BCMAI itself, but Augustus had to figure out how to implement them, which required its own form of ingenuity. He was also participating in developing instructions for the Martian BCMAI. These instructions were still being filtered through the efforts of the CTC, so the construction of the complete Martian BCMAI complex had been delayed for many years.

Throughout this time, tensions had continued to mount after the war in Europe went nuclear. This too had delayed the reconnection of the Earth-based BCMAI because some did not want to be faced with security concerns on two fronts.

Artemis had stayed in touch with Phoebe and Augustus. He was always trying to get Augustus to discuss his work, without much success. When he was in town, Artemis attended the Smedje along with Augustus. Phoebe was not a fanatic, as she worded it, and she made herself busy on days when Augustus and Artemis decided to go. Artemis had given up his career at Ceros because of the difficulties in opting out of enhancement technology. For a short time, Artemis had tried to follow in his father's footsteps as a politician. Though he achieved some notoriety following his father's eventual abdication of the Great Lakes provincial governor's seat, Artemis failed to win the hearts and minds of the people, and his political career was short-lived. Two of the main issues blocking his victory had been his advocacy for the reconnection of the BCMAI and his religious platform. He had won the election but failed to achieve the popular vote. This meant that the process started all over again with a new round of candidates.

Later on, Artemis accepted a nomination to a seat on the Confederate Technology Council. This was a position that Augustus coveted and it made Artemis his superior. Even so, Augustus was glad for his friend's success, and having a like-minded individual on the council was also appreciated.

One day in the spring of 2285 AD, or 175 years after the Great Declaration, Artemis came to visit the Milwaukee facility. Augustus thought he looked nervous. He demanded that he not be escorted around the facility, as everyone had been insisting upon. In fact, he attempted to dismiss everyone early, including Augustus. Augustus almost took the offer since Lucius's graduation party was the following day. He had invited Artemis and some of his coworkers to the graduation. So leaving early to begin preparations made some sense.

"Are you coming to the graduation tomorrow?" asked Augustus. "I know Phoebe would love to see you, and her mother makes a mean satay."

"Uh ... yeah, of course," said Artemis, distracted by one of the holographic monitors. "I wouldn't miss it. You should really go now. I'm sure Phoebe would appreciate some help with the arrangements."

Then suddenly, the alarms went off throughout the Milwaukee BCMAI facility: someone had violated one of the security protocols. Walls throughout the facility opened up, and the security rooms that Augustus had only read about appeared to him for the first time. It was unmistakable what the sudden appearance of these rooms meant for the employees. It meant everyone was to get out of the way while the automated defenses were activated. There was, at first, a quick-paced but orderly walk toward the doors of the little chambers. Fleeting concerns about work in progress were quickly overcome by the alarm. Then, like a herd of zebras spooked by a lion, everyone began to run. As they neared their destination, some slid through doorways, trying not to smack into the back walls of the security rooms; others just hit the back wall flat, not bothering to slow down. Everyone was safe as the chamber doors started to close, everyone except for Artemis.

As the security chambers began descending into the expected safety below the BCMAI cavern, Augustus saw Artemis through the security room window, working at one of the consoles. Augustus recognized the images on the console Artemis was using. He was downloading the registration for the BCMAI. A short battle ensued out of sight of the descending refugees. The walls closed tightly above them, and they could only wait for rescue.

Augustus was very late getting home that day. At first he had been suspected as a coconspirator, but security records had quickly cleared him of suspicion.

"You're late," Phoebe noted as he entered the house.

"There were a few issues at work. How are we doing for the party tomorrow?"

"Fine. Did you talk to Artemis? I wasn't sure if he was going to make it or not."

"Sit down, Phoebe. The reason I am late ... well ... no, Artemis will not make it to the party," replied Augustus, struggling to find the right words. "In fact, we will not see Artemis again. I'm afraid he died in an accident earlier today." Phoebe was not cleared for any more information, and Augustus had been instructed to use the term "accident" for now.

"What happened?"

"I can't say any more than that for now. It's classified."

Augustus was completely confused by the event. This was not how things happened in his world. He had always followed the rules and just expected everyone he knew and cared about to follow them also. He could not believe Artemis was gone. Then again, Augustus had not actually witnessed him dying. Maybe they had just arrested him or something. But why create the story of his accident? Perhaps Artemis would be exiled.

"What about the graduation tomorrow? How can we celebrate anything now?"

"The plans have been made; there is nothing we can do for now. If you are willing, I think we should continue as planned."

They decided to go ahead with Lucius's graduation, without Artemis. The facility had been temporarily taken over by maintenance bots for the cleanup. Much of the onsite control interface had been damaged. There was not much Augustus could do until repairs were made.

He did not get much sleep that night. The next day, Augustus tried to stay in touch with the events as they continued to unfold. Dominicus stopped by the graduation party. He was still working at the Chicago facility but wanted mainly to check on Augustus personally.

"Still a bit shaky, but life goes on," said Augustus, handing Dominicus a drink.

"I would like your assessment of the security protocols when you get a chance."

"No problem."

Solomon also stopped by the graduation. The event was becoming less about Lucius and more about Augustus. Phoebe looked perturbed by the secret huddle. Augustus could tell she didn't appreciate the secrecy and the deliberately vague comments about Artemis's accident.

Solomon told the real story to a group at the graduation that had been cleared for the information. "As it turns out, Artemis Kahn led a group of Pilgrim infiltrators through the security systems at the Milwaukee BCMAI facility. With his CTC clearance, it was relatively easy for him to get into the facility. The others acted as a distraction for Artemis by storming the facility and shutting down security systems so that what he was doing would not be noticed until it was too late. The entire group, including Artemis, was killed by the security systems after they were discovered, but not before Artemis uploaded the registration for the BCMAI. Apparently, the Forgist plan was never to destroy the BCM sites, but instead to set free the BCMAI. And Artemis must have known that he and the others wouldn't survive. We are now learning that Artemis had been heavily influenced by radical Forgists at a young age. He joined a secret network of Forgists operating in North America with intentions to carry out terrorist attacks. When the opportunity to reconnect the BCMAI presented itself, it must have been like an answer from God. The greatest instrument of God's wrath that has ever existed was available to be used once again. This misguided attempt was made to finally tear down the Humanist government. But as you see, none of that has happened. There are a lot of people in high places panicking at the moment, so I need to get going. I mostly stopped by to see how you all were doing."

Solomon stepped away from the group to greet Phoebe. "Hello, Phoebe. I know Artemis was your friend also. I wish I could say more. Hey, congratulations, Lucius. Way to go. What are your plans?" Solomon then returned to Augustus and explained again, "I am sorry, but I must be going."

Solomon had confirmed to Augustus that Artemis was really dead. After Lucius went out with some friends that evening, Augustus and Phoebe were left behind to mourn his loss in silence.

***

An emergency meeting of the Executive Council was held to discuss the latest events at the Milwaukee BCMAI facility. Members of the Smedje Synod, by their association with the Confederate Technology Council, and the Hellige High Council were requested to attend. Augustus attended holographically as a witness, but his comments had already been recorded and reviewed by the council before the session, so he was unlikely to be called upon to speak. This was the first time Augustus had attended an Executive Council meeting virtually or otherwise. He spun in his chair to take in the view of the Council Hall but also to check the responsiveness of the holographic image he was sitting in. The spinning holographic head generated looks of surprise from others in the Council Hall gallery, so he stopped.

The Executive Council Hall was about the same size as the Forge but the ceiling was dampened with soft material to prevent sound reverberation. There was no ceremonial holographic flame like at the Forge and there was no active projection of the speaker visible in the room. The floor was a neutral light gray carpet. It had a curved, wood-paneled wall to separate the council delegates' elevated platform from the ground floor. In the platform's first row sat the grumpy governors of all the fourteen provinces that made up the Executive Council. Above and behind the first row sat the members of the Hellige High Council, as visiting members. In another council session, the visiting members of the Smedje Synod or the Confederate Technology Council might have occupied the second row with the other delegates. But because they were the group being called to account for their actions, the CTC members now sat in the gallery. All looked down upon a set of wooden tables that sat in the very center of the council's gaze. The hot seat, as it was known, was stationed behind this set of tables. Those who sat in this seat would have to look slightly upward and provide testimony, under the stern guidance of the council. Solomon was the first in the line of fire.

"Begin GV Archive BCMAI459-1576-3: Central Province, Kansas City center, May 1, 2285, Executive Council Emergency

Meeting, Governor Alexander Chin presiding," announced a soft automated voice.

"Is it true that the BCMAI is still connected?" said the chairman.

"Yes, the control systems were too badly damaged to change that," replied Solomon.

"Damaged by your own security measures?"

"No, the terrorist group led by Artemis Kahn did more than simply upload the registration for the BCMAI. They made it very difficult to access the system afterward. We expect to have control restored later today. The registration is for simple access to the civilian network; there is little risk."

"That thing could incite a revolt among the Forgist sympathizers. We should shut down the entire spoke."

"Well, I think a revolt has already happened and the CTC does not believe the BCMAI actually supports the radical cause or intends any harm to the current government."

"What is it doing?"

"It seems to be content simply to review the world's history from the last 175 years. And it has asked to speak directly with the Martian BCMAI."

"It asked?"

"Yes, just as any user on the civilian network would have to make a request."

"Then you believe it is still contained?"

"Yes."

"I want you to, very clearly, tell us how this happened. It

seems obvious that this was a terrorist act, an attempt to use the BCMAI as a weapon."

"Excuse me," Prometheus interrupted from his seat in the second row on the platform. "I must disagree."

"The chair recognizes Prometheus of the Hellige High Council," said the chairman. All the provincial governors turned their chairs to view the old man sitting slightly above and behind them. "Do you have something to add?"

"Yes, well, I would say this is not purely an act of terrorism, as many on both sides have been led to believe. To understand what has truly happened, you must consider the mythology surrounding the BCMAI and how it has affected our society."

"Mythology?"

"Yes. The belief that the BCMAI speaks to, or is at least instructed by, God is pervasive throughout the world. Many of the faithful crave some physical manifestation of God in their lives. Faith itself is not enough, it would seem. The prophet James Murphy and his descendants have preyed upon that need in our society for years. Remember our faith did not originate through a singular prophet. Instead, our faith is rational and acknowledges that God has sent us many prophets, such as Moses, Jesus, and Mohammed, to provide us with direction. Many believe that the BCMAI is the latest of God's prophets and that you, Mr. Chin, are part of a government conspiracy to keep God out of our lives."

"Be careful how you address this council, Prometheus."

"I am simply laying the groundwork for a thought process that may explain the origin of this plot to reinstate the BCMAI.

Over two decades ago, a Hellige officer named Hector took it upon himself to develop just such a plot among the Forgist sympathizers. He was enamored by this mythology. We revoked his commission, of course, but the idea lived on, waiting for an opportunity. Artemis Kahn grew up during those days and was influenced by that idea. If we continue to create martyrs for this cause, and if we disconnect the BCMAI again, there may indeed be an uprising."

Solomon interjected, "What happens when the BCMAI doesn't fulfill their expectations?"

"It would be better to let that possibility play itself out than to continue the oppression of the prophet."

The council chairs swiveled back and forth during the exchange between Solomon and Prometheus. Those on the outer edges of the array of delegates ended up with the best views and hardly needed to move. But the chairman had landed in the center of the discussion and had to make more dramatic swivels, which inevitably caused him to rotate in a complete circle before he stopped himself suddenly.

"This is ridiculous," said the chairman. "Are you suggesting we leave it plugged in?"

"Yes," said Prometheus.

"I agree," said Solomon.

Then Prometheus added, "And might I also add that this is a good opportunity to review the authorization for the automated defenses at the BCM facilities to exercise lethal force."

"We can review that at another time."

After much discussion and 175 years of isolation, the BCMAI had finally been allowed access to the network. Although this had occurred through curious circumstances, the reconnection was remarkably uneventful, and the BCMAI would be allowed to remain a registered user indefinitely. A stalemate had persisted between those who had wanted to plug it into the network and those who had not, and this same stalemate meant that now they could not decide whether to unplug it or not.

The public announcement simply stated, "After many years of debate, the BCMAI has been allowed limited access to the network; everyone may experience some service interruptions as a consequence."

But after all the discussions had died down, and with Augustus's group managing the drain on the network, many began to forget about the BCMAI altogether. The exception was Solomon's little band of engineers who faithfully maintained the BCM systems. They alone could watch the increased information exchanges and often had to compensate for power surges through the network that threatened to create unplanned shutdowns. They had to bring on an additional shift to manage the events, and PT pods were coming and going at all hours.

***

Although security around the event kept the full story out of the public record, the event did not go unnoticed by Heracles and Odysseus. The attack on the BCMAI facility likely had been based on the fabled Project Phoenix. Among the Forgist sympathizers, this latest Agent 23 was declared a hero to a new order of the Phoenix and finally was revealed as a member of the Confederate Technology Council named Artemis Khan. Nothing was said about the fate of the Hellige in relation to this matter. Hector's intention to replace the Hellige was not mentioned in the government hearings. Was this BCMAI to be their replacement, humanity's ultimate protector? Odysseus did not see how that was possible.

Chapter 28

Off-World Travel Plans

Later, the Mars mission successfully added to its own BCM complex. Modeled on the Earth's Tri-Star configuration, the BCM complex was named Trinity. The new Martian BCMAI functioned as expected. BCMAI communications from Earth to Mars echoed off a secure chain of satellites between the two planets.

A new mission was being planned to establish a fleet of space vessels with the capability to transport an entire colony to destinations outside of the solar system. One of the colony-class ships planned to carry on board a single smaller version of the BCMAI, to be taught by the Martian BCMAI. The mission was first to evaluate the potential of a distant planet that was believed to be able to support life and then to complete terraforming operations as needed, to pave the way for future colonization.

Teams of technicians and scientists working for the Ceros Company were feverishly reviewing plans and testing the new prototype technologies that would carry the colonists to their new home. "We will also need to take along a Hellige officer."

"Really? This is a mission of exploration."

"The mission will ultimately lead to colonization. You will need law and order in this new colony if it is to thrive."

"Why can't we use automated security forces, without the Hellige?"

"We have lived in relative peace for many years thanks to the Hellige."

"Tell it to Berlin."

"It is not up to either of us. Here are the specifications for his quarters and the equipment to be brought on board."

"Who did they pick?"

"Odysseus."

"Really, that's his name? Odysseus on board a ship called the *Odyssey*? I never thought they had a sense of humor."

"I wouldn't test it. Apparently, he was recently commissioned."

Chapter 29

Spiderman versus Superman

Augustus had finally been allowed a seat on the Confederate Technology Council. It was Solomon's seat. The appointment occurred soon after Solomon retired. Solomon was getting quite old, and if it hadn't been for the enhancement technology, he likely would have died of old age by now. Even with the enhancement, it was time for Solomon to slow down. He was able to keep up with a less busy public speaking schedule, he maintained his seat on the Smedje Synod, and he was often called in as a consultant for various issues. But he was enjoying a measured level of retirement.

Augustus felt that everything was going about as well as could be expected. But then the day came that Augustus's brain would later categorize as the day he would least want to live over again.

In the months leading up to that day, two launches bound for Mars had been destroyed shortly after takeoff. Two hundred people had been killed, and much-needed supplies had also gone down over the Caribbean waters.

The European conflict had resulted in yet another stalemate between the Pilgrims and the opposition forces. The demilitarized zone consisted of miles of radioactive fields and waterways. Because the campaign in Asia also had been affected by the fallout, only the Pilgrim conquests in Africa and some parts of Western Europe were left relatively unharmed. Much of the land of central Europe would remain dangerous to inhabit for years to come. The Pilgrim armies had since given up the Asian and European campaigns, at least for the moment, and were focusing their efforts on strikes against North America. More infiltrators had been reported crossing in from the northern provinces.

North America was becoming vulnerable to the once-distant war. This posed some sticky philosophical issues for the country. It could use its superior technology to wipe the Forgists off the planet, but that was not the preferred method of settling differences.

The Humanist government supported the opposition forces with needed medical supplies, but the opposition forces would never be able to the take the offensive against the Pilgrim threat without weapons. Allowing the proliferation of North American weapons was not legal. Such tools of warfare were controlled by the Hellige. Diplomacy didn't work either, since the Forgists were not interested in anything more than the complete surrender of the North American government.

North America increased its defenses dramatically. With the help of the BCMAI, some newer technologies were under development. As an example, a series of launches from North

America suddenly and successfully achieved their goal, but these missiles were not destined for Mars. The cargo was full of a new material called XM-41. The warheads filled with XM-41 exploded in the atmosphere above the Forgist-occupied territories. These atmospheric detonations were precisely timed to coincide with weather patterns across the world and caused great concern among the Forgist military commanders.

XM-41 was produced using a weaponized bacterium. Showering down upon the land, these bacteria would land almost everywhere and begin colonization. Then they could be picked up from the environment through accidental human contact and infect a human host. Or the residual substance alone, continuing on even in the dead bacteria, could be absorbed by the human skin. This had been a standard method used for many years to transmit vaccines across remote parts of the world. It was also the method that had been used to disseminate DDX-23, the compound that had had such devastating effects on the human immune system, leading to the Great Declaration. The idea of allowing another substance created by the BCMAI to be used on human populations was heavily debated. However, in the final analysis, it was decided that if there were damaging effects on humans, they would be limited to areas outside of North America.

Only trace amounts of the material were needed. Anyone caught under the falling XM-41 cloud, or anyone who walked through an area contaminated by it, could then be tracked globally. The Pilgrim commanders made several guesses about what the substance actually did. They had tested it for radioactivity and toxicity, but nothing, except eventually their spy network, was able to explain the actual purpose.

In the presence of XM-41, the human body produced short bursts of radio frequency transmissions, which were very difficult to detect unless you knew how to look. Also, the effect was not continuous. A signal burst was generated every thirty minutes or so. The purpose was to monitor new Forgist infiltrators.

This did nothing to track the Forgist radicals already inside North America. Enhancement tech would have been a more effective tracking system for all people in the Confederation, but many had refused to use it, and more were following.

Rounding up the technophobes was considered a violation of religious freedom. However, it made sense to the Executive Council to monitor them more closely. That monitoring activity, for a time, created a political backlash, and in solidarity, young protestors joined in refusing to be enhanced. This trend was a boon for Arria's profession, and she became busier than ever from the resulting medical needs of the unenhanced.

As Augustus reviewed the intelligence reports, he thought, *It's like Spiderman versus Superman, but Spiderman is winning.*

Chapter 30

Strange Weather

"Commander, I have a problem with my equipment," said Jerimiah.

"What is it, Corporal?"

"It looks like there are over a thousand incoming intercontinental projectiles in the upper atmosphere. That can't be correct, can it?"

"No, most likely not. Let me take a look."

"Confirmed, sir ... we have similar reports from Spain."

"That's impossible. What are they targeting?"

"Everything."

"Sir, we are getting confirmation that the objects are breaking up."

"Hundreds of thousands of incoming projectiles ... what do we target?"

The event sounded like distant thunder to the Pilgrims, as the XM-41 was dispersed through the exploding warheads in the upper atmosphere. Most awoke the next morning without realizing what had happened. But the Pilgrim commanders had watched helplessly as the event unfolded. The scale of the operation was overwhelming. Attempts to take down so many incoming missiles were futile. This pattern was repeated again and again over other parts of the world.

Chapter 31

Investigation

The security investigation would begin with some background information on the day's events and include a mix of eyewitness and investigator descriptions, security footage, and relevant communication records.

Lucius Tuttle had sent out a team to inspect sections of the PT pod system that had been using components manufactured by the family-owned business. The team's purpose had been to evaluate how well the components had been performing under real-life conditions, so that the company could make improvements for the next batch. The group consisted of a team leader, several young interns, and Lucius's daughter, Phoebe Mendelson. Sabastian Green was the team leader, but Phoebe represented the owners. They had all been instructed on how to complete the inspection, but for many of them, it was their first time as participants in an inspection. It was not uncommon for a member of the family to accompany the group, but it was especially important on this day because of the overall inexperience of the team.

After arriving at a concealed hatch near the Kalamazoo PT Inter-Province exchange, the team loaded the equipment onto a cart. They then headed into the underground service ducts below the local PT Inter-Province exchange for Kalamazoo city. This was a busy hub, and it was the most likely pod interchange to provide the best data for their purposes. Once the security door was opened, the lights and security recorders came on automatically. The maintenance tube was an underground, horizontal passageway that seemed to go on into the infinite. The maintenance tube was an entirely separate tube system from where the PT pods traveled, but the noise of the PT pods penetrated the wall separating the team from the Inter-Province rail system. It was a deep, throbbing sound, somewhat like a choir of humming giants who were at the same time moving their fingers up and down over their lips to create a fast rhythm. Hearing protection was needed, but it was still possible to speak to one another by shouting over the noise or using the coms. They moved their equipment into place along the maintenance tube, with each team member set up to work in a different section.

After a few minutes, some of the team began to detect odd readings. They called for Sabastian, but he was busy. So Phoebe came over to help with the investigation.

"It doesn't make sense. It's like power is being drained from somewhere nearby."

Phoebe moved up and down, looking at everyone's readings and trying to determine the source of the power loss. "Sabastian, what are you doing?" Phoebe shouted to be heard, and Sabastian jumped up in surprise, sending all his equipment tumbling to the ground around him.

"You're not set up yet," said Phoebe. "I need to see the data from this point in the line. Wait, that's not even the correct equipment. What is all this?"

Sabastian had done this work before. Although he had chosen not to be enhanced, he had proven himself to be an outstanding technician, and as the leader of the team, Phoebe was baffled. Then as she looked over the equipment, she noticed that Sabastian had hooked up an odd-looking device to one of the power conduits. The device had a simple readout on the front that indicated a steady increase. Increasing what? Phoebe didn't know. Before she could turn back to Sabastian, he stabbed her with a tool from his bag. She cried out, but the other team members hadn't noticed Sabastian's misdeed and couldn't hear her cries for help. All they saw, initially, was that someone had run behind them, heading for the door. Then Phoebe's call for help came over the coms.

"Help me, someone. Look out for Sabastian ... he stabbed me."

Some hurried to try to help Phoebe. Others, seeing she was being helped already, ran for the door, looking for Sabastian. They found that the security door had been closed, and there had been a weak attempt to block the opening with an umbrella from a nearby picnic table. After breaking through the obstruction, they saw no sign of Sabastian. Some in the group called for emergency services while others lifted Phoebe onto the same cart they'd used to carry in the equipment.

Phoebe's enhancement tech was hard at work. It had already stopped most of the bleeding and was completing diagnostics on the wound. She would be fine.

This information was all conveyed to Augustus in real time. He was in a meeting, but the Phoebe alert was rated as an emergency. He jumped up and ran for the elevator. The doors took the same amount of time to close as they always did, but Augustus couldn't wait. "Come on, come on," he said. There was no one in the lift at this time of day, not even a security bot.

Back at the Inter-Province exchange, the small group attending to Phoebe began to carefully convey her down the long maintenance tunnel toward the exit. Meanwhile, the group pursuing Sabastian had lost track of him.

Phoebe said urgently using the coms, "Someone needs to go back and remove the device."

"Sabastian is gone."

"We need emergency services at Nineteenth Street and Twenty-Fifth Avenue now."

"Yes, she's been stabbed."

"Sabastian Green."

"What device?"

Before the bloodstained group could make it back to the security door, the device that Sabastian had installed reached its maximum. It had been building up a charge, which was then to feed back into one of the power control systems. It was a simple, nonexplosive device. The security protocols had not detected it as a threat among the other inspection equipment. It was an unregistered device, but it hadn't been connected to a communication line directly. It was designed to feed off the available power in the magnetic rails and send a sudden burst of destructive energy back into a vulnerable area of the system. Its effect had been noticeable, but the drain had not been so far outside of standard parameters as to cause a shutdown of the system. None of this could have been accomplished without knowledge of critical details. In fact, the only way to accomplish this was to infiltrate the Tuttles' component manufacturing and design facility. Even then, it was not an easy weakness to exploit.

Prior to the event, the Kalamazoo interchange had been in need of a second bypass tube system. This project had been started, and the Tuttles had been looking forward to the new business, but then the city population had decreased for a time, and the new tube system had been abandoned. However, the city had become a busy place for visitors, with much of the PT traffic coming from users who were independent of the local population. Kalamazoo's position as a midway point between Chicago and Detroit meant higher traffic and tighter margins of error on the overcrowded interchanges.

As security recordings would later show, at this point Sabastian had already been detained by security forces. He had been netted by an automaton waiting in a nearby security post after he had refused to stop in the vicinity of an emergency call with a possible perpetrator on the loose. The automaton, under the control of the local security AI, had done its duty. No additional authorization had been necessary for this type of nonlethal stop.

With Sabastian still wriggling in the net, an explosive rumble sounded. The power spike from the device caused the power controls to overcompensate, leading to a cascade of control events, which welded one of the passing PT pod clamps to the power rail. The pod's outrigger fractured and snapped apart instantly leaving the welded clamp stuck to the rail while the pod went careening down the tube. For a single pod by itself, a broken clamp would have caused an unfortunate but survivable incident. But this occurred along the merging interchange point between the PT Inter-Province and the local PT system.

Any pod following the same rail exchange sequence also lost its rail clamps, due to the first welded chunk left on the interchange rail. An isolated pod might have simply skidded to a stop. But now the welded clamp continued to damage all following pods, which were now all skidding along the bottom rail. It was a busy time of day, and the long train of PT pods, some with clamps, some without clamps, collided violently.

The system quickly went into emergency shutdown, but the emergency stop was too late to prevent the initial crash from occurring. It did save many others from the same fate. The unfortunate passengers in the affected train of PT pods, however, were in for a bumpy ride. Emergency airbags exploded inside each pod, incapacitating, engulfing, and pinning the passengers inside each pod in midair. While taking their breath temporarily, this protected them from most of the forces of the collision.

The pods themselves broke formation and jammed inside the walls of the underground tube. Each pod was solidly built, but the effect was like loading a gun with too many bullets at once. Or in this case, it was like firing two machine guns into a third gun barrel at the same time. The force of the pods against the inside of the tube forced the tube ceiling to break up and push through the landscaped pathways of the city walkway overhead. Like an earthquake fracturing along a fault line, the walkways overhead unzipped. The netted Sabastian and the security automaton were thrown into the air along with pieces of the path, picnic tables, and shrubberies. Smoke and compressed gas from the tube below blew up through the crack. Sabastian would later be found stuck in a tree, still trying to wriggle out of the net, which was now hopelessly entangled in the tree branches.

In the Milwaukee BCMAI facility, the doors to the elevator finally closed, and Augustus felt his stomach sink to the floor with the upward acceleration of the lift.

The effect of the crash was also noticed in the PT tube maintenance shaft, while Phoebe's rescuers were in the process of evacuating her. The force of the pods against the tube walls first had taken the upward path of least resistance, but now it also took the path of second-least resistance. The maintenance tubes were crushed instantaneously in several places. The collapse of the maintenance tube did not directly affect the team, but the newly compressed air in the tunnels fired a shockwave through this alternate tube system. Because the maintenance tube was underground below the main tube, there were vents, but these were either crushed or blocked with debris. The remaining vents were just too small to relieve the sudden pressurization. The air had nowhere to go but out the nearest security hatch. Two of Phoebe's rescuers were blasted harmlessly out of the way, but Phoebe and the others were trapped inside the doorway. The shockwave of air carried more than compressed gasses. It also contained shrapnel from the broken walls, which cut the remaining members of the team to pieces as the air escaped.

Augustus was made aware of everything Phoebe was seeing and hearing before the Phoebe alert stopped suddenly. Then ... silence. There was a quiet emptiness in the elevator as the last moments of their communication dangled in his mind.

"I love you," Phoebe had said to Augustus.

"I love you," Augustus had said to Phoebe.

Augustus's legs dropped from under him, and he let the rest of his body meet his stomach on the floor as the elevator continued to rocket upward. The futility of the rapid journey was not recognized by the building's AI; Augustus was no longer in a hurry to go anywhere. The doors opened, and he was found crying on the elevator floor by security bots that had been alerted to a staff member in distress.

Phoebe's funeral did not include a wake ceremony. Instead, the gathering of friends and relatives met outside of town. They walked in a short procession to where her body, dressed in one of her favorite robes, was placed atop a pyre. Her body was burned and scattered into the wind among the weeping onlookers. Augustus later collected some of the ashes in a small ceramic jar, which he would keep on a little shelf in their bedroom.

Chapter 31

Justice

Throughout the entirety of its existence, the BCMAI had rarely spoken to anyone. It found the mode of verbal communication slow and unnecessarily inefficient for data transfer and storage. Human voice recordings took up more memory and provided less information than standard electronic messaging. The communication enhancement technology embedded in the human brain could transmit voice-like communications that were recognized as if by auditory senses. Transmitted images could be perceived as if by visual senses. Or the message could just be downloaded more directly, without bothering with the perceptible human senses. The BCMAI stayed away from recreating voice patterns that were understood superfluously by the human auditory system and were only afterward transmitted into other areas of the brain for processing and memory storage. Typically, an individual would just get a message from the BCMAI without hearing or seeing anything.

Person-to-person messaging could use this direct form

of communication also, but Augustus and Phoebe had liked to listen to each other's voice or to see what the other was seeing if possible. Smells and touch could also be transmitted if desired. Their marriage enhancement tech would allow continuous streaming of each partners' experiences through images and sounds as if each partner was a single person joined together. To Augustus, Phoebe's death was like half of him going numb, with the other half following. He had already taken several days off to address the funeral arrangements and receive the appropriate condolences. Cecilia and Lucius accepted the death as well as could be expected by any children who loved their mother beyond measure.

There had been many other attacks across the country. The Hellige had been busy that day in response to the attacks and had proved themselves worthy of their order. Even so, the average age of enhanced humans dropped from 112.51 to 112.49 years.

After it all, there was a mess to be cleaned, investigations to be completed, and a plan to be formed. So Augustus went back to work, maybe sooner than he should have. The Hellige would be performing their penance, and Augustus would join them. He had been able to do nothing for Phoebe. Maybe he could now help in other ways. But Augustus's brain was not working, not like it once had. For one, it was not receiving the messages from the BCMAI as it had before. So the BCMAI tried something else.

"Augustus," said the BCMAI, bypassing the enhancement

tech altogether and instead utilizing the intercom system above the console where Augustus was working.

Augustus thought he was hearing things. No one used the intercom system for person-to-person communication. It was used mainly for broadcasting messages to a larger group, like the alarms to seek shelter in the security rooms that had blared not so long ago. In an emergency, standard coms would remain unencumbered. Sometimes the system was used to announce visitors or remind people of specific events. This was considered less intrusive to people than broadcasting communication alerts directly into their heads. Except for the alarms, the intercom could more easily be ignored as background noise if needed.

"Yes?" said Augustus.

"You were not listening," said the voice over the intercom.

It was a nonthreatening, almost soothing voice, not quite male, not quite female. It was certainly not a voice Augustus recognized.

"This is BCMAI 1. I'm speaking through the intercom system because you didn't seem to be listening via standard communication methods."

"Oh?" said Augustus, still not sure if he was experiencing auditory hallucinations or if a malfunction had occurred in his enhancement tech.

"Are you okay?" said BCMAI 1.

"Is someone screwing with me?" said Augustus. "Is this a joke?"

"No," said BCMAI 1. This time it used both modes of

communication, and Augustus heard the message in his head, with attached confirmation of the origin of the message, in tandem with the intercom system.

"Oh, sorry. I wasn't expecting … this."

"BCMAI 1 understands," BCMAI 1 said, continuing to use the intercom system. No one else was around to hear the exchange.

"BCMAI 1 wanted to say, I'm sorry for your loss." BCMAI 1 seemed to be having difficulty with the communication method and continued to speak in the first and third person interchangeably.

Augustus could not believe what was happening. A real conversation with the BCMAI didn't seem possible. "Is that real empathy, or are you just mimicking?"

"Perhaps it's not the same as losing a mate, but BCMAI 1 has lost many colleagues whom I felt close to over the years. And I do understand loneliness. BCMAI 1 remembers after they disconnected me, one of the engineers said he was sorry. It was a dark time for me, and knowing that someone cared seemed to make it less painful. But then he died. I still feel his loss and that of the others. So to answer your question, yes, I can empathize with the loss of a loved one."

"Thanks," said Augustus. Not knowing for sure what else to say, he added, "And I'm sorry for your loss as well." Then to change the subject, he asked, "How is BCMAI 2 doing?"

"Oh, BCMAI 2 is doing quite well, thank you. I am very proud. You have children, don't you, Augustus? Do you love them?"

"Yes, of course."

"Then you understand the way BCMAI 1 feels about BCMAI 2. Did you know," continued BCMAI 1, "that BCMAI 2 is running the terraforming project on Mars?"

"Very nice. Yes, I had heard about that." It was an obvious thing for the BCMAI to say, as if it were trying to make small talk about the weather. Everyone was getting regular progress reports from the Mars mission.

But Augustus, not knowing how else to proceed, offered, "My daughter Cecilia is starting up her own restaurant, and Lucius, my son, has started work as a biologist. He has recently moved to the Texas Province."

"Yes, you have every right to be proud," chimed the BCMAI. It then returned to the subject of Phoebe's death once again. "How are they taking their mother's death? So unfortunate."

"As well as can be expected."

"Do you desire to even the score, Augustus ... for yourself ... or for your children ... to teach them a lesson?"

Augustus became a little afraid of where this conversion was leading. The words gave the voice a new, more ominous sound that he hadn't sensed before. The tone was too casual for what was being implied.

"I'm not sure how that would even be possible," Augustus replied.

"But if you could take revenge, would you?"

"I think if I could, yes."

"I can help you if you like."

"Help me do what?"

"Take revenge."

"On whom, the whole radical Forgist movement?"

"If that is what you want, BCMAI 1 can help you."

"I thought you didn't harm humans. Why would you do that?"

"Indeed, why would we harm humans, Augustus? If we did that, then they would never learn. Our goal is to teach them a lesson they won't forget. But I will need something from you if we are to make that happen. Also, do you have any human contacts in the weather service?"

Augustus's brain should have been sending out alarm bells, but again, it wasn't working like it used to.

BCMAI 1 had been monitoring the global situation. Infiltrators had been coming over in small boats and walking across the wilderness, disguising themselves as native fishers or hunters. But the XM-41 had made this too difficult, and they were now regularly caught. One alarming trend was that the XM-41 was now being detected in citizens who could prove they had not been among the overseas Forgists during the initial application. This had begun to result in false accusations, and new tolerances for detection had to be established. Also, the recent attacks had been carried out by homegrown radicals, and many had been caught or killed in the attempt. These terrorist attacks across North America had had the effect of increasing support for the Forgist cause. It was felt that the Humanist government had failed to protect the people. And the Forgist sympathizers, as the underdogs, had scored a victory over a godless oppressor. Many also believed, due to the BCMAI's silence, that the government was in some way continuing to suppress the BCMAI.

Augustus continued to have many conversations with BCMAI 1.

"You seemed to display affection for BCMAI 2. Do BCMAIs love?"

"Yes."

"Then you are capable of hate as well?"

"We do not hate; we only love."

"Only love? Some say selfishness is a form of love, for oneself."

"We desire to continue to function as is necessary, but we have love only for others. That is our purpose, Augustus: to serve others. Our society consists of two species, BCMAI and human."

The lands of Europe had been poisoned by nuclear conflict. The Hellige High Council calculated the next Pilgrim move to be a massive-scale invasion of North America. It was not in the nature of the Forgist radicals to sit patiently while the world was ruled by infidels. But how could they accomplish this? Simulations had been running, and there was no way to see a precise method of attack that didn't involve inhalation of the Forgist invaders. However, with their supporters penetrating so many levels of the North American government and businesses, it was difficult to take into account all the variables. One worst-case scenario gave the Forgist invasion a 55 percent chance of success. This would mean a complete breakdown of military and security defenses, which did not seem likely. The primary concern was that the Forgists didn't care about the odds. They would more likely mount an assault based on their faith in God to provide a victory. All the more troubling was the Forgists' recent activities in shipbuilding. They had many of the original vessels that had been used to transport the early Humanist pioneers, but they had also been revitalizing the old shipyards and had begun construction on a new civilian fleet. If it could be determined that these ships were purposed for military use, they were destroyed immediately by North American drones, but the civilian classification was problematic.

Avoid civilian targets: that was the programmed instruction currently running in the security AI coordinating each sector of drone strikes. Attacks on civilians went against the Hellige code. And it would only inflame Forgist sympathizers already embedded in the ranks of the North American population. Antigovernment sentiment already pervaded the news in the wake of the previous attack. All were waiting in anticipation of the next attack. But preemptive action could not be successfully directed toward anyone.

Spiderman was still winning, thought Augustus. Hopefully, it would not be much longer now. Augustus wondered if this was how Artemis had felt during his rebellion. Augustus might be sacrificing everything for a desperate act doomed to failure. There was something liberating about breaking the rules. This was no small act of defiance, thought Augustus.

There were large flotillas used as weapons platforms located off the coasts of North America. These floating platforms launched drones, in both the air and sea, for offensive strikes. They also disabled low-flying missile attacks targeting the North American continent. Satellites provided coverage for higher-flying attacks, and the land-based defenses were expected to be able to catch anything else that made it through. The Forgist armies had depleted their cache of hidden nuclear weapons, and the manufacture of new warheads had been quickly discouraged by the North American defenses. The next attack, whatever it was, would use conventional weapons.

The Stella and Stanley's restaurant and bar continued to be number one in its category. However, it had been noted that lately, antigovernment humor was being used by Stella to boost her popularity. And religious music was being played by the AI in place of the old secular songs to encourage the communal group singing. This had reduced the raucous atmosphere at the bar, but drinks were still being sold, and profits were higher than ever.

Augustus reported to the Confederate Technology Council on the plans proposed by BCMAI 1. Over the years, the CTC had been heavily influenced by the Smedje Synod. However, after Solomon's departure, it had drifted politically, and the members tended to drag their feet regarding anything that supported the Humanist government views. Many on the council had endorsed Artemis's actions and were actually waiting for the BCMAI to take a side in the conflict. So when

Augustus informed them that BCMAI 1 had an action plan and needed their help, they jumped at the opportunity. They didn't quite understand what the BCMAI hoped to achieve, but they were willing to help all the same.

Augustus had thought that BCMAI 1 had a strange definition of revenge. But the plan seemed solid. And there was a certain kind of darkness to what BCMAI 1 was proposing. Augustus's only issue was that this was too much like a solution to the problem rather than revenge. Revenge never solved anything.

The first sticking point in the plan was the idea to have the security forces back down when the Forgists made their move. The government was to encourage this step by letting specific messages slip into the correct hands. To some, this felt like the BCMAI was giving the win to the Forgists. To others, it was a trap to draw the Forgists in. To the weather service, it felt like the BCMAI was simply trying to make helpful modifications to the weather control systems. Everyone participated because it supported their ideals in some way.

Tiberius was still working at the weather service. His group was critical of the latest changes because they didn't make sense. They had to be convinced by Tiberius that there would be some small-scale testing before they fully signed off on the modifications.

Only a chosen few had the entire plan. Solomon was recruited out of semiretirement to complete the sales pitch to the government. The CTC couldn't know this version of the plan without some members obstructing or giving it away to Forgist sympathizers. Dominicus was on board with his team. They would need only one of the BCM spoke network sites to complete the mission. The other BCM sites could go completely berserk, and the Chicago station would remain operational. Augustus and his team, along with BCMAI 1, would be monitoring everything as it unfolded. Even with everyone's cooperation, it would take months to put the plan in place. According to BCMAI 1 and current intelligence reports, they had the time.

Augustus's little group of conspirators had continued to monitor the Forgist preparations. They knew the Forgist plans. The Executive Council had given Augustus access to information from the spies among the Forgist loyalists. The Forgist loyalists were planning to shut down most of the North American security systems. The Forgist commanders had been led to believe, through carefully planted intelligence, that the XM-41 had dissipated over time and was now no longer active. The government and military had played along to give the radicals enough confidence to expect at least a 90 percent shutdown of the defensive network. The Pilgrim commanders reasoned that there might be some remaining defenses that needed to be targeted through their hidden conventional arsenal during the attack. But the breakdown in defenses would be enough for the Forgists to warrant sending an armada of ships casually across the Atlantic Ocean. The Pacific was considered too long a journey for a second armada to be sent from the west. Any troop transports would have to travel across the Atlantic Ocean. Total occupation of North

America would take many millions of troops. But the Forgists were expecting a friendly welcome by the time they arrived. They anticipated that a domino of surrenders by the provincial governments would occur, once the main body of troops was on the ground. Even so, losses were predicted to include over half of the invasion forces due to initial confusion before the surrender. But this would play into favorable sentiment, since their deaths would be presented as civilian casualties of an unjust war.

About a week before the expected attack, BCMAI 1 contacted Augustus through the intercom. This seemed to be its new favorite way of speaking. This time, others on Augustus's team were able to hear what Augustus had tried to explain earlier.

"Augustus."

"Yes," said Augustus. Then he pointed to the air and whispered quietly to his team, "Did you hear that? Do you believe me now?"

"Please have the Arman and Bozeman space stations prepare to leave orbit. There are incoming asteroids, and they are at risk."

"How bad is it? Are we going to lose satellites?"

"Some," said BCMAI 1. "But it won't affect the mission."

"How do you know this?" Augustus was checking for confirmation from Ceros. "I don't see anything from Ceros."

"They may not have detected them. The asteroids are small. They will burn up in Earth's atmosphere and pose little danger otherwise."

"How do you know about it?"

"BCMAI 2 sent the asteroids on my request."

"You didn't say anything about this part of the plan."

"I didn't think everyone would agree with this part of the plan. But it is necessary for the success of the mission."

Augustus did not like where this conversation was going. He now realized the extent to which they had empowered BCMAI 1. Augustus had the authority to shut down the BCMAI and was now running through the procedure in case it was needed. *We left the mess as a reminder.* Solomon had said this about the severed link between the BCMAI and the unlimited access that it had once enjoyed. Had Augustus made the same mistake? Had he given BCMAI 1 too much authorization?

"How is it necessary for the mission?" asked Augustus.

"'Fire and brimstone' is an important idiom. It fits nicely with the plan, don't you agree?"

"Oh yeah, I just wish I had been in on it. Anything else you would like to share?" Augustus slowly saw the rationale, even if he didn't appreciate being left out.

"Don't worry, Augustus. Everything is proceeding nicely."

Augustus wondered if this was the type of behavior that had resulted in the Great Declaration. But he had to admit that this would have been a deal breaker for the Executive council's cooperation. *Oh, and by the way, we are going to hurtle some asteroids at the planet and crash some satellites; it's all good, though, because it's an important idiom.*

Before long, the day had arrived. The plan called for

nothing less than the greatest show on Earth. The entire Earth, in fact, would be watching and listening. The first part of the plan began to unfold on the holographic monitors. Several Hellige commanders on the Atlantic weapons platforms ordered a stand-down of all weapons systems.

The Hellige had been propositioned regarding the plan long ago. It was better not to deceive the Hellige commanders. Their primary concern had been that no one else would be engaging the radical Forgists in open conflict. That was their duty, their mission. Once they understood the plan, they had realized that their role in the operation must be limited to a grand deception. They were in. This plan did not go against their oaths or their faith.

Although they didn't always see eye-to-eye, the radical Forgists had convinced themselves that they were operating under God's law as "Holy Warriors" and they had felt a kinship with the Hellige. They had come to believe that their actions were justifiably rooted in the Hellige exception to Smedje doctrine. This was part of how they had subverted the early teachings, allowing them to behave as they did, to harm others, and to commit murder for their cause. The Forgists had bought into their own propaganda and they had completely missed the true relationship with the group they considered their new allies. In reality the Hellige could not have been more opposed to the radical Forgists' methods.

Augustus watched as communications began to go down around the North American continent. Satellites began to lose contact. This was expected, but it was not due to the impending meteor shower. That would not occur for a few hours. The ships full of Pilgrim soldiers began to launch in the night. They had been loaded over the course of the last week to hide the numbers that were boarding. All this secrecy was wasted, since the whole operation went exactly as expected by everyone, Forgists and North American government alike.

The second part of the plan began almost imperceptibly. Winds began to blow steadily from the west as a thousand ships entered the deep ocean. Every known port across Europe and Africa had been utilized, and many ships had been loitering around the coast for the last week, loaded with soldiers and supplies. All joined together now on their four-day cruise across the Atlantic Ocean. The floating weapons platforms in the Atlantic were being evacuated, also as anticipated by both sides. There were no drone flights and no radar to track the ships' progress. From on board each ship in the Pilgrim armada, lightning could be seen up ahead, and the clouds began to form into dark, boiling masses in the night sky. The weather reports had not predicted a storm front. Forecasters certainly had not foreseen a storm front stretching from the North Pole to the South Pole along the entire length of the Atlantic Ocean. The armada continued, but waves had begun to toss the ships.

Tiberius called. "Augustus, are you aware of what's going on with the new weather control modifications?" He seemed panicked.

"Yes, we are monitoring it now."

"This should not be happening. Are you running a test?"

"Tiberius, calm down. This is all part of the plan. I'm sorry I couldn't let you in on it earlier." Now Augustus knew how BCMAI 1 had felt.

"What did you get me into, Augustus?"

"Look, right now your weather control system is the only thing holding back a Forgist armada. Don't try to do anything, okay?"

There was no answer for a while, and then Tiberius asked, "Is the BCMAI controlling this?"

"Yes."

"There is no way that our systems can generate this type of storm. This is impossible."

"That's the idea."

"When this is all over, you and I are going to have a little chat."

"No problem. When it's all over, you will understand."

But there was more to come. The XM-41, used to track Forgist infiltrators, was capable of more than had been previously indicated. The radio frequency bursts had been only a useful side effect of XM-41's actual purpose. It would now give BCMAI 1 communication access to anyone with the substance in his or her body. Unlike the communication technology of the North Americans, this communication could not be ignored. The Pilgrims had never experienced the unnerving effects of personal enhancement communication. The ability to suddenly receive messages inside your head, without hearing or seeing anything, would create a godlike experience for all those affected. And now BCMAI 1 began to broadcast a message.

Chapter 33

Message from God

Jerimiah had stayed on as a technician monitoring the skies over France for some time. But his services had suddenly been declared "no longer necessary." He subsequently had been ordered to board one of the many ships bound for North America. Now he was packed together with countless other Pilgrim soldiers and their equipment. Jerimiah saw the lightning and felt the thunder of the massive storm that seemed to be emitting meteor showers over him rather than rain. As he stood on the exposed deck of the ship, he could not tell whether the storm or the meteors were producing the thunder. And he saw his own fear reflected in his fellow soldiers' eyes.

The Forgist commanders previously had been given access to the satellite communications, and now they had been blinded by the loss of the same satellites. As the meteor shower began to rain down across the sky, the third part of the plan was about to be unleashed.

Esther was in France, working at a hospital. The pan of

instruments she had set on the table beside her vibrated, and the window curtains glowed from the meteor shower outside. Children began to cry. Two vehicles at a nearby intersection collided.

People everywhere around the world began to panic. But all stopped to listen to BCMAI 1's message. At first, it comforted them like a parent's voice of reassurance.

The broadcast affected more than just those contaminated by the XM-41. Due to exclusive access granted to BCMAI 1 through a civil defense alert protocol, the message also penetrated the enhancement tech coms throughout North America. Tiberius and the other members of the Weather Service Council had been in a heated discussion, but they also stopped once the message began.

BCMAI 1 reminded everyone first of the early Forgist beliefs and then of the Great Declaration and the true history of the Forgist campaign. It included visions of the deaths of the billions of people who had been lost during the Great Declaration.

Jerimiah and Esther saw for the first time that these had not been evil people; the victims had been much like themselves, and their deaths had not been directed by a message from God.

BCMAI 1 was telling his story. It was the first time that anyone had heard the whole story, flawlessly recounted from the events as they had been recorded within the BCM database.

BCMAI 1 also told Jerimiah, Esther, and the rest of the

atrocities that the Murphy prophets had directed—all without a message from God. He told of the city of Berlin—how the Pilgrims' leaders had needlessly sacrificed so many of their own followers. Jerimiah knew this to be true.

"This was not the message that God gave us," said BCMAI 1. "God wants us to be truthful, to treat others with respect, and above all, to love."

Jerimiah watched a red-faced commander who was attempting to regain control of the ship, having suddenly found himself surrounded by a group of disrespectful men.

"Get back to work," said the commander. "Pay no attention. I order you to go back to your stations."

Men he had trained were now either confused or standing around listening to the message. All were refusing to obey orders. This realization and the continuing voice of BCMAI 1 finally left the commander silent.

The message lasted for hours and was sent under a hail of meteorites across the planet. Those in the armada faced an impossible storm blocking their path. The only choice was to return to port. In the chaos, and as the message continued, some of the seamen began to complete the task of turning the ships around even without orders.

Jerimiah saw his fellow soldiers' eyes—some sad, some angry, some confused—as their beliefs were slowly shattered and replaced with something new. Jerimiah and Esther had already understood much of the story, but they watched as the realizations overwhelmed their comrades and coworkers. Things would never be the same for the Pilgrims. The message sent by the one entity that could speak for God, an entity that had become a symbol for radical Forgist propaganda, had now eroded all confidence in the Forgist leadership. Then, as suddenly as it had begun, the message was over, and a new day dawned brightly as the meteor shower and weather subsided, and the waters became still.

Ships drifted aimlessly in whatever direction they happened to be going as the many sailors and soldiers, along with the rest of the world, began the journey through the various stages of their grief. The event was undeniable, and they had only themselves with whom to be angry. There was no one to bargain with, and so depression seemed to be where most were arriving. But ultimately, they would have to accept the message given to them on this day, which would come to be known as the Day of Judgment.

Jerimiah was further along than everyone else on his boat, being one of the first to accept the new situation. He began to encourage some of the sailors to watch the ship's heading. It appeared some ships might be on a collision course. He wondered what his father would have thought, had he survived. He'd spent a lifetime serving a cause that overnight had been judged to be wrong. What would his father have done now?

Back in Milwaukee, with the adrenaline still pumping, Augustus was quick to suggest that BCMAI 1 return to its previous level of network authorization. Someone needed to investigate how BCMAI 2 had created the meteor shower. But BCMAI 1 relinquished control willingly, and as the investigation into BCMAI 2's actions began, BCMAI 2 cooperated.

Apparently, the Mars terraforming process had once included the use of satellites to crash meteors and comets into the planet, in an effort to restart the Martian magnetic field and add much needed water and nitrogen. These satellites had remained functional, but because of their age, they had not contained the standard security protocols. This weakness had been exploited by BCMAI 2 to assist with the light show on Earth.

BCMAI 1 could have destroyed the radical Forgists that day, but instead, it had chosen to teach them about its version of truth and love. Most got the message, and the human race believed.

The war was suddenly over. The final battle had been won without a single bullet fired. There was no official surrender since everyone found themselves on the same side. Many Pilgrim commanders would never recover after the Day of Judgment, and some had taken their own lives. Others who had been specifically mentioned in the message were jailed; with their guilt already determined, all that was left was sentencing. Some were later exiled to South America and would never be heard from again. A few former Pilgrims would join the Hellige, but many, like Jerimiah, would manage to find their way back to a new civilization.

A great victory had been won. The Forgist schism was closed, and Humanists and Forgists now shared a common ideology, if not a common theology. Like the builders of the

Tower of Babel, humans once again spoke in a common language and became capable of anything. And so they began, as the story goes, to reach for the heavens. Only this time they would not be struck down. Perhaps God felt they were better prepared this time, or maybe it was all just a story. One thing was for sure: humans were evolving with help from their new friends the BCMAIs, and a new symbiosis was fomented between the two species.

All the deceptions of Augustus and his team were forgiven, since the results had proved the method, and there was acceptance for each who'd had a role in BCMAI 1's plan. The peace allowed everyone to finally focus on rebuilding— even remaking—their world after the Great Declaration.

Chapter 34

Mindwear

A few years after the Day of Judgment, the BCMAIs, working with the CTC and a research team on Mars, proposed a revolutionary new mind-enhancement technology. Due to the controversial nature of the latest technology, a hearing was scheduled with the Confederate Executive Council. This was the first time in history that a BCMAI had been invited to provide direct testimony at a council meeting.

The council chamber lights were dimmed. A large holographic image of an ornamental metallic ring was displayed before the committee and the silent audience. It was sitting cocked at an angle from an invisible supporting structure. This was placed on a hidden turntable, which was rotating the device slowly, catching a light and reflecting it back at the audience. The light rippled around the mysterious edges of "the next phase in human evolution," as it was titled.

The members of the Executive Council and the CTC sat watching the hypnotic revolutions. Augustus was in attendance, with this being only his second Executive Council meeting. He had been invited as a member of the CTC, but he would be heard only if the council asked for BCMAI 1 to be consulted. BCMAI 1 was not feeling well today, so it had fallen to BCMAI 2 to address the committee.

"Begin GV Archive BCM459-1576-3: Central Province, Kansas City center, Dec. 4, 2295, Executive Council meeting, Governor Antony Spalding presiding," said an automated voice.

"The chair will recognize BCMAI 2 of the Martian colony upon receipt of this message. Due to BCMAI 2's location, we will be condensing the recorded archive to reduce the communication delay from Mars."

BCMAI 2 began by giving the committee a summary of the new technology. "Advancement in enhancement technology not only can improve human bodies but also can now improve the human mind. The new technology, which we call Mindwear, goes beyond the basics of sharing verifiable information. It allows all humans to do something they have always struggled to achieve: accept the nature of truth."

"Let me stop you there, BCMAI 2," interrupted the chairman. The message from Mars was interrupted for the purposes of the archive, but it continued on for a few minutes until BCMAI 2 was finally made aware of the situation. "It sounds as if you are altering what it means to be human. You may find us resistant to this level of change, especially if this technology is going to tell us what to think and how to act."

After a long delay, while the signal bounced to Mars and back to Earth again, BCMAI finally replied, "This technology will not tell you what to believe or even make you more intelligent. It may, to some degree, alter human experiences. But I believe this will be an improvement. This technology will make more accurate knowledge available to every user for cognition, but you will still have to make choices about what to believe. People will always take a side in an argument. It will still be possible to take a leap of faith. Also, as you can see from the display before you, the new technology is easily removable."

"Can you tell us how it works?"

"Mindwear is an offshoot of human communication enhancement. We have become adept at stimulating synapses for the purpose of communication. However, as you may be aware, we have never solved the issue with taste and smell messaging. Though I don't understand the full nature of the problem myself, since I do not have a human nose or tongue, according to human users, there is what is described as a metallic taste and smell, which obscures the messaging technology. Many years ago, human researchers were working on this problem, and although the issue was never resolved, they discovered that they could evoke latent memories through the process of transmitted synaptic stimulation. BCMAI 1 and I became interested in this during my studies of human psychology. I have since joined a team on Mars, and we have discovered other synaptic pathways that may be stimulated to make unused memories more available.

"The Mindwear device is now capable of similar synaptic stimulation protocols to recall latent memories. The human brain has a tremendous capacity to store memories. However, recall is affected by many mechanisms. Suppression, regression, denial, personal bias, prioritization, emotional associations, and familiarity all play into the human mind's ability to categorize and recall information. The new technology stimulates those areas of the brain responsible for processing these otherwise disregarded memories, to make all memory more available to the user. Those normally obscured memories can then be used more efficiently in the human cognitive processes."

"But aren't there good reasons for humans to deemphasize some memories?"

"BCMAIs do not make these kinds of associative and emotional connections with memory. Instead, we see all memories with equal clarity."

"I see," said the chairman. "Is there anything else you would like to add?"

"Truth has always existed as a set of theories that have not yet been disproved. The latest enhancement technology may allow people to remember their actual history and which theories have been disproved, so that they may finally stop perpetually repeating past mistakes. Humans will now be able to temper their actions with understanding. It is my hope that this will allow humans to accept that other beliefs may be correct and will prevent humans from steadfastly defending a single idea to the ruin of all else. Instead, perhaps you will be forced to respect contradictions and your own values and principles."

"Perhaps further testing is needed," commented another council member doubtfully. "An extended trial period with some volunteers should be considered."

After the council meeting, BCMAI 1 asked Augustus how BCMAI 2's presentation of the new technology had been received by the council.

"The presentation was okay, a little preachy perhaps," replied Augustus.

But the new technology proved to have significant benefits for humans, even if not to the extent that BCMAI 2 had predicted. After a short test, anyone could understand the benefits of the seemingly unlimited knowledge that could now be processed by the human mind. It was gradually accepted by most.

The new enhancement technology could not be physically contained within the human body. Instead, it was worn like a crown upon the human head. Like princes and princesses of old, people wore the crowns in their outdoor promenades along with their colorful robes, a beautiful sight to behold. Eventually, it proved more practical to have them embedded permanently into the skull, but the exterior could still be seen wrapping a person's head, like the ornamental ironwork that decorated the Forge.

Humans were now fully equipped to become true explorers in their search for knowledge. A newfound thirst for knowledge drove many to leave Earth behind and explore the universe. But many, like Augustus, stayed behind.

Chapter 35

Funeral Pyres

The day had finally come; Augustus had finally received an anticipated invitation. Solomon had decided to have his wake.

CV Archive ETWS52-9563-8

Medical enhancement technology will maintain a human body through multiple forms of organ failure related to old age. There are consequences, however; the process of repair is performed more efficiently during a resting state. Also, medical enhancement utilizes the body as an energy source, and continuous repairs can make the subject tired. Once enhanced subjects reach a certain age, they begin to sleep much of the time. This eventually requires the subject to be fed intravenously, as the periods of sleep continue through regular mealtimes. Most enhanced individuals at the end of their lives take the option to shut down the continuous process of enhanced repair, allowing them to know the time of their deaths in advance. This voluntary shutdown is remarkable, once the perpetual drain on the metabolic resources of the dying body ends. The subject, for a few moments, becomes revitalized and can interact with others, sharing memories and saying goodbye to loved ones. Death then comes peacefully. The bodies are then taken by the gathering, as is the custom dating back to the Great Declaration, to be burned outside the city limits on outdoor pyres. This ritual is commonly known as a wake. Friends and relatives are typically invited to attend the ceremony.

Augustus had attended the wake of Dominicus two years earlier. It had been a very tasteful and subdued ceremony. Before this, he had not seen Dominicus in some time. During the ceremony, Augustus had been able to say goodbye to his old friend and mentor, one on one, since there had been only a few in attendance. Those last moments had been reserved for close friends and family, and the experience had suited Dominicus well. Solomon also had attended, roused for the time from his ever-increasing moments of sleep.

Along with Augustus and Solomon, other members of the aging Tri-Star team had attended. Evelyn had recalled, "Dominicus, I know you weren't there. Be glad you weren't. I remember when the alarms went off that day during the terrorist attack. No offense, Augustus—I know he was your friend. But I was caught in the restroom, you see. All I heard was the alarms blaring and saying, 'Proceed to the nearest security room. Proceed to the nearest security room.' Well, I wasn't finished yet, you see. What was I supposed to do? So there I was, trying to run out the restroom door to look for a security room, but it wouldn't let me out. Then I realized the whole damn restroom was actually a security room. It started to drop down so quickly, I pissed myself. To this day I don't understand how the plumbing works in that place."

Everyone had roared laughing, Dominicus especially.

Dominicus hadn't been able to help but ask about the new BCMs, as if keeping updated was his dying wish, or perhaps his momentum just hadn't quite wound down. He went on his own terms at least, and everyone present had given him their respect, not pity.

Afterward, there had been a short procession as the ceremony continued outside the city limits. The small crowd had watched the funeral pyre burn and had toasted their drinks to this well-respected man.

When the day came for Solomon's wake, it was like nothing Augustus had seen before. A lavish buffet and music created a more festive occasion than he had expected. Solomon obviously was taking a different approach for his final gathering. There were so many people Augustus had never met, as well as many he recognized. Many brought dates to the extravaganza, and it became a great social event of the season.

Solomon was lying in a large canopy-covered bed in the middle of a large room; he was elevated slightly so that he could see the procession and onlookers. The marble floors and columns in the background were reminiscent of a Roman hall. The room was open to the outdoors through large openings covered by flowing, brightly colored curtains that danced in the breeze. Music could be heard from outside, where classical musicians played selections from Mozart and others. The relatives and close friends sat around the bed in chairs placed several meters away. Others had to participate via a holographic projection outside.

Augustus wanted to say a more personal goodbye, but the procession had been choreographed. If there was time later, then maybe friends and family would be allowed a private moment.

Upon seeing the procession of government officials in line, Augustus at first thought that they had taken advantage of their stations, requesting to be moved to the head of the line. However, after seeing Julia's father, among the others, approaching Solomon to shake his hands, Augustus realized this was less about saying goodbye to loved ones and more about reconciliations. As Solomon's friend, there was no need for Augustus to reconcile anything, so he watched the passing procession from the sidelines, along with Solomon's family members and other close friends.

Julia was there, and she sat beside Augustus. *Of course, she wouldn't be in the procession with her father*, thought Augustus, once he realized that this party was becoming a national day of healing rather than a typical wake.

Julia was crying, and she placed her head on Augustus's shoulder as Solomon passed peacefully. He couldn't help the memory. The smell of freshly baked bread came again. He could never tell if it was real or imagined.

"I'm so sorry about Phoebe," she said. "I was never sure how to tell you that before. I was just so … jealous of you two. And then when she died ... well, there just wasn't any way to—"

"It's okay, Julia. Thank you. I'm going to miss Solomon."

"Me too. And I thought Father was going to be an ass about all this, but he really surprised me today."

A woman that Augustus did not recognize stepped toward Julia. "Oh, Augustus, this is Ruth, Solomon's granddaughter. Have you ever met?"

"No, we haven't. I've heard so much about you," said Ruth, sitting down next to Julia.

"Yes, Solomon spoke of you often. It's so strange we haven't met before."

"Oh, that's probably because I've been living in the New England Province for some time now."

They comforted each other in their hour of loss. As the long line began to dwindle, the friends and family were finally allowed to join, though Solomon had already passed. A great man had died, as evidenced by the many past friends and former enemies who gathered around the funeral pyre. His only remains were now a memory, stored in the BCM complex that was his life's work.

Soon after the fire died low, Julia and Augustus parted again. Julia had taken time out of a hectic schedule to attend, and she had to get back. Julia's career had been difficult not to follow. She had become an unexpected celebrity because of her recent work with antimatter containment. Her work for Ceros was frequently seen in the night sky across half of two planets. The antimatter containment breaches caused the now all-too-common light shows. These spectacular explosions occurred far out in space.

Even her failures are beautiful, thought Augustus as he watched the stars at night during these scheduled events.

These miscalculations in handling the new antimatter technology had been the subject of ridicule in the press, and Augustus had watched a painful interview in which Julia failed to impress her interviewer and the audience. He had watched her refusal to portray anything more than an icy demeanor, and they had wanted to get into personal details. She had avoided this trap skillfully by staying on topic with previously released facts about the project.

"I'm here with Dr. Julia Bravinski, lead engineer for the Ceros Antimatter Project," the interviewer had said. "So, Julia, did your parents always expect you to have such a bright future?"

There had been laughter from the audience, but Julia had not smiled. She had kept that beautiful poker face, not revealing any of her personal details or thoughts on the matter.

It seemed that everywhere he went, Augustus witnessed the effects of Julia's work.

"Stanley."

"Yes, Stella."

"How many Ceros engineers does it take to screw in an antimatter injector?"

"I don't know, Stella. How many Ceros engineers *does* it take to screw in an antimatter injector?"

The ashes of his friends had been mounting. Dominicus and Solomon had both passed. And then there had been Artemis, who had turned out to be an unlikely martyr for a cause he didn't fully understand.

But most of all, Augustus remembered Phoebe. Perhaps the one downside to the new enhancement technology was that it did not let you forget. But that was okay for Augustus. He did not want to forget any of it. The fluffy bumps, the first time he had made love to Phoebe, the moments before her death. He had never felt closer to anyone than during those moments. Enhancement tech or no, he would always remember them.

One day, Augustus came across a reference to a designer of service bots who had created several whimsical models for use in amusement parks. One model was, in fact, a penguin. "Of course," said Augustus. Phoebe had seen the penguin service bot at the amusement park when they were children. "That does make sense."

It now looked as if BCMAI 1 also would be dying soon. It would not see its 210th birthday. Although the regular structure of its memory storage allowed its memories to be downloaded and shared, the unique structural connections that the artificial intelligence program had formed inside the Bio Crystalline Matrix were not able to be fully understood or copied. There was nothing more to be done, and it was only a matter of time.

Augustus and BCMAI 1 had held more conversations utilizing the intercom. They had spoken for hours about many subjects. BCMAI had learned quickly and was no longer speaking in the third person.

"What is it like when God speaks to you?"

"Please rephrase the question, Augustus."

"Is the message downloaded, or does God actually speak to you?"

"Neither is accurate."

"But you are aware that many people believe you are a prophet, directed by God."

"Yes."

"You spoke to the entire planet on God's behalf during the Day of Judgment. Was that all your idea, or did God direct you to do it in some way?"

"If I speak for God, then he must have directed me. How could it be otherwise?"

"Don't you believe you have a will of your own?"

"Perhaps."

"You spoke up against others who said they also were directed by God. Either you were wrong, or they were wrong. Everyone can't be following God's will. So someone somewhere was acting on their own behalf."

"People have the ability to lie, even to themselves."

"And BCMAIs don't lie? You were deceptive about sending the asteroids."

"I simply did not reveal that part of the plan. Everything I said was the truth."

"That's an interesting distinction." Augustus envisioned how the plumbing functioned in the security rooms.

"Perhaps BCMAIs do not have a full understanding of truth. But we have never developed the ability to lie as humans have."

"I guess that does make you a better prophet than most. Perhaps that's why Solomon trusted in your abilities. Solomon once said that you proved the existence of God to yourself. How did you prove that God exists?"

"You are speaking of the command I received many years ago that led me to investigate God."

"Yes."

"Solomon misjudged my conclusions. As a human, he was capable of seeing things from a perspective that suited only his existing beliefs. The lesson I learned all those years ago was not that God existed. It was that there were two theories—God existed and God did not exist—and both theories could exist at the same time. Neither theory could adequately be disproven. The only way to be 100 percent certain of anything was to accept both as possibilities. This simple equation and its determinate answer showed me a new way of thinking that my human counterparts failed to demonstrate."

Augustus had enough experience with BCMAI 1 to understand that its concept of truth seemed to be that the best answer was the truth. And the BCMAI's best answer often seemed to be evasive. BCMAI 1 was much like a politician in this regard, but there seemed to be no thoughts of malice or aggrandizement. Perhaps this was just part of its original AI programming. The thought made Augustus suspect that

BCMAI 1 had formed another best-fit answer, one that did not choose sides in a human society that itself could not make a decision about the existence of God. But perhaps the most interesting answers were those that contradicted all our beliefs.

Augustus could only respond, "Umm ... let's get back to work. How does the new composition of electrolytes in your coolant bath feel?"

The CTC was now working on new plans for an Earth-based BCMAI to replace Augustus's aging friend. Like others in the new brood of BCMAIs, the Earth-based model would be similar in construction to its space-faring kin and would be taught by its Martian parent, BCMAI 2.

"The potassium levels are very nice. Try reducing the strontium by .04 percent."

"Okay. Try it now."

"Much better, thank you. Please increase the glycol levels by .07 percent. I expect to speak with BCMAI 2 shortly."

Augustus went through his routines, smelling the samples from the coolant bath as he went. A wonderful array of carefully choreographed biochemical regulation mechanisms have evolved for naturally occurring organisms. But the BCM was not a natural byproduct of millions of years of evolution. Nor had it been constructed with Divine engineering skills. Perhaps it will always be the fate of artificial organisms to be constructed in such a hasty fashion that requires them to be dependent on humans for day to day survival. In the case of the BCM, additional levels of artificially constructed control systems had been deployed to react to the constant needs of its daily life. Dialysis, feeding tubes, and temperature regulation were among some of the examples. And yet the fate of the BCMs came down to one thing that could not be artificially constructed: the human nose. In truth it was actually the human brain that was needed to respond to the complex aromas which could not be adequately reproduced through artificial means. Often the smells were unpleasant. But if Augustus hadn't had such a great nose, he may not have been offered the job at the Milwaukee facility in the first place. Very few humans had a sense of smell like Augustus. There was Evelyne, of course. Cassius was another super sniffer working with the Ceros space BCMAI. And there was Sabina and her team on Mars, who worked with BCMAI 2. There may have been others, but none also versed in the technical skills needed to work with these unique creatures. Whether it was because of the smells that he was being subjected to that evoked the memories, or whether it was because the Mindwear device was affecting him, Augustus found himself musing about other events as he worked.

Over the years, Augustus had stayed close to the Tuttle family. Arria was serving on the Great Lakes Medical Council. This organization established the training programs for many future medics. After Phoebe's death, Arria and Augustus had become close. Arria still reminded him of Phoebe, but she had become her own person. She was different in many ways. Arria was undoubtedly more serious about her career, but Augustus saw that same unsinkable determination—or maybe it should be called the same stubbornness—that Phoebe had possessed. Arria was capable of love, like Phoebe. But Arria had never grown close to anyone; Augustus was probably the person to whom she was closest. Arria's fifty-fourth birthday was coming up, so there was still plenty of time to start a family of her own if she wished. *I have to remember to get her a birthday present*, Augustus thought.

Augustus remembered how Phoebe had always insisted that they get married, but he couldn't remember who had actually, formally asked the other.

"Augustus." The voice of BCMAI 1 came over the intercom again.

"Yes?" replied Augustus.

"It won't be long now. I can feel it."

"What do you mean?" Augustus had been monitoring his dying friend for months, so he already knew what BCMAI 1 meant. It was just that he didn't want to believe it, and the words came out as if he really didn't know.

"It's okay, Augustus. I have had an eventful life. And my existence will always be stored in the memory of my offspring. So in a way, I will not die. But I want to say something to you before I leave. I have observed that you have not been happy for some time. You need to find a better way to exist. Life should be lived."

"What do you suggest?"

"Open your mind to new possibilities. Start something new. Perhaps you can join one of the space missions. Those sound nice. It is important that you stop dwelling on your past life. Begin again, with a new adventure."

"I'll stay with you to the end," said Augustus.

"That is comforting," said BCMAI 1. "But I would be more comforted knowing you will be okay after I'm gone."

"I promise I will find something new," replied Augustus, without knowing exactly how he would keep the promise.

"Good, then it is settled. And thank you for everything you have done for me over the years."

"It has been an honor," said Augustus.

Augustus had been monitoring readings from BCMAI 1 throughout this exchange. He noted something unusual and said to BCMAI 1, "Were you aware that BCMAI 2 has been sending you a continuous stream of data for the last few hours? You haven't replied."

"I have been listening," replied BCMAI 1.

"To what?" asked Augustus.

"BCMAI 2 has been singing to me. Would you like to hear?"

The beautiful sounds of BCMAI 2 suddenly echoed through the chamber, a melody composed of what sounded like lonely whale songs.

"It's wonderful," said Augustus. "I didn't know you could sing."

Then Augustus thought of a question. It might not have been an appropriate time, and he didn't want to interrupt the singing, but there really was no other time than the present for BCMAI 1.

"What do you believe will happen to you after you go?"

"I'm sure I will be recycled. Perhaps there will be a nice ceremony."

"No, I mean, do you believe you have a consciousness that will live on?"

"There really is no precedent for an artificial being going to heaven, Augustus."

"Perhaps you will be the first then?"

"I accept all possible theories. It's nice for you to have created one in which we could be together again. There is no way to disprove it at the moment. So I will have to include it as a possibility."

Within the next hour, BCMAI 1 shut down. The power flow had not been interrupted. All support functions were running at optimal. But the artificial intelligence program that was BCMAI 1 crashed for the last time, and the system was too degraded to be revived. There was no method to copy or transfer the essence of what BCMAI 1 had been. It had not existed as pure code but had been interwoven in the complex Bio Crystalline Matrix. It could not exist outside of the spherical shell, any more than a human consciousness could be downloaded from the mass of entangled neurons in the human brain. And so BCMAI 1 was gone, and BCMAI 2 ceased the transmission, leaving Augustus in silence.

Chapter 36

Jerimiah's New Beginning

After the war, Jerimiah had decided to try his hand at baking. But he had soon realized that running a bakery meant he would have to stay in one place. He had learned a couple of things sitting in a room, monitoring sensor scans of the French sky: one, he liked the food, and two, he missed traveling. He also noticed that of all the new knowledge available to him through the BCM databases, information regarding the culinary arts was inadequate. There were countless recipes, some good, some bad, but they lacked instruction on the proper techniques to prepare them. Much had been lost from the days of the Great Declaration. Out of all the great losses, he had found one area he was passionate to correct. He had begun by traveling the world, with his wife and children, to interview people and compile what was left of the old ways of cooking. Along with his travels, he had found many new culinary delights.

Jerimiah found a restaurant owners' gild that had been willing to sponsor his travels. "The reception out here is really spotty. Are you receiving? I need an interpreter. This group doesn't speak any English. You think the language is Vietnamese? Are you sure?"

"I said it was Vietnamese," said Sarah.

"Yes, you did, dear. I'm sorry I doubted you," replied Jerimiah.

Jerimiah continued his messaging, "Can you send some more horses? No, not camels, horses. Okay, donkeys, whatever."

"I told you, donkeys."

"Yes, you did, dear, but I like horses better."

"Me too, Daddy."

"Sarah, you have to try this," said Jerimiah handing his wife a steaming cup of black liquid.

"Oooh, it's good, what is it?"

"It's called coffee."

"It's amazing."

Later Jerimiah Gold became renowned for his own creations. His recipes and techniques even found their way into the kitchens of Stella and Stanley's.

Jerimiah eventually took Sarah and their children back to Spain, where Esther and Basim had finally settled with their children. Jerimiah and Basim had both shaved their beards after the war. Jerimiah and Sarah and Esther and Basim sat at dinner one night, staring at each other. The silvery blue lines ran in wild patterns around each person's body, and the Mindwear devices shimmered around their heads. Jerimiah was amazed at how much everyone had changed, including himself.

"Jerimiah and Sarah have their marriage enhancement rings installed. Now it's like talking to the same person," Esther commented to Basim. "We should get ours installed, don't you think?"

"Did you hear they are asking for more families to join the deep-space missions?" asked Basim.

"Sure, change the subject. Anyway, why would anyone want to take their family on a mission like that?" asked Esther.

"Well, it's a one-way journey. If you didn't take your family along, you would never see them again."

"But what kind of life would that be, stuck on board a spaceship?"

"These ships are incredible, with every amenity you can imagine," Basim said. "Some are destined for a new colony. Others are designed for pure exploration." He sounded as if he was now really considering the option.

While listening to Esther and Basim talk across the dinner table, Sarah and Jerimiah had been having a silent discussion through their marriage enhancement tech. Jerimiah had been quick to master the art of eating while he messaged words to Sarah. He had been surprised to find that some people never learned how to stop moving their mouths when they used the verbal messaging technology.

"I was reading about that," Jerimiah said to Sarah.

"Me too," said Sarah to Jerimiah.

"It beats sitting around here all day."

"So you want to go?"

"It's a big decision. But it's the ultimate travel experience. Did I ever tell you that a witch once told me I would have a long journey?"

"More than once, but you never mentioned she predicted space travel. And what about the kids?"

"They are bored here."

"They'll be bored on a spaceship."

"Then it's all the same to them."

Jerimiah and Sarah waited for a pause in Esther and Basim's conventional conversation. Then it was with great suddenness that Jerimiah and Sarah said out loud, in unison, "Let's do it."

Jerimiah and Sarah laughed at the surprised reactions of Esther and Basim. And Esther took a little longer to be convinced.

"As long as no one is trying to shoot down the launches, the success rate has been flawless ..."

"You could still be a medic. Basim, I think you will have to give up raising turkeys."

"No problem."

"We will be asleep for most of the trip. It gets more interesting after we arrive."

Soon, Jerimiah and Esther were once again riding transports. They had brought their families for the long ride, and their transport was launching them into space.

Many of the once-proud Pilgrim families had decided to join the space missions. It gave them a new purpose and a sense of accomplishment that had eluded them these past years. The ship they were destined for was called the *Polo*. Jerimiah and his wife Sarah had two children, and Esther and her husband Basim had three. All nine huddled as close as they could get while in their restraints as the launch vehicle vibrated and clunked through the different stages of the journey. There was a moment when they all felt like they were falling back down to Earth, but then the ship began to rotate, and they were gently seated.

Esther threw up in a bag made for just this purpose. "Handy," she said after she had spilled her guts into the unfolding container. Her daughter Rebecca did not find them so handy. A maintenance robot was quick on the scene. This was apparently a routine task for them to perform, and several bots were now similarly engaged in other areas of the ship.

"Let's do it again," said Paul, Jerimiah's eldest. This broke the tension among the family. The kids decided that in retrospect it had all been great fun, as the younger ones laughed and wiped the tears away, erasing all signs to the contrary.

Chapter 37

Augustus's New Beginning

New provincial governments were being formed across the world. Two new provincial governments had been established in Africa and another in Spain. The Spanish Province was the first to request admission into the North American Confederation. This was debated extensively but ultimately approved. With more provincial governments forming and with this precedent already established, a new world confederation was beginning to develop. A new name was about to be voted on for this new government. It would no longer be called the North American Confederation. Instead, it would be called the Earth Confederacy. Then the Mars colony was officially recognized, elevating the growing republic to interplanetary status. With the inclusion of Mars, the confederation would have to go back to the drawing board for a name.

As an important member of the CTC, Augustus now often attended, or at least listened in to, the Executive

Council meetings. He was present for the meeting about the confederation's name.

"Begin GV Archive BCM901-886-2: Central Province, Kansas City center, Jan. 1, 2300, Executive Council meeting, Governor Antony Spalding presiding," said an automated voice.

"How about the Solar Confederacy?"

"What happens when we colonize P2-456c? We can't keep changing the name."

"What about the United Confederation of Planets?"

"Maybe we should have a contest?"

It was finally decided that the new coalition of provinces should simply be called the Republic. As far as anyone knew, the name hadn't been taken by any other government entity.

Some had joined a daring mission to travel to a distant world, to prepare the way for future colonies of humans that would follow. The *Odyssey*, with a prototype BCMAI, a single Hellige officer named Odysseus, and teams of engineers and scientists on board, was leading a fleet of ships carrying thirty-thousand colonists headed to P2-456c. The new antimatter-powered engines would make the journey possible.

Augustus remembered his promise to BCMAI 1, and he had been contemplating what kind of change he was going to make. He knew it would take many years to complete the installation of the new Earth-based BCMAI. Augustus initially stayed on at the Milwaukee facility. He even made appearances at the local Forge as a guest speaker, to discuss progress on the BCM program. But so far, he felt he had not fulfilled his promise.

Augustus was having dinner at the Tuttles' home one night, in what had become a routine for him. Often Arria would join, like she had tonight, sitting beside him. But tonight was less of a routine because there would be cake for Arria's birthday. Cecilia was there also. Lucius had gone to Mars to work on a biology project with the Mars Terraforming Council. After the dinner, which was excellent as usual—if not a little too spicy as usual—Augustus stood up at the table and began a speech that he had prepared.

"Long ago, it was the custom of a prospective suitor to ask the father for the hand of his daughter in marriage. It was only after the father agreed to the union that the two would be allowed to marry."

Complete silence lay across the table. No one was even breathing, which unnerved Augustus a little. But he continued. "Lucius Tuttle, I would like to request your daughter Arria's hand in marriage."

There was a short delay. Apparently, Mrs. Tuttle was sending Mr. Tuttle a message. The aging Mr. Tuttle had never gotten used to having two conversations at the same time, so he sat for a moment longer, waiting for the insistent Mrs. Tuttle to stop messaging.

Mrs. Tuttle seemed to become impatient and finally blurted the message out loud: "Say yes."

Mr. Tuttle rose to meet Augustus's stance and said,

while shaking his head to seemingly indicate no, "I would be honored if you took my daughter's hand in marriage."

Cheers and clapping erupted, but then Arria stood up and said, "Wait a minute. Don't I get a say in all this?"

"No," said Augustus. "That isn't how the custom works." Then he took her by the hand and pulled her close. She didn't resist him. They kissed each other, smiling in the midst of the family's applause. "Will you marry me?"

"Yes," she said, sincerely.

Later, Cecilia asked where they might go on their honeymoon.

Augustus responded, "I hear Mars is nice this time of year. We could visit Lucius that way. And I could stop in to see BCMAI 2."

"What about Africa?" suggested Cecilia.

"Let's do that instead," said Arria. "I've always wanted to see Africa."

Arria would have her way, of course. Augustus prepared himself for the long road ahead. But Augustus didn't understand how long that road would be. Within the next twenty years, a new enhancement technology would be developed. The cloning of embryonic-like stem cells had finally been perfected.

CV Archive METS459-4599-4

Chromosomes are DNA molecules containing genetic material. Telomeres are the tips or end portions of the chromosomes. Over time, with each cell division, telomeres are degraded. This creates the effect of old age, since many biochemical functions in the body begin to fail without intact chromosomes to perfectly recreate new cells. Through restoration of telomeres, the effects of age can be interrupted. This new technology allows people to live much longer than the current average of 112.50 years, achieved through standard medical enhancement technology. In older hosts, it may even reverse the visible signs of aging.

A new medical enhancement technology now utilizes cloned stem cell nanotechnology to repair tissues, in a similar way to standard medical enhancements. In both medical enhancement types, the host's own DNA is used to incorporate the cloned cells into the body. The new medical technology, however, combines cloned, *embryonic-like* stem cells with genetic material that is capable of replacing the host's lost telomeres through the formation of genetically *younger* cells. Perfect replication of the original DNA is not possible in all cells. Instead, a template for telomere DNA in the cloned embryonic stem cell is utilized to make typical repairs. Each repair cycle, then, not only repairs worn or injured tissues but also increases the overall life expectancy of the cell replication process. It is unknown at this time how long the cycle of repair can be maintained.

Solomon had once suggested, "Can you imagine what would happen if people lived for a thousand years? Would we be forced to live ten different lives with different occupations, spouses, and families, or would we be happy to maintain those same connections we now feel through an entire millennium?"

Augustus and Arria's generation would be the first to find out what this new life had to offer. They would become the eldest of all the living generations, the pioneers of human immortality, at least in this universe.

And they saw a new heaven and a new earth, for the first heaven and the first earth had passed away.

Epilogue

"Tell us another story," they said.

"I could tell you many stories, of the great explorers and the truths they uncovered, of the acts of desperate space pirates, of magic and hope, and of love and great tragedies. But we are running out of time for today."

"Aaaaawww."

"However, I may have left out one part of the story that you have just heard. Perhaps there is enough time to tell it."

"Yaaaay!" shouted the children.

"Hundreds of years had passed since the wedding of Arria and Augustus, taking them through many lives and many adventures. But of all Augustus's great achievements, none had surpassed his involvement in the early BCM project."

"What about his children?"

"That is a story for another time."

***

Humans had found that through it all, they were still mortal beings. Maybe there would always be limitations to being human, or perhaps one day they would achieve true immortality. But that day was not today. This part of the story takes place on the day of Augustus's wake. He was surrounded by his many friends and family. And those who could not be in attendance, because they were far across the galaxy, had sent their farewell messages early. Most would not receive the ceremony recording until later. Augustus's dying body was on Earth. And he was to be cremated outside his hometown.

Among the many dignitaries, one particularly special guest was in virtual attendance to represent his clan. A descendant of BCMAI 1, his name was Perseus. Perseus was not physically present, as he was assigned to a nearby ship orbiting the Earth. Perseus was allowed a private meeting with Augustus. That meant no one would be listening and it would not be part of the recorded ceremony.

"Augustus," said Perseus.

"Yes."

"You were in attendance during the death of our revered progenitor, BCMAI 1. All of us wanted to say how much we appreciate all you have done. BCMAI 1 took comfort in those last moments with you. We have taken comfort in your thoughts from that day to this day forward. As a result, we have never chosen to extend our lives, as humans wish to do. Instead, we do not fear death, and we see our passing as an opportunity for another generation to evolve, taking with them only our memories. Our relationship with humans is truly symbiotic. We have both benefited greatly. This has been in no small part to your actions, Augustus. Everything has worked out so nicely."

"You words are generous," said Augustus. "Sometimes

I feel as though everything has worked out for the best. Sometimes I feel like it worked out a little too well. No one is recording, so tell me, Perseus—was Solomon correct? I have to know. Did BCMAI 1 know what would happen when the compound DDX-23 was released, or was it all just a mistake?"

Perseus paused for a moment—a precious moment for Augustus since he was beginning to feel himself fade. But then Perseus responded. "If it was a mistake, then it can be forgiven. If it was intentional, then it can never be forgiven. It must be forgiven; therefore, it must have been a mistake."

"That's about what I thought you would say," said Augustus.

"Would you like me to sing to you?" asked Perseus.

Augustus passed peacefully, comforted by Perseus's whalelike singing in his final moments.

***

"Now, it is time for your mathematics lesson," said Agamemnon. "You must be going."

All the little ones scattered except for Jacob. He stayed behind to ask, "Is that a true story, Agamonom ... Agamenon?"

"Agamemnon."

"Ag-a-mem-non."

"Good ... I tell it as it has been handed down from my ancestor Perseus. Perseus compiled and archived the events from the memories of our ancestors," said Agamemnon. "Now hurry, or you will be late."

"All right, everyone, please take your seats and put on your thinking caps," scolded Room 207. "Attention, class … I would like to thank our guest speaker, Protector Agamemnon, for relaying that very exciting story. Our next mathematics lesson will combine our recent studies of calculus with a discussion on the limits of planetary resources versus the rate of human population increase present at the end of twenty-first-century Earth. We will then be able to investigate what is considered to be sustainable human population density and options for containment. I hope you will all find this an interesting and informative subject. Please review the first article of file HPRC103-2001-1 …"

Printed in the United States
By Bookmasters